The Return of the Heir

THE RETURN OF THE HEIR

A Guardians of the Isles Romance

Gerri Russell

TULE
PUBLISHING

Dedication

To all those who have experienced trauma in their lives and still believe in hope. You are the best of humanity, and a brilliant example of the resiliency of the human spirit. Much love to you all.

THE RETURN OF THE HEIR

Some say it is a blessing, others a curse that the triplets, Alastair, Tormod, and Orrick, born to the laird of the MacLeod clan arrived on the eve of Samhain, the darker half of the year when the barrier between the human world and the fairy world breaks down. For some it is a time of celebration. For the MacLeods, it is a time to be wary. The fairies have interfered with the Clan MacLeod before in centuries past . . .

PROLOGUE

G WENDOLYN HARRIS STOOD alone outside the doorway of the chapel at Dunvegan Castle. It had been three years since the MacDonalds had raided their village and killed everyone except her sister, brother, and herself. Why they were spared when so many others perished that day, including her parents, made no sense.

In the days after the raid, there were times when Gwendolyn had wished she and her siblings had been killed. Death would have been preferable to the pain and sorrow they had experienced wandering through their lifeless village. It wasn't until the MacLeod clan had arrived and helped them bury the dead—then taken them back to Dunvegan Castle—that hope for their future had taken hold.

Much had happened to Arabella, Samuel, and her in the past three years, but nothing more exciting than what would occur in a matter of moments when she would become the wife of Alastair MacLeod. The clan heir. The three of them would truly become a part of the Clan MacLeod, and all their troubles would be behind them.

A nervous fluttering took flight in Gwendolyn's stomach as she peeked inside the chapel doorway, trying to catch a glimpse of her brother and sister. They should be standing near the front, yet she couldn't locate them. With a frown, Gwendolyn shifted her attention back to the hallway where she stood, waiting for Norman MacLeod to escort her down the aisle to join her life to his son's. Just thinking about being near the elder laird sent a shiver down her spine.

Since arriving at Dunvegan, she'd come to know why others referred to him as "Wicked Man" MacLeod. For daily he abused all those in his path—servants, clan members, his wife, and especially his own children. Even so, Gwendolyn and her siblings had kept their heads down and tried to only think of how grateful they were to him for taking them in when they'd had nowhere else to go.

Bringing her thoughts back to the present, Gwendolyn forced herself to stand taller and breathe slow and deep, keeping her excitement and her nervousness in check. It was hard to imagine only three days had passed since she and Alastair had been betrothed, on her sixteenth birthday.

The announcement and the signing of the betrothal document had come as a surprise to both herself and Alastair. They had spent some time together over the past three years, mostly at meals, and a few times alone in each other's company. But they were essentially strangers, who were now thrust together at his father's insistence.

Gwendolyn peered once more down the long aisle in the chapel to the man who waited for her there. Alastair MacLeod could only be considered breathtaking to anyone with eyes. The morning sun streamed through the chapel's stained glass window to highlight the shining darkness of his hair and revealed the hint of a wave in its thickness. His sideburns accentuated the high cheekbones of his slightly elongated face, and the hollowed line of his jaw. His shoulders filled out the midnight-blue surcoat and tunic with a power and grace that rippled clearly from every taut inch of muscle; his legs, long and lean, peeked out from beneath the hem of his tartan in such a way that made her heart beat faster.

In spite of all that, it was his eyes that commanded most of her attention. They were dark, and at this moment, as dusky as the dark brown mane of his hair, and they were focused on her. When a genuine smile of appreciation touched his lips, Gwendolyn drew a startled breath.

An arranged marriage such as this was not uncommon. Her own mother's marriage had been a prudent union between two clans with no thought whatsoever to affection, or whether the two parties concerned would eventually tolerate each other. Her mother had been happy enough until the day her marriage to a Harris ended her life because of a feud with a rival clan, the MacDonalds.

Her throat tight, Gwendolyn stepped back, out of view, trying to collect herself. Would her own marriage be similarly cursed? Or was Alastair's smile a sign that theirs would be a different kind of union?

Suddenly footsteps sounded, coming swiftly towards her. She drew a deep breath and braced herself for the arrival of her soon-to-be father-in-law. Gwendolyn turned to greet him—but it was not Norman MacLeod who reached for her. It was not the Wicked Man MacLeod who clamped a brutal hand over her mouth to stifle her scream. She had never seen this man before, but she could tell he wasn't a friend to the MacLeods. Her captor hauled her backwards, out of the hallway and out to the rear courtyard.

She tried to wrench away, but he was too strong. No one was around to witness anything since they were all packed into the chapel, waiting for her to marry the heir. She dragged her feet, trying to make it difficult for the brute who held her tightly in his grasp. Desperation brought a cold sweat to her skin as he pulled her to the wall of the rear courtyard that faced Loch Dunvegan.

Her captor's hold on her lessened, and she twisted out of his grasp. She drew a ragged breath of the sea air even as her back pressed against the wall that separated the castle from the cliffs of the sea loch. She had nowhere to go but over the ledge. She turned to scramble up the wall when the whisk of drawn steel filled her ears.

A firm hand dragged her down, then thrust her backwards. She hit the wall hard as the deadly edge of a knife pressed against her neck, stilling her movements. "What do you want?"

"Take off your gown."

Fear and desperation rose in Gwendolyn. She'd avoided all the unwanted attention that had come her way over the past few years, only to lose that battle now, on her wedding day, with a man who was not her intended spouse? Her anger flared as she twisted in her attacker's arms and slammed her knee into his groin.

He groaned and hunched forward. Gwendolyn jerked away, racing back towards the castle. Her only hope was to either alert others to her attacker's presence or find somewhere to hide.

"Get back here or your brother and sister will die."

He was lying. He had to be, but then she hadn't seen either of them in the chapel. She kept running even as the sound of footsteps sounded close behind her.

"I have them locked away. Stop, or I'll kill them both."

Gwendolyn stumbled, and turned as the man advanced on her, his dagger poised to strike.

"That's better," he said as he came close. "Now hold still or I'll slit your pretty little flesh." With a flick of the dagger, he caught the bodice of her gown and sliced it all the way down to the hem. Gwendolyn's knees started to wobble as the weapon gleamed in the morning sunshine.

"Take me to my brother and sister."

"Only if you do as I say." He once again caught her against his chest and held the blade to her throat as he dragged her back to the cliff's edge. She felt the dagger dig deeper into her flesh and the warmth of her own blood trailing down her throat. At the edge, her captor stopped and peeled her gown from her then wiped the bodice against her neck, smearing the fabric with the bright red blood. From his sporran he withdrew a sheep's bladder filled with a dark red liquid. With his dagger, he pierced the vessel and doused her dress with the additional blood.

Fear rippled down her spine. "What are you doing?"

"Making it appear as though you jumped. Once Alastair finds your dress along the shoreline, bathed in blood, he will assume you are dead and won't turn the countryside upside down looking for you."

She stared into her captor's hostile face. "He hardly cares enough for me to go to such trouble."

A wicked smile came to the man's lips. "He would if he knew a MacDonald, his most hated enemy, had taken something that was his from him."

"Why would you do something like that?"

"Men have gone to war over far less."

Gwendolyn blinked hard to stop the tears that threatened. "You mean to start a war with the MacLeods?"

"Not until you steal the Fairy Flag, their most valued treasure, and give it to my clan. We will use the luck of the Fairy Flag, and any magic it contains, to smite our enemy once and for all."

Gwendolyn had been shown the Fairy Flag shortly after

her arrival at Dunvegan. Norman MacLeod had taken her to the drawing room where the MacLeods kept the flag, hanging between the seaward-facing windows. He claimed the length of magical silk had been given to the MacLeods by a daughter of Oberon, king of the fairies. The fairy princess had imbued the flag with the power to overcome an enemy or a hardship when it was unfurled and waved three times. Doing so would bring the fairy legions to the flag bearer's aid.

The legend also claimed the magic of the Fairy Flag could only be used three times, after which it would return to where it came from, taking the flag bearer with it. The flag had already been put to the test twice before when the MacDonalds invaded with overwhelming numbers. At the waving of the Fairy Flag, the tide of battle turned and the MacLeods were saved from destruction.

As the memory faded, Gwendolyn stiffened. "Why would I give you anything that might help you win such a war against the MacLeods?" The MacDonalds had killed her clan and left her and her siblings orphans.

Her captor leaned in closer as the knife bit deep once more. "Because if you don't, you and your siblings won't live to see another sunrise."

"How can I trust you have them in your possession? Am I simply supposed to take your word for it?"

A hint of a smile pulled up the corners of his lips. "Somehow, I knew you'd want proof." He reached into his sporran once more and withdrew a length of pale blond hair with the ribbon Arabella had worn earlier still tied about it and placed it in Gwendolyn's hand. Next, he removed a lock of hair that was the same golden brown as her brother's.

Gwendolyn clenched her fingers around the proof that he had her siblings, the two people she loved most in this world. "Why capture me? Why fake my death?"

"I've seen the way Alastair MacLeod looks at you. You are important to him. And by taking you away from him on the day he believes you will become his, I hurt him, I hurt the entire clan. Only they will not know it was I who took you from them. I'll make it look as though you chose to end your own life rather than marry Alastair MacLeod."

Bile rose up in Gwendolyn's throat. "Isn't taking me from Alastair punishment enough?"

"The punishment hasn't even started." Her captor released the blade at her throat but in the next moment he reached up and grabbed a handful of her hair.

Gwendolyn cried out as he tugged at the length then sliced through a section of her golden-blond hair. With a satisfied smile, he released her and clutched the strands of her hair in his fist. Gwendolyn's hand lifted to the blunt section of her abused hair.

"Now that you have the means to falsify my death, let me and my siblings go. We will leave. We'll go far away. No one will ever find us."

"I'll put you where no one will find you," he said with a

terrifying smile. "But first, while everyone is crowded into the chapel, you must go and steal the Fairy Flag. Quickly, before you are missed." He grabbed her arm and shoved her in the direction of the castle.

"Nay. If you want the flag, you'll have to steal it yourself."

"If I stole the Fairy Flag, I would be forced to eliminate the guard who stands vigil beside it day and night. Is that what you want? To kill one of your soon-to-be kin?"

"You think I can talk the guard away from his duty to steal the flag for you?"

Garrick gave her a slow nod. "You've proven yourself to be a clever girl over the years that you've lived here. Why else would a nobody from a distant clan be marrying the heir to the MacLeod chiefdom?"

Gwendolyn glared at her captor. "I did not manipulate him if that is what you are insinuating. Besides, the Fairy Flag was given to the MacLeods by the fairies. Will the magic work for anyone else?"

"No one knows the answer to that question, because no one but the MacLeods have ever used the Fairy Flag. But even if the magic does not work for us, our possessing the flag will keep the MacLeods from using it when we do finally attack."

Agony rocked Gwendolyn. Her wedding day was over. Her life as she had known it was over. If she stole the Fairy Flag from the MacLeods, and gave it to their enemy, she would forever alter the course of the Clan MacLeod.

"Enough stalling," Garrick growled. "Do what I ask or there will be dire consequences for you and your siblings."

CHAPTER ONE

THE SCOTTISH SKIES overhead were grey and tumultuous as Alastair MacLeod reined his horse to a halt, forcing everyone in his company to do the same.

"Why are we stopping when we are so near our goal?" Graeme Duff, the captain of his guard, asked.

"It has been five long years since I've seen the golden stone of Dunvegan Castle."

"Are you having second thoughts about returning?" Graeme asked.

"Nay. I'm ready for this challenge. Four years of studying diplomacy at Edinburgh University and a year abroad in the foreign service have forged me into the man I am today. Those skills will serve me well as clan chief."

"Then why the sudden hesitation?" Graeme asked.

"I am ready to lead my people. That is not the issue."

Graeme frowned. "Then what is?"

"Memories. Memories of my mother's death, my father's dominance over us all, and—" Alastair cut off his words. He hadn't spoken Gwendolyn's name aloud since the night she vanished.

Graeme nodded in understanding. He had been at Alastair's side that fateful day. "That was five years ago. You have moved on with your life."

"Aye, in some areas," Alastair agreed as he continued to stare into the distance. "But not in all. I can no longer pretend I didn't run away from my duty five years ago."

Graeme's frown increased. "It wasn't just you who ran away. Tormod and Orrick left as well, and for similar reasons to your own. The three of you came into this world together, but of the three, you are the one who will lead all of the MacLeods into the future. You made the best of a bad situation for your siblings. Before you left, you made certain Callum and Rowena were safely tucked away at school until your father died a year ago."

Aye. He'd made sure his siblings were nowhere near their father. But since his father's death, Callum, the youngest of the five siblings, had come home to run Dunvegan. He had pleaded with Alastair many times to return from his diplomatic post in France. He'd gone there to try and determine if the heir to the Scottish throne had enough backing to risk the Jacobites starting a war with England.

Alastair stared at the hulking four-storied mass of golden-brown stones, which his mother, Janet, had always hated. His father had merely laughed and said all great men lived in such places. It had been the seat of his father's power and his uncontrollable rage. For his mother, Dunvegan Castle had become a prison she had never been able to escape. The pain of loss pierced Alastair's chest, mixing with the anger at his father that never seemed to abate. Dunvegan was the heart of the MacLeod clan, no matter what horrors had happened within its walls.

In the distance, Alastair could see the gate at the drawbridge opening. Callum had obviously seen their approach.

"Your brother seems eager for your return," Graeme said cheerfully. "What did that final missive say that finally called you home?"

Callum had not called Alastair out for what had happened in the past, but as the man responsible for the perils to come. "'The Isles and her people are in danger. If you do not step up to this moment, then all shall be lost,'" Alastair recited as he turned his gaze on the man beside him. "Regardless of what Callum said, you and I both know war is brewing. The most urgent threat is a war amongst the clans. The MacDonalds are gathering power and the allegiance of many of the smaller clans on the Inner Hebridean isles. Soon, they will rise up against the MacLeods. We must be ready when that time comes."

"Agreed." Graeme cast his gaze over the men behind them. "The men are ready."

Alastair tightened his lips. It was time to put aside all the bad memories and his broken heart and do what was right, for his kin and all of the innocents who would be caught up in the coming conflict. It was time to take his rightful place not only as clan chief but also as a Guardian of the Isles.

"Whether you want to acknowledge it or not, the time away has been good for you. You are a different man now, one who will be embraced upon his return."

The thought of being welcomed at his home brought a bittersweet feeling to his chest. Alastair glanced back at the castle in the distance. He had come back to Dunvegan to accept the role of laird, but he was also determined to strengthen his clan, to prepare the men for a coming war of the clans, if his plans to find a diplomatic solution failed. One way or another, he would revive the strength of the MacLeod clan.

"Let's proceed," he said to Graeme as he signalled his men. "I'm coming home to change the future of our clan. From this day forth, we shall be known as both warriors and diplomats." Alastair flicked the reins, setting his horse in motion once more. His men followed. The silence of the next several minutes was broken only by the clop of the horses' hooves on the hard, rocky surface of the trail. As they neared the gates, Alastair could smell the tang of the sea beyond the cliffs. He'd missed the smell of the sea. The scent filled him with memories of a happier time before his father had taken that blow to the head that seemingly overnight had changed him from a strong leader to a man filled with rage and suspicion.

A few years later, he and his brothers had only been nine

at the time, and unable to do much to help their mother when their father tossed her in the dungeon and left her there to die. Alastair's hand drifted to the dent in his skull given to him by his father when he'd tried to free his mother. His father had left him unconscious for days and by the time he'd regained his senses, his mother had died. The pain of her loss had dulled over time, but the anger over his father's cruelty remained.

Alastair's gaze shifted to the Fairy Tower on the south wing of the castle. The tower was named such because the clan used to keep the Fairy Flag there before the new keep was built. Since the time of her death, his mother's spirit had haunted that place: The Grey Lady, the castle residents called her for the grey gown that floated around her as she moved amongst the empty spaces in the tower chambers. No one in the castle went to the Fairy Tower anymore.

It was no wonder his mother's spirit still remained with them. Alastair had always wondered if it was to watch over the children she'd left behind, or to further irritate their father. The man had been enraged the first time he'd seen her floating around the tower. He'd bolted the doors to the Fairy Tower shut and forbad anyone in the castle from going there.

Alastair shook off the memory. The rest of the castle residents were waiting for the eldest son's return so they might flourish once more as they had before his father's accident. He tightened his fists around the reins in his hands. As the first-born triplet, it was his duty to bring harmony back to their troubled corner of the world and lead his clan into the future.

As Alastair and his party crossed over the land bridge leading to the entrance of the castle, he turned his gaze once more to the Fairy Tower. The sole, usually shuttered, window in the tower was open, and in the empty space a ghostly face he'd thought he'd never see again appeared for only a heartbeat.

A cold chill crept up Alastair's spine. "It cannot be."

"What cannot be?" Graeme asked as they rode into the front courtyard.

Alastair blinked and searched the window again. The wooden shutters were in place and appeared every bit as undisturbed as they had been since his father sealed the tower nine years ago. Had he only imagined seeing Gwendolyn? Was his conscience so guilty over her loss that her image had come to mind when he returned to the last place he'd seen her alive?

The day she'd disappeared, he'd lost a part of himself. He blamed himself for her leaping to her death. In the five years he had been gone from this place, he'd learned to accept her absence in his life. But the very thought of her brought back pain, joy, and regret. He forced the emotions from his thoughts as they entered the courtyard. His youngest brother, Callum, stood in the shadows created by the arched entry to the elaborately carved front door.

They brought their horses to a stop and dismounted. Several servants stepped forward to take the horses from him and his men. Alastair nodded a greeting to the men and murmured his thanks, as his attention fixed on his brother. Callum was no longer the awkward youth he'd left behind five years ago. There was no denying he was a young man now at nineteen years of age. Alastair had always thought Callum bore a striking resemblance to their father, but now he could see that his brother had their mother's eyes and her kind smile as he stepped forward.

"It's about time you returned home." Though the words were harsh, they were softened by his soft brogue and by the hint of tears in his grey eyes. Callum took another step closer and suddenly enveloped Alastair in a fierce embrace. "Welcome home, Brother."

Alastair's arms wrapped around him and gave his brother an equally fierce hug. "I'm sorry it took so long. I needed that time—"

"It matters not. You're home. We have much to discuss." Callum released him and took a step back. "Come," he signalled towards the door. "Now that you are here, there is a small matter you need to handle straight away."

"What is that?"

Callum opened the door and moved up the stairs. Alastair followed as Callum headed down the hallway. As they drew closer to the great hall, the sound of a scuffle and men shouting came from within. Drawing his sword, Alastair stepped quickly into the chamber and came to a sudden stop in front of a pile of his men and his sister Rowena beside them wailing, "Get off him!"

"What in God's name is going on?" Alastair could feel his pulse pounding at his temples. The men in the pile continued to ignore him. Fists flew against an unseen enemy. Alastair's gaze narrowed on his sister as she pulled at one man's arm, trying her best to minimise whatever was happening here. *Rowena? Rowena was here?*

Alastair moved to her side. "Why aren't you at that fancy school where I left you?"

Rowena released the man's arm and straightened. Her gaze filled with surprise at first, then shifted to anger. "I left Miss Doddie's School for Girls last year. I graduated and decided to come home instead of becoming a tutor for some English lass."

"Why wasn't I told you'd returned?"

If possible, her back straightened even more. "You treated us as if we were unimportant, so that is the way I decided to treat you."

"Now see here, Rowena—"

She cut him off with a gesture of her arm. Her eyes glinted fiercely. "You and I can squabble later. Right now, get these men off of him."

"Off of whom?"

"The man I'm going to marry."

"What? When? Oh, good Lord." Alastair signalled to his

men behind him to help break up whatever was happening. One by one, his other clansmen were drawn back until a lone figure remained huddled in a ball against the planked floor.

"Marcus, are you well? Did they hurt you?" Rowena surged forward and helped the young man to his feet.

"It would take more than that to hurt a MacDonald," the young man said as he straightened his vest and jacket.

Alastair's senses and his sword were trained on the dangerous man before him. The MacDonalds were their fiercest enemy. "What happens here?"

Everyone started talking at once.

Alastair whistled shrilly. "Silence. One at a time, please." He turned to Thomas Becks, his steward, who had watched the brawl. The man Alastair had always thought of as a second father had aged. His head was fully grey, but Becks still had the same wisdom in his eyes. His welcoming smile brought out more distinctive lines about his eyes and mouth. "How did this man enter the castle?"

"Good tae have ye home, m'laird." Becks cleared his throat as he addressed Alastair. "Yer sister has taken a fancy tae this man. We forbad the two of them tae see each other, but she dropped a rope from the north tower and allowed him tae climb right up."

Alastair sheathed his sword and rounded on his sister. "So, this was not an attack on the clan. Why would you do such a thing? You know the history of our two families."

"We were in the process of capturing him when you arrived," Innis, one of the castle's warriors, interjected with a tug on Marcus MacDonald's arm. "We were going to tie him up and shoot him for daring to enter our domain."

"Nay!" Rowena shrieked, clinging to Marcus's other arm. "He meant no harm to any of you."

"He's a MacDonald. Treachery runs in his veins," a voice rang out from the gathered warriors.

Marcus's nostrils flared through a hot gust of indignation, but the interloper held his tongue.

Alastair pressed his fingers to his temple, fighting back a sudden throbbing there. He had wondered what kind of greeting he would receive, but this was nothing like he'd imagined. Instead of stepping into a fray, he'd formed a thought to head to the Fairy Tower and figure out why he'd imagined seeing Gwendolyn there. "Return him to his clan before this escalates any further."

"Alastair, please," Rowena whispered. "Do not send him away. What if these men kill him?"

"Kill me?" Marcus surged forward. "I would like to see them try."

"No one has any desire to kill this man." In a similar situation, Alastair was certain the MacDonalds would not spare a MacLeod, but for some reason his sister seemed fond of the lad. Alastair flattened his lips as he gazed at the warriors who were now his men even though he hadn't seen them in years. Amongst them he recognised four he could trust. "Emery, Innis, Andrew, and Tully, can you give me your oath that you will escort this MacDonald, unharmed, back to where our land meets theirs?"

"Aye," the men said in unison as they moved forward to extract Rowena from the man's arm. Her cheeks paled as the four men led the intruder outside.

"He will be safe, Sister. You have their word." Alastair held out his hand. "Come, we have much to discuss."

Instead of accepting his hand, Rowena gathered her skirts and raced out of the great hall, then up the grand staircase.

"Becks, how long has this thing between my sister and Marcus MacDonald been going forward?"

Becks pursed his lips. "None of us truly ken fer certain, m'laird. But this isn't the first time we've caught him in the castle."

Alastair's headache throbbed more intensely. "Let me get this straight." He looked over the remaining men gathered before him. "This has happened before and none of you thought to do anything about it before tonight? Why stop him now and not then?"

A warrior he knew as Mackie stepped forward, his cheeks reddened. "Because we knew you were coming home and didn't want a MacDonald to be the first thing you saw. We want you to stay. You belong with us. We need you here."

Alastair felt an ache somewhere within him that had nothing to do with his long journey here. *You belong with us.* How long had it been since he'd belonged anywhere?

"He's right." Callum's brow furrowed. "Every year you

were gone, things kept getting worse. Then Father died and things deteriorated even more. So much is wrong, and none of us know how to fix any of it. We need you now more than ever."

They all looked at Alastair expectantly, as if he could simply say something and everything would improve. He frowned. What the hell could he say that would make them feel as though he knew what he was doing? "Close the gates. After I speak with Rowena, I'll meet you all back here and you can explain to me all that has happened in the past five years."

Before any of them could respond, he strode down the hallway and raced up the stairs, taking them two at a time. He'd fled his obligations, however temporarily, to have a serious discussion with his sister about bringing an enemy into their home. At the top of the stairs he paused, gazing down the hallway towards the south wing and the Fairy Tower beyond that.

Once again, in his mind's eye he saw the face, framed in a thick cascade of golden hair, that had haunted him for years. A delicate nose, wide-set blue eyes that were neither light nor dark—more like the colour of the sky at twilight. Shaking the thoughts of the past away, he turned and headed down the north wing to his sister's bedchamber and the duties that lay ahead.

He had to live in the present if he were to resume his rightful place as heir of the Clan MacLeod.

CHAPTER TWO

RESTLESSNESS SWEPT OVER Gwendolyn as she moved to the single window in the tower where she and her brother and sister had been held hostage for the past five years. Those years had been long and hard, and at times her brother and sister had wanted to give up and let the cold take them when their prayers and pleas went unheeded. But Gwendolyn was not about to give up. She clung to the tattered shreds of her pride, honour, and courage no matter how hopeless things looked for the three of them.

But today, something was different. Garrick was more agitated than usual. Something had changed. Garrick held himself more stiffly, his features were tight, and his shallow breaths were followed by a gusty sigh. He was irritated, but about what? She and her siblings had done nothing to provoke him. They never did. It was why they were still alive.

Gwendolyn curled her fingers into a tight ball, trying not to let hope blossom. She'd imagined changes in Garrick's behavior before, only to be disappointed in the end. And yet, when the sound of horses approaching came to the tower,

Garrick disappeared, and she couldn't hold back the flowering of hope inside her chest.

Their captor never seemed to be spotted by any of the castle residents as he moved about, even in the daylight, stealing food from the kitchen for them and clothing from the residents as her siblings outgrew their garments. She'd assumed he had found some sort of secret passageway to move about the castle without being seen. And if it weren't for the chain at her ankle that kept her tethered to this place, Gwendolyn would have disappeared, along with her siblings, years ago.

Over the years, not one of the castle residents came to the Fairy Tower, removing all hope of rescue. The old laird had put such fear into the hearts of those who lived at Dunvegan, threatening death to any who tried, that ever since Norman MacLeod had died, no one but Garrick entered the tower.

Moving the pelts Garrick had given them aside, Gwendolyn stood. The chain was just long enough to reach the window if she stretched her body forward. Grasping the wooden shutter, she shifted it aside and drew a deep breath of the salty air. A breeze stirred, touching her face and throat with its cool breath, pressing the muslin underdress against her breasts. Garrick had given her the plain dress after he'd taken her wedding gown from her. He'd slit her bloody dress in half, making it appear as though it had been caught on the rocks as she'd jumped from the cliff. Garrick had wanted a plausible explanation for the MacLeods to find her dress but not a body. Then, after she'd stolen the flag for him, he'd brought her up to the Fairy Tower to be chained alongside her siblings. It seemed like only yesterday. . .and yet, judging by marks she and her siblings made upon the tower walls, she knew it was not.

After Garrick had secured her in her chains, he'd taken the flag and had never returned to the tower with it again. She had assumed he'd passed it on to whatever contacts he had within the castle staff and smuggled it out of Dunvegan, delivering the priceless artifact to the MacDonalds. Gwendolyn released a soft sigh of regret as she continued to gaze through the single window in the tower. She'd had no choice but to steal the flag and hand it over to the enemies of the MacLeods.

"What do you see, Gwennie? Tell us," her now fifteen-year-old sister, Arabella, asked with longing in her voice.

Gwendolyn looked at the hills in the distance. One of her only pleasures when Garrick left them was to look out the window and tell her brother and sister, who could not move as far as she could, what she saw. "Healabhal Mhor and Healabhal Beag look particularly fine today." The flat-topped hills known as the MacLeod's Tables dominated the skyline for miles around.

"You tell us about those hills all the time," her brother Samuel replied in an ever-deepening voice. At twelve and a half, he was quickly becoming a young man.

Gwendolyn's throat thickened at the thought of all they had suffered over the years. The weight of her guilt for not being able to free them was almost harder to bear than the chain at her ankle. Forcing a lighter note into her voice she said, "Well, let's see. . . The heather is in bloom. Can you smell the honeyed scent?"

Both her brother and sister closed their eyes and drew in a deep breath. "Aye," Arabella said with a smile. "It's sweet and a little spicy at the same time." As soon as she drew in a breath, she started coughing, producing a rattling in her chest. Gwendolyn swallowed hard. The sound was growing worse. Next time Garrick came to them she would plead with him to bring her honey and whisky with which to treat Arabella's cough.

The increasing sound of hoofbeats brought Gwendolyn back to the situation before her. Turning to the window, she looked again, this time a little closer to the castle. Were the MacDonalds finally attacking the castle now that the old larid was dead? They had the Fairy Flag. If the flag's magic worked for them, then the MacLeods didn't stand much of a chance in holding them back. She stood on her toes, trying to get a better view. "There are men on horseback, twenty or so of them." Twenty men? Even with the Fairy Flag in their possession that hardly seemed like enough men to over-whelm an entire castle.

"Perhaps they are why Garrick left us in such a hurry," Samuel said.

"Perhaps," Gwendolyn acknowledged. A moment later, the men did something unexpected. Not advancing, they simply waited atop the ravine that separated the rest of the isle from the basalt rock on which Dunvegan perched. At high tide, the ravine would be filled with water, but the tide was out and the drawbridge had been lowered. The barrier would have been raised had it been the MacDonalds come to attack. Not the MacDonalds then. Someone else was heading for Dunvegan.

The company of men started moving towards the gate. At the sight of a dark head leading the group, a shiver rippled down Gwendolyn's spine. *Alastair?* The man she was once supposed to marry had returned to Dunvegan. He and his men were moving swiftly now, across the drawbridge. The late afternoon sunshine highlighted the luster of his dark brown hair and showed the definitive outline of his muscular body.

Then, just before he reached the courtyard, his head lifted to gaze at the tower window. She could feel his gaze connect with her own. She forgot to move, forgot to breathe, just for a moment before she slammed the shutters closed and drew back into the shadows of the tower in a sudden panic.

"Gwennie, what is it? What did you see?" Her sister's face drained of colour.

Gwendolyn stood there a moment longer, perfectly still, every muscle rigid with tension, before she finally drew a breath, then another. Her heart thundered in her chest as she turned towards her brother and sister who stared back at her expectantly. She'd never thought she'd see him again. Pain and pleasure twisted inside her in equal measure. "Alastair MacLeod. . .has returned."

Arabella's eyes widened. "He's come to save us."

Gwendolyn turned back to the window. Even if Alastair hated her for what she'd done to him, she could at least try to save her siblings. She drew a deep breath, ready to scream for help as she opened the shutters. The men had passed over the drawbridge and were no longer visible. Her breath left her in a rush. She had screamed out this window for years, only to not be heard. She shut the window and held back a sob, trying to put on a brave face for her brother and sister. "They are gone," Gwendolyn whispered. "Why would Alastair look for me? He thinks I'm dead."

"Then he'll be pleased when he discovers you are not." Arabella came towards her, reaching out her hands. They were chained on opposite sides of the tower, and could touch each other now that Arabella had grown.

Gwendolyn wrapped her fingers around her sister's, accepting the comfort she offered. Her sister's fingers were chilled, as they always were at this time of the year. The changing of fall to winter would bring the hardest-to-endure months in the cold and lonely tower. "Please wrap yourself in your pelts, Arabella. Your cough is growing worse every day."

Garrick had provided them with pelts and blankets years ago, but it was barely enough to keep them from succumbing to illness. Arabella had had a cough last winter that had returned over the past few weeks as the nights turned cold.

Arabella released Gwendolyn's fingers and did as instructed, huddling into her makeshift bed for warmth.

"Do you think Alastair will come to the tower?" her brother asked hopefully. "If he does, he might find us. He'd never leave us here. We would be saved."

Gwendolyn forced a calm smile to her lips for her siblings' sake as she moved back to her corner of the tower. "Let us find comfort in that thought, shall we? Tell me once again what you will do, Samuel and Arabella, when you are finally free?" It was a game they'd played for years. It was the one thing, thinking about the future, that brought any animation to their faces. The answers were always the same. They wanted to be outside, to remember what grass smelled like, to feel the rain upon their faces, and feel the crash of the surf at their ankles. They wanted to eat marzipan treats and sleep on a huge bed with a soft mattress stuffed with feathers. But they never mentioned going home. For they had no home to return to since their parents and most of their clan had been slain during the raid on their village.

She and Alastair had met eight years ago when his father had brought them back to Dunvegan. They spend little time together since Alastair was training to become the next laird, and she was learning how to run a household the size of

Dunvegan. But at meals they often sat together and had gradually come to know each other better.

Against her better judgment, Gwendolyn had fallen in love with Alastair years back, when they'd met each other by chance along the shores of Loch Dunvegan. That night she'd seen not just tolerance in his eyes, but actual affection. Though, that was before she'd betrayed him and his entire clan.

Arabella and Samuel continued to discuss their hopes and dreams with each other, no longer needing Gwendolyn to interact with them, which came as a relief since she needed a moment to ponder all that had just happened.

Alastair MacLeod had returned. Garrick MacDonald had been waiting for this moment for a long time, ever since he'd had her steal the Fairy Flag. What were his plans now? Would he immediately attack the MacLeods and use the flag and its supposed fairy magic to ensure the MacDonalds' success? Or would he wait?

If he chose to wait, could she somehow warn the Mac-Leods of what was to come? She glanced down at the chain about her ankle. She'd spent the past five years trying to hack through the thick iron with a small dagger she'd managed to steal from Garrick. She'd also tried picking the lock and sawing through the chain portion that tied her to the wall. All her attempts had caused no damage to her bindings and had only dulled and pitted the blade of the dagger.

Garrick had never threatened them physically, except for

a time two years ago when he had consumed too much ale
and tried to force himself on her. Somehow she had managed to wrap her chain around his throat, and pull it tight.
Her anger gave her the strength she needed to fight him as he
clawed at the chain. With what little breath he'd had left, he
begged her for mercy. She'd thought about killing him then,
but when he'd gone limp in her arms, she'd relented. It took
so long to regain his senses that she'd thought life had fled,
until he drew a deep breath and slithered away from her.
Since that day, he hadn't come close enough for her to try
something similar again.

During their entire imprisonment, Garrick never released
them. Not even for them to bathe or relieve themselves.
Instead, he provided water, soap, and bathing sheets once
every month for them to clean themselves and a chamber pot
that he cleaned occasionally himself since no one else knew
of their presence in the tower.

No one, that was, except the Grey Lady. An icy chill
whispered through the dimly lit tower that had nothing to
do with the coming season. A frothy grey mist swept across
the floor then gathered into a more solid shape until the
image of the woman appeared before them.

Arabella gave a little yelp as she always did when the spirit arrived.

"It's all right, Arabella. She will not hurt us." Gwendolyn
had long ago given up trying to comfort her sister with
anything but words. The spirit hadn't hurt them in the five

years she'd been coming to them. The lady never said anything. Gwendolyn wasn't sure if she could actually talk. But whenever she did show herself, she stared at them and thoughts came into their minds, as though she had planted them there.

"What do you want, Lady Janet?" Gwendolyn asked as the woman stared at her from only a few steps away. The mist that surrounded her lessened and her image became much more solid than it had ever been before. Though she'd tried it before, many times, Gwendolyn reached out to touch the specter before her, wanting to find it solid. As always, her fingers chilled and slipped right through what should have been the woman's left arm. Gwendolyn's shoulders sagged as disappointment rippled through her.

"What do you want?" Samuel asked, rising to his feet and scowling at the woman. In the past year, her brother had become far more aggressive towards the woman when she appeared. His fear of the ghost had faded, and he'd taken on the role of protector of his sisters. "Have you finally come to free us?"

If only I could.

Gwendolyn heard the words in her mind as she studied the image before her. "Your son has returned to Dunvegan. Does that have something to do with why you are more. . .solid?"

The Grey Lady floated closer until Gwendolyn was engulfed in an otherworldly mist. A chill crawled across her skin. *Danger! You must escape. Help my son.*

Gwendolyn's hands fisted in the fabric of her dress. "How are we supposed to do that? I've been trying to set us free for five years." She thrust her leg and the shackle that surrounded her bruised ankle towards the ghost. "I cannot slip from my bonds as easily as you slip through walls."

I will help. I will find a way. And with those words, the Grey Lady disappeared.

Arabella gasped. "Did I hear her correctly? Did she say she would finally help us?"

All the tension in Samuel's body left him and he sagged against the tower wall at his back. "That is what I heard, too."

Freedom.

At the thought, the tightness in Gwendolyn's chest lessened for the first time in years. She had no idea how the Grey Lady could do anything to help them, but Gwendolyn latched onto the thread of hope as she turned towards her brother and sister. Their eyes were bright and wide, echoing her own tentative hope that they might yet escape the tower before the days turned cold and the darkness of night after night lingered all around them. They would leave the castle and go far away until all the danger was far behind them.

The sound of familiar footsteps on the stairs broke through her thoughts. The sound grew louder until the bolt on the door slid aside and Garrick entered the chamber carrying a bundle of cloth. Instead of avoiding her as he usually did, he came right towards her. Gwendolyn's heart started pounding wildly.

Garrick gave a low laugh. "Thought I'd never touch you again, did you?"

She grabbed the length of chain between her hands. "Don't come any closer."

Samuel sprang forward, as far as his chain would allow. His eyes narrowed on Garrick as he swung his arms out, trying to grasp Garrick in some fashion. "Keep your hands off my sister."

Arabella rose and stretched forward as well, trying to grab hold of their captor. While the siblings were barely able to touch each other, there was a small area in the very center of the tower where Garrick could stand and not be reached by one of them.

Unfortunately for them, he knew exactly where that spot was located and stopped there. He threw the bundle of clothing in Gwendolyn's direction. "Put these on."

Gwendolyn clenched her jaw as she glared at the man she'd come to hate over the years. "I will do no such thing."

A smug smile came to his lips as he drew a flintlock from his belt and pointed the barrel at Arabella. "You will do exactly as I say, or Arabella dies."

Gwendolyn's fingers went numb and the chain fell from her hands to rattle against the wooden floor. She'd wondered for years why he kept them alive. Surely it would have been easier to kill them and be done with his revenge. There was obviously a reason he needed them alive, but she wasn't going to risk Arabella's life to confirm her suspicions. "Lower the weapon." She reached down, and with trembling hands lifted the bundle of cloth to her chest. "I'll do as you say."

"I thought you might see reason." His voice was mocking and slightly amused as he returned the pistol to his belt.

Gwendolyn unfurled the bundle to reveal a grey dress that was several years out of style. Perhaps it was one of Lady Janet's old dresses? "Why do you want me to wear this?" she asked, trying to keep the quaver from her voice.

"Because tonight you are going to haunt this place and scare that bastard, Alastair MacLeod, and his men right into my trap."

Now was not the time to be meek. She had to stand up to Garrick even though she felt small, nervous, and completely inadequate to meet this sudden challenge. "What do you mean?"

He waved the pistol at Arabella again. "Put the damn dress on."

Gwendolyn hurriedly slipped the dress over her head. The hem pooled at her feet. Janet had obviously been several inches taller than she was. The bodice gaped at the bust, and the waist settled around her hips. Her healthy figure had vanished when she only ate enough to keep herself alive. She gave everything extra to her siblings to allow them both to grow and thrive.

"Turn around," Garrick demanded.

"Why should I—"

He waved his pistol more forcefully at Arabella. "I was raised never to strike a woman, but over the years you've aroused a great violence in me that I'm finding hard to ignore right now. If you think I won't shoot her, you're wrong."

Gwendolyn raised her chin in defiance. "The sound of gunfire will alert everyone in the castle that something is happening in the tower. They will come to investigate."

"And find all of you dead. Now, turn around."

"Why haven't you killed us before now?"

"Because I needed you alive and cooperative when the MacLeod returned home. I want to hurt him as much as he and his clan hurt me. The three of you were obviously important to him for him to rescue you all those years ago and then to agree to marry you, Gwendolyn."

She wanted to argue that Alastair's attachment to the three of them was not that strong, but to do so might threaten their lives just as the hope of rescue had presented itself. With no real choice, she did as Garrick demanded. The chain at her ankle rattled against the floor with her movements. The sound of the chains had never been loud enough to bring anyone to their aid.

He was behind her in a lightning-swift motion. He grasped her arms and tied them behind her back.

"Untie me or I'll scream." Panic rose as she felt the rope tighten, rendering her helpless.

He turned her to face him. "You've screamed before, and everyone merely assumed it was the Grey Lady haunting the tower." His tone was silky with menace.

"Please untie me. I'll cooperate with whatever it is you want me to do."

"You'll cooperate all right." He shifted down to her feet and pulled an iron key that was tied to a loop on his belt. He inserted it into the shackle at her ankle and it came free, rattling against the floorboards.

Gwendolyn drew a sharp breath at the unexpected action. Instantly, her leg lifted and hovered above the floor without her doing anything. Free from the heavy shackle and chain, it felt as light as air. She forced it back to the ground and shifted her weight upon it. Tingles of sensation shot up her leg as she took one uneven step and then another. "Why after all this time are you releasing me now?"

He gave her a wicked smile as he draped a sheer and billowing cloak about her shoulders, then fastened the clasp in the front. "Because you are going as Lady Janet to the new keep to haunt those who have just returned to the castle. I want them so scared they will leave once more. Keep yourself from being recognised or your siblings will pay the price."

"How am I supposed to move about the castle without anyone seeing me?"

He grasped a piece of parchment and unrolled it before her. "This is a map of the castle and all the secret passageways I've discovered over the years. You'll be able to move about with ease. Quickly, memorise the details."

"If that is what you wish, then I will do it." She could barely force the words out through the tightness in her throat. He didn't leave her much of a choice. But once she was out of the tower, she would think of some way to free her brother and sister as well. "Untie me."

"Nay."

Gwendolyn frowned. "Will I not need my hands to open doors?"

"You're a clever girl. You'll overcome the challenge."

"You promise not to hurt Arabella or Samuel?" She wished she could stop shaking. She'd been dreaming of leaving this tower for years. . .but not under these circumstances.

"Only if you force me to do so." He opened the tower door, and she peered out into the half-light of the spiral stairs leading up to their prison. The air was lighter outside the tower room, fresher, with a hint of a tang that brought back memories of wading through the tide along the shores of Loch Dunvegan.

Gwendolyn paused as a thought struck her and she turned back to her captor. "What if the Grey Lady disapproves of me haunting the castle in her place?"

"Then you'll have more than just your siblings to worry about." He shut the door.

Gwendolyn drew herself up. She mustn't be a coward now. This might be her one chance to gain their freedom.

Taking her first tentative steps on legs that were weak and unsteady, she began her descent.

She had no idea how to free her family, and she had no idea how to haunt a castle even though she'd been watching the Grey Lady do just that for the past five years. In either case, she had better devise a plan, or the situation she'd thought couldn't get any worse, would become even more perilous.

CHAPTER THREE

A LASTAIR KNOCKED ON Rowena's door. "Rowena? May I come in?"

"Nay." Her voice was tight. She had obviously been crying.

"Please? I've missed you, Sister." Alastair leaned against the door. This was not how he wanted to renew his relationship with his sister. "I would very much like to talk with you." The door opened so quickly, he stumbled forward before he caught himself.

"What if I have nothing to say to you?"

He offered a tentative smile. "Then listen, because there are many things I need to say to you. But first, I must apologise."

She crossed her arms over her chest but moved aside so he could enter.

He moved to the chairs near the hearth and took a seat, patting the cushion beside him. "I am sorry I had to send Marcus away temporarily until I can understand the situation better."

"Temporarily?" She took the seat beside him but her face

remained impassive.

"How did you two meet?"

She pursed her lips, as if deciding whether to tell him or not. After a short pause, she sighed and said, "I was walking alone along the shore of the loch when he appeared. I did not know what to make of him at first. He looked like he'd just washed ashore from a shipwreck."

Alastair wanted to ask why she was walking anywhere unescorted, but he held his tongue, hoping she would continue.

"It turns out, he had been out sailing in a small boat he'd built himself. The boat capsized and he'd swam ashore only moments before I found him."

"Why was he out on the water?" Had he been trying to spy on the MacLeods for his clan? Alastair fisted his hands then forced himself to relax. He was here to mend fences with his sister, not create a deeper rift. She obviously cared for the lad.

"He was testing a new sealant he had created for sailing vessels that can fix breaches in the hull while the vessel is still in the water."

"If his boat sank, then obviously the sealant didn't work."

Rowena smiled. "It did work, but by the time he got the sealant in place, the boat had taken on too much water. He couldn't bail the water out fast enough by himself. He was able to recover the boat the next day, and the two of us tried to replicate the experiment. With the both of us to bail the water out, the boat stayed afloat."

This time Alastair couldn't fight his clenched fists. "Nay, Rowena. You cannot put yourself in such dangerous situations."

Her expression tightened and he saw pain in her eyes. "You cannot come back here and tell me how to behave and who I can see after leaving me alone for so long. Besides, I was perfectly safe. In case you forgot, I know how to swim."

He winced internally as he recognised how much pain lay under her words. "It wasn't my intention to come back here and tell you how to live your life, but I hope you will give me the chance to be your brother again—someone who cares about you and your welfare."

She looked away for a moment then returned her gaze to him. "I can agree to let you be my brother as long as you don't tell me I cannot see Marcus anymore. I truly care about him."

"Would you agree to supervised visits?"

"Perhaps."

He knew his sister well enough to know that was all the commitment he would get from her until she got over her anger at him. "I brought you a gift from my travels. Two gifts actually." He lifted the small parcel on his lap and handed it to her.

"You cannot buy your way back into my good graces."

"One part is a gift. The other a request."

With an arched brow, she accepted the package and untied the string. She set the package in her lap as she unfolded the muslin wrapping to reveal a length of yellow silk and a green box. At her questioning gaze, he prompted her to open the lid. From inside, she withdrew a small crystal vial with a gold cap. Instantly, a floral scent filled the room.

"You brought me perfume?"

"From France."

She removed the cap and drew a deep breath. "I smell jasmine, roses, patchouli, oranges, and vanilla." She replaced the lid and smiled. "All right. I forgive you for leaving me behind for five years."

"I would love to hear more about your time away at school," he prompted.

She set the bottle of fragrance aside. "Perhaps later. Right now, I'm more interested in why you would bring me this." She lifted the silk from the package. "It resembles the fabric of the Fairy Flag."

"Which brings me to my request. Now that I am home, I need to ready the men for a potential war with the clans. It would be easier to rally their spirits if the Fairy Flag were once more in its place of honour in the drawing room for all to see."

She frowned. "It looks nothing like the Fairy Flag."

"That's where you come in. I would like you to embroider the fabric so that it resembles the original."

She straightened. "You know I don't sew that well. Nor

is it as aged or distressed as the original."

"You may bring one person into your confidence in order to see the task done. I am willing to pay them handsomely to keep their silence."

Rowena's brow furrowed. "Why would you want to fool everyone into thinking the flag has been returned?"

He hoped he could explain things in a way that would make her understand what he knew in his gut to be true. "The flag is such a part of our clan identity. Simply having the flag in our possession, magical or not, has helped us turn the tide in battle. I fear without it, we will fail no matter how well-trained the men are."

She nodded. "It has felt like something was missing in our lives since it was stolen."

By the MacDonalds he wanted to add, but knew that comment would not help his cause given his sister's attachment to Marcus. "Will you do it? Will you help me create a replica to take the flag's place until I can get the original back?"

"You intend to steal it back?"

"I intend to bring the Fairy Flag home. One cannot steal back what rightfully belongs to them, only return it." At her nod, he continued, "Will you help me and keep this secret between ourselves?"

After a short pause, she nodded. "I will ask Roberta, our laundress, to assist me. Not only is she loyal to this clan, she is a wonder with a needle. If anyone can distress the fabric to look aged, it would be her."

"Thank you, Rowena." He stood and moving to her side, pressed a kiss to the top of her head. "I am so happy to see you, and I am proud of the strong, determined woman you've become."

"Even if I want to pursue a relationship with someone you disapprove of?"

"I trust you, and because of that, I am willing to get to know him better during supervised visits."

She nodded. "I've missed you, Alastair."

"It is good to be home again." He left her then, feeling cautiously hopeful that his plan to strengthen his clan mentally and physically might work after all. Still not ready to return to the great hall, Alastair wandered up to the one place where he felt truly at home.

The cool night air washed over Alastair as he stood atop the battlements of the old keep. He drew a deep breath of the familiar salt-scented air and felt himself slowly relax as he looked out over the silvery-grey waters of Loch Dunvegan. This was his special place—a place where he had come for years to escape his father's dominance and to clear his head. Despite the fact his father was dead, the man's spirit, it seemed, still lingered every bit as much as his mother's did. The minutes passed by in silence as the grey sky faded to an inky black.

"I thought I'd find you here." Graeme's voice came from behind Alastair, breaking into his thoughts. "Everyone is waiting for you in the great hall. Mrs Honey has cooked a feast befitting the prodigal son."

Alastair couldn't help but smile as he turned to his friend. "I can only imagine." Mrs Honey's way of showing love was through her cooking. "I needed a moment after speaking with Rowena. She's convinced she's in love with that MacDonald boy."

"He's hardly a boy."

"You know what I mean. What if the MacDonalds are only using her to get to me and infiltrate our clan?"

Graeme lifted a brow. "Are you so certain the lad isn't truly in love with your sister?"

"How could he be? Our families have been rivals for centuries." Alastair sighed. "I knew coming home would be hard, but I thought the demons I would face would be less tangible—the memory of my father, the spirit of my mother, and my own pain over losing Gwendolyn on our wedding day. Not enemies amongst us and poor security by untrained men." He gave a soft sigh. "I'll find a solution to Rowena's infatuation, and all else that needs set right."

"None of that sounds very diplomatic. Didn't you come here to be a peacemaker?" Graeme asked.

"I thought the peace agreement would be between the MacLeods and the MacDonalds, not members of my own family and clan."

"Needless to say, you've got your work cut out for you, but then again, you were never one to give up no matter how difficult the task."

Alastair turned back to the balustrade, his gaze shifting to the south and the Fairy Tower. Had his mind been playing tricks on him when he'd seen Gwendolyn's face in the window? What other explanation could there be?

Aye, he wasn't one to give up, but sometimes things ended whether he wanted them to or not. "Let's go. I've been out here too long as it is." He'd barely finished the last word when a chill ran up his spine. Someone was watching them. He could feel it in his bones. And he didn't like it one bit.

He looked down. At the base of the old keep he saw a grey cloak as it rippled around a feminine form. He'd only returned to Dunvegan a few hours ago, and already the spirits of the dead were making themselves known. A sudden chill gripped him. Was he the only one who had seen Gwendolyn and now his mother? "Graeme." Alastair pointed at the specter in the distance. "Do you see her too?" *The Grey Lady had never appeared outside of the old keep since his father murdered her there.*

"Aye. Could it be your mother has broken the chains that bound her to the old keep for so long?" Graeme came beside him and stared at the figure below as it flowed across the front courtyard and towards the new keep.

Alastair narrowed his gaze, trying desperately to see the woman's face. Yet all he could make out was a corona of bobbing golden-blond curls beneath the hood of her cloak. The night air became suddenly cold. As cold as the grave. He shook his head, dispelling the memory of Gwendolyn's hair. "Come, let's see who or what this is." He turned towards the doorway leading to the stairs, with Graeme following close behind. The two of them emerged from the stairway and rushed outside. The old keep was separate from the new keep. Quickly, Alastair raced towards the front of the castle where he had spotted the figure. Seeing no outward sign of the woman, he moved towards the entrance of the new keep. As he placed his hand on the latch, Alastair heard the howling of dogs, far off, and a short, shrill scream, choked to silence before it reached its crescendo.

His breath caught. Though the sound had been a scream, the tone was not unfamiliar to him.

Gwendolyn.

"Your mother's voice sounds different than I remember."

"That wasn't my mother. It appears Dunvegan is now haunted by the spirits of both my mother and my once betrothed."

Graeme startled. "I don't know much about ghosts, but if Lady Gwendolyn died on the rocks below the castle, why would her spirit linger here?"

Alastair jerked around. "How am I to know? But I saw her, and I heard her voice only moments ago. I am convinced of that."

"Is there anything to be done about either spirit?"

Alastair's hands fisted at his sides. "I used to find my mother's presence here comforting. Mayhap in time I will feel similarly about Gwendolyn."

"You're certain she died the day of your wedding?"

Alastair inhaled sharply, his muscles stiffening as his gaze swept the hazy darkness settling about the castle. "All that remained of her on the rocks below was her bloody and tattered wedding gown and a bloodied lock of her hair. 'Twas high tide that day. I always assumed her body was swallowed up in the waters of the sea loch."

He turned back to the door and pulled it open as all his frustration coiled in his stomach. Mrs Honey might have prepared a fine meal to celebrate his return, but he was almost certain he wouldn't be able to consume one bite. "Let us leave these ghosts behind and make our way inside."

"The entire household came out to celebrate your return."

"Then let's not keep them waiting any longer," Alastair said as he took the stairs to the first floor of the castle two at a time, heading for the great hall.

Before they entered, Graeme stopped Alastair with a hand on his arm. When he turned to see what his friend wanted, Graeme simply smiled and said, "I always knew you'd be a fine laird."

"Thank you for that. You're always at my side, aren't you?" Alastair said as they entered the chamber together.

"Always."

They were barely through the threshold when several dozen men and women came rushing to greet them.

"So, then. Ye've come home." Mrs Honey was the first to step close with a crooked smile and her eyes shining bright. "'Tis about time. We've missed yer comely face nigh these long years."

Alastair drew into an embrace of the woman who had spoiled him with treats from her kitchen all through his youth. "Not as much as I've missed you."

An eruption of cheers rang out as others came forward, offering greetings and hearty, shoulder-thumping embraces. Alastair smiled easily. It was good to be home and surrounded by those who loved him. Yet, even as he celebrated with his men and his servants, Alastair kept his eyes trained on the two women who stood apart from the others.

Alastair excused himself and made his way to where his sister stood beside his chatelaine near the head table. "Mrs Morgan, you haven't aged a day since I left." Her hair was still a vibrant red and her face, though lined, retained a hint of youthfulness. "You are just as beautiful as ever." Mrs Morgan was a short firebrand of a woman who barely reached the height of Alastair's chest. But her lack of stature never seemed to stop the woman from bending people to her will.

"A fine welcome home fer a lad who never bothered tae send a single scrap of a note tae let us ken how ye faired. If it were up tae me, I'd send ye back tae France until ye learned some manners."

"Mrs Morgan." Alastair laughed. "I'm glad to see you

haven't changed a bit. Still running the place like a sergeant, I see."

"Someone had tae." She wagged her finger at him. In response, he gathered her in his arms and twirled her so hard and fast that her black bombazine skirt belled up, revealing the stockings tied around her knees. "Enough. Ye rascal. Put me down before ye break this old woman."

Alastair set her down with a smile. "I missed you too."

She straightened her skirts with a scowl that became a smile. "Ye better take yer place at the table so Mrs Honey can serve ye the meal she's been preparin' all day."

Alastair turned to his sister and offered her his arm. "Shall we, Rowena?"

She accepted his arm and allowed him to escort her to her place beside him at the head table. Callum sat on the other side. Alastair relaxed into his chair and served first Rowena, then himself from the platter of meat and vegetables that had been set before them. Callum served himself next.

"Has anything strange been happening around the castle since I left?" he asked his brother and sister.

"Such as?" Rowena asked, forking a piece of roasted mutton into her mouth.

"Strange noises? New apparitions?"

"Old castles are filled with strange noises," Callum said.

Rowena set her fork down as she tipped her head to the side, thinking. "I've only seen Mother's ghost on occasion in the window of the Fairy Tower. But she's been very active these past five years."

"How so?" Alastair asked.

Rowena met his gaze. "Everyone here has heard the rattling of chains and odd knocking sounds coming from the tower all times of the day and night."

"Do you ever hear screaming coming from the tower?"

Rowena shrugged. "At times. That and crying, but we all assumed it was the Grey Lady."

Alastair stiffened. "Do you ever go to see her?"

Rowena frowned. "Nay, never. Father forbad us from doing so."

"Father died over a year ago."

Rowena flinched at the force behind the words. Callum's featured hardened.

"You've never been tempted?" he asked the two of them in a softer tone.

"We never thought about it, even after Father died. He was adamant that no one should release Mother," Callum said.

Rowena looked away. "I am not so brave as you, Alastair."

He took her face in his hands and turned her gaze back to his. "You are braver than you think. Aren't you the one who thinks you fancy a MacDonald?"

A hint of a smile pulled up the corner of her mouth.

He released her. "Have you ever seen the ghost of Gwendolyn roaming the castle grounds?"

"Nay." Rowena's smile vanished. "Nor along the shoreline." She moved closer. "Why, have you seen her?"

"I thought so, in the window of the Fairy Tower when I arrived and not long ago in the front courtyard."

Rowena's eyes went wide. "Perhaps her spirit needed you to be here for it to materialise. You left right after she fell to her—" Rowena stopped abruptly. "I'm sorry, Alastair. I did not mean to upset you."

"You didn't," he lied, trying to stem the pain rising in him. "I can't bring her back, and I've stopped punishing myself for something that feels like it happened half a lifetime ago."

Rowena brought her cool hand to cover his. "It would be understandable if it took some time to set her from your thoughts now that you are home."

Alastair pushed his chair back from the table and stood. "I am not going to live in the past," he said more forcefully than he intended. At his outburst, a hush came over the chamber as all eyes turned to him. Irritated with himself, he turned to his sister. "Let's start by opening the Fairy Tower once more."

"Are you serious?" Callum asked as he stood.

"But Father forbad it," Rowena said again and stood as the blood drained from her face.

"Father is no longer laird. I am. If I want the Fairy Tower opened, it shall be opened. For I have no fear of ghosts."

Even as he said the words, a chill rippled down his spine. He had a healthy respect for otherworldly beings, but he would not allow them to stop him from doing what needed to be done.

Graeme, who was seated two seats down, stood. "The men and I shall support you in any endeavor you choose."

Alastair strode through the great hall until he stopped before an arrangement of battle weapons upon the far wall. He reached up and drew a battle axe down, then hoisting it over his shoulder, he exited the chamber and headed for the main staircase. He flung open the castle door and moved quickly towards the doorway to the Fairy Tower with the rest of the castle at his heels, a cacophony of voices coming from the crowd.

"He'll set the Grey Lady free," someone called out.

"'Tis his mother. Why should she not be allowed to roam the castle as she would have while she was living?" a female voice countered.

"What if there are other spirits?" someone cried from the throng.

"Or fairies."

Alastair stopped and turned to face the crowd. Everyone had now fallen silent. The residents of the castle looked at him with both expectation and fear. At the sight, guilt swamped him that he was only now returning as laird. There was an obvious need for leadership. A bigger need for reason, and for someone to wipe away the stain of his father's ruthlessness. "Our dealings with fairies are in the past. And as for the Lady Janet, she was only ever gentle and kind during her life. Why would she be anything but the same in her afterlife?"

Determined to proceed, he turned back to the door and, raising his battle axe, swung it down once, then twice against the iron chains and the stout lock that barricaded the door. The screech of metal against metal filled the night air, followed by the clang of the iron as it fell to the ground, released from its duty of keeping the castle residents out of the tower. Seven years had passed since his father had placed the chains there in an effort to keep the ghost of his mother inside.

Tonight, she would be freed, along with any other spirits who had taken up residence in the castle. An excited chatter built behind him as the others waited for the doors to open. Gripping the wrought iron handles, Alastair forced the wooden doors to part. A thunderous boom reverberated through the emptiness as the doors hit the stone walls of the tower.

Still clutching the battle axe, Alastair drew a sharp breath and stepped into the darkened tower. Excitement wedded with hesitation made his breath catch. The harsh tenor of his breath echoed loudly all around him. Faint moonlight streamed through the open doorway, illuminating only a couple of feet in front of him. The scent of undisturbed air, heavy with dust, filled his senses.

Behind him, light flared. Alastair turned to see Graeme coming towards him with a torch in either hand. "Here, take this." Graeme handed him one of them.

Flickering light splashed across the ground floor of the tower, revealing only an empty space. They waited as a silent group, peering into the dimness for the oft-seen flash of grey, to hear the low moan, to spy the edge of a not-quite-seen face marked by a silver tear, but no manifestation came.

"Sorry to disappoint all of you, but there are no ghosts here to greet us," Alastair said for the benefit of the crowd behind him.

There were groans of disappointment and the sound of shuffling feet as many of those who had followed returned to the main keep until only he, Rowena, Callum, and Graeme remained.

"Mother's not here?" Rowena's voice filled with disappointment and a hint of fear.

"Not unless she has taken up residence in one of the upper chambers," Alastair replied. "Shall we go and see?"

"I'm up for it," Callum said with an eager smile.

"That's what you wanted, wasn't it? To prove that Gwendolyn is not here?" Rowena asked.

"Perhaps neither Mother nor Gwendolyn are here any longer. Perhaps Father's death and my coming home set them free. Come." He stepped towards the stone staircase that led to the first floor. "I'll go first. Stay behind me, and Callum and Graeme will follow behind you."

As they approached the spiral stairs, the torchlight twisted and danced upon the stone walls and created writhing spirits on the floor in front of them. Rowena grasped hold of the edge of her brother's shirttail and followed.

Alastair used the torch to burn through the cobwebs that had formed over the years. He took the steps upwards as cold dampness seeped into his bones. On the first floor, he let the light splash across the chamber, only to reveal dust-laden furniture that had been long forgotten. The thick scent of undisturbed air came to his nostrils. "Empty as well." He moved back towards the stairs when a strange sound, like a muted rustling of chains sounded from above.

"Someone or something is here," Graeme whispered, holding his torch out in front of him.

A strong sense of premonition made Alastair's skin tingle. The unusual sensation knocked him off-kilter, but he held tight to the torch in his hand. Suddenly, a flash of light as bright as lightning from the sky pulsed through the room. Alastair shielded his eyes from the unearthly brightness as a prickle of ice touched his cheek. Alastair shivered at the unexpected sensation and drew a breath and held it, centering himself and his emotions as he prepared for whatever came next.

The light softened. The chill vanished, replaced by a delicate caress that filled his body with an overwhelming sense of peace and tranquility.

"You were right, Alastair. Mother's here." Rowena's

voice was no longer fearful. Instead, it held the same calmness he experienced.

A mist gathered in the corner of the chamber and grew denser until the image of a woman appeared. Her dark hair, soulful grey eyes, and ivory skin were as he remembered. It was not fear that filled him in that moment, but a deep yearning for the woman this apparition had once been. "Mother."

She said nothing, and yet he felt words form in his mind.

I've missed you, Alastair, Callum, and Rowena. I've missed my children so much.

Rowena sobbed softly as she released the death-grip she'd had on his shirttail. "We've missed you too, Mother. We're so sorry Father not only robbed you of your life, but also that he locked you away from us."

At the sight of his mother, Alastair's chest tightened. He didn't understand what was happening, but he didn't need to. That some part of his mother still remained in this world brought warmth to his chest. "Are you alone here in the tower?" he asked. "Is Gwendolyn somehow with you?"

As soon as he asked the question, his mother's image grew more faint. The air in the chamber became chill and she floated towards the stairs.

"She wants us to follow her," Rowena said.

Alastair turned to his sister and brother. "Stay here. We have no idea what awaits above."

"Don't be absurd. We wouldn't miss this for anything."

Rowena moved past him and up the staircase after her mother. "This is the most exciting thing to happen around here in ages. I'm glad you opened the tower. It's time to release the secrets of our past."

Alastair scrambled to catch up with his sister, with Graeme and Callum trailing close behind. He and Graeme did not expect warfare in the ancient tower, but neither of them wanted to leave Rowena unprotected either.

They followed their ghostly mother up to the second floor when they heard faint voices calling out. *Help us, please. Help us.*

"What was that?" Callum asked. "It didn't sound like a ghost."

Just then, a massive armoire leaning against the wall pitched towards Rowena. Alastair shot forward, dropping his torch and the axe before sweeping her out of the way. The heavy wooden furnishing crashed to the floor with a thud that echoed through the otherwise undisturbed chamber. The brittle wood splintered and sent large chunks flying. Alastair covered his sister with his body, sparing her injury even as a few splinters pierced his flesh.

"Are you both unharmed?" Graeme asked as he removed chunks of wood from Alastair's back and legs.

Callum came to his side. "There's blood on your shirt, Alastair."

"'Tis nothing. Only splinters." Alastair pulled back from covering his sister, then stood, before helping her to her feet.

"I'm sorry to have forced you to the ground without warn-ing, but that heavy armoire could have seriously harmed you. Are you well?"

Rowena shook out her skirts and ran a hand across her bound hair. "I'm fine, but why did the armoire fall? And don't blame this on Mother. She was already up the next staircase when it tilted in our direction."

"It wasn't our mother, but someone of this world. I felt more than saw someone move past us in the shadows. Did you get a look at them, Graeme?"

"Nay," Graeme said as he retrieved the battle axe from beneath the shattered wood. "My focus was on the two of you. But I also saw something slide past, heading down the stairs."

"Go after them, Graeme and Callum." Alastair picked up the fallen torch. "Rowena and I will continue here."

Graeme handed Alastair the battle axe, then headed down the stairs in pursuit. Their assailant had a significant head start, but any information Graeme or Callum could glean would be most helpful.

Alastair turned his attention to the spiral stairs where his mother's spirit waited. Her hands were clenched and a worried expression lingered in her eyes. "We are both well," Alastair assured her.

At the words, his mother nodded, then turned and start-ed up the stairs once more.

Follow.

The word filled his mind as he clutched the torch and the axe in his hands and, this time, took to the stairs before Rowena. Their mother slipped right through the door at the top, leaving him and Rowena outside the bolted and locked barrier. Had his father installed this obstacle? It had never existed when Alastair had explored the tower as a child. He passed the torch to Rowena. "Stand back."

Once his sister had taken several steps back down the stairs, Alastair raised the battle axe over his head and brought it down hard against the lock. It shattered and fell with a clang against the wooden floor. He quickly slid the bolt back and raising the axe once more, prepared himself to greet whatever secrets were hidden inside.

CHAPTER FOUR

ALASTAIR CLUTCHED THE handle of the battle axe in his hands and opened the door. The wooden barrier struck the opposite wall with a loud thud as he stepped into the darkness and froze. The first thing that came to him was the smell of decay and unwashed bodies. The second was the sight of his mother's ghost hovering over a young woman huddled against a wall, shivering in the cold night air. The third was that of the boy who stood against the opposite wall with the heavy chain in his hands. "Who are you? What are you doing in the tower?"

"Drop your weapon," the boy said with a tremble in his voice, though he appeared ready to deflect whatever blow might come his or the girl's way.

For a moment, Alastair and the boy stared at each other without sound or movement before Alastair set the axe aside, then took a torch from his sister's hand. He held the light closer to the young woman and studied her face. Could the face in the tower window have been hers? His gaze lowered to take in the rest of her appearance. "My God," he breathed as he noted the shackle at her ankle, and also the boy's. "You are not here of your own choice. How long have you been held prisoner here?"

The boy dropped his chain, his gaze shifting to the wall beside him. "Most of our lives, it seems."

Alastair held the torch closer to the stone that had been scraped with lines. "Do those etchings mark the days you've been here?"

"Aye," the boy replied hesitantly as his gaze shifted back to Alastair.

The boy stared at him as though taking in every detail of his person and his dress as though he were a curiosity, which for this child he was exactly that. Alastair's heart clenched. The boy and girl had been in the tower for years. But who were they? The boy appeared to be around eleven or twelve years of age. The girl perhaps fourteen. They were both familiar, yet he couldn't recall where he knew them from. As the girl continued to shiver, Alastair removed his surcoat. "Here, this should help keep you warm."

She flinched away as she stared at him with wide eyes, then her shoulders relaxed. She nodded and allowed him to drape the heavy garment around her slender shoulders. "Thank you, sir," she replied, her teeth continuing to chatter.

Alastair knew he should get them out of there, but instead he simply stared at them, unable to do anything more. Both the boy's and the girl's golden hair was dull and matted with filth. Their skin was grey and their flesh, that should have been healthy and vibrant, shrank from their bones, leaving them gaunt. Deep purple smudges ringed their eyes and their hands were stained black.

Rowena stepped into the chamber, flooding it with light. "Has our mother been protecting you?"

"The Grey Lady?" The boy shrugged. "She has not hurt us, which is what we feared at first."

"She is kind," the girl said. "Though she cannot talk, she sings to me by putting the words and the melodies in my head."

"Aye, and then you sing them to us, over and over again," the boy complained with a dramatic roll of his eyes.

Sing them to us? The boy's words would imply a third person. Or did he mean his mother's ghost? Alastair's thoughts were broken by the sight of the Grey Lady as she circled the girl in a flitting, almost jubilant way. Then, in a burst of brightness, she vanished, leaving stunned silence in her wake.

"No matter how many times she does that, I'm still amazed every time," the boy said.

"Aye," Alastair breathed, relieved to hear his mother's ghost was more calm than angry. She had every right to be a bitter and enraged spirit after the way their father had treated her at the end of her life. But it was always his mother's way to find the good in everything, no matter how terrible it was.

Rowena stepped forward, her gaze narrowing on the girl. "Is that one of my old dresses?"

The girl's face paled to a ghostly white and shivers racked her frail body once more.

At her continued shivering, something inside Alastair finally broke his fascination at the horrors before him. "I am certain she had far greater need of the garment than you did, Rowena."

"I agree," Rowena said, coming to the girl's side and placing a gentle hand on her arm. "I have many more gowns we can have fitted for you until we can make new ones that are yours alone."

The girl's eyes widened. "Are we to leave the tower?" Speaking sent her into a coughing fit.

Alastair's lips tightened grimly. "Aye. We need to get you out of here." He handed the torch to his sister and picked up the axe once more. "Put your foot out," he said to the girl.

Instead of doing as he'd asked, she made a barely audible sound as she cowered in fear against the wall.

Alastair cursed himself for a fool. What did he expect? The girl had been treated as nothing more than a caged animal for years. "I should have explained myself better." He softened his tone. "I intend to break the chain from the shackle at your ankle so we can take you back to the castle. There, we will free you from the iron band."

Her eyes grew wider, revealing a piercing shade of blue. "You'll take us to a place that is warm?"

The colour was unique, and so familiar. . . Alastair wondered about where he'd seen such colour before as he nodded.

The boy crossed his arms over his thin chest. "What about our sister? How will she know where we are?"

Alastair frowned as his gaze shifted to a third empty shackle that lay against the floorboard along the opposite wall. "Your sister?" He'd been right in thinking a third person had also been here.

"Gwennie," the young woman said. "We won't leave without her."

Gwendolyn? Alastair inhaled sharply, his muscles stiffening warily as his gaze flew to the young woman's face. "Gwendolyn is alive?"

"Aye."

The news brought the same bittersweet sensation to his chest as it had when he'd first seen Gwendolyn, barefoot, her clothes torn, and her hair in disarray, amongst the ruins of her village. In the days following her disappearance on their wedding day, he'd been desperate to find any evidence to suggest she might still be alive. He'd searched the shores of the loch for hours, he'd prayed to a god who rarely listened to his pleas, he'd fought his own brothers when they'd begged him to acknowledge the truth—that she was dead. "Where is Gwendolyn?"

"The man who captured us took her. He's forcing her to haunt the castle just like the Grey Lady."

Alastair stepped closer. "The Grey Lady is dead. You said Gwendolyn was not."

The girl flinched against the wall. "Don't hurt us."

Alastair mentally cursed and forced himself to step back. The things these three must have endured over the years. . . "I promise never to hurt you." In a calmer voice, he asked, "Do you know who locked you in here?" He crouched to his knees, looking into her eyes. He had to gain her trust.

"Garrick MacDonald."

"Nay," Rowena gasped from behind him. "It can't be true. Not Marcus's clan."

"He told us his name on more than one occasion. 'Tis Garrick MacDonald. I promise you." The girl studied Alastair's face. The fear in her eyes faded, and she offered him a faint smile. "I remember you now. Gwennie told us stories about you over the years, about the day you two were supposed to marry. The day Garrick kidnapped all of us. She called you her *grá geal*."

Her bright love? "Why would Gwendolyn consent to playing the part of a ghost?"

"Garrick threatened to kill me if Gwennie didn't do as he asked."

Alastair tensed. "Where is Garrick now?"

"When he heard someone coming, he fled," the boy said.

The villain who almost crushed his sister with the armoire belowstairs.

"Alastair, if what they say is true, it's more important than ever to get them out of here before he returns." A tremor sounded in Rowena's voice.

Alastair turned to his sister. She must be devastated by the news. "I'm sorry, Rowena—"

Her features were tight as she shook her head. "My feelings on the matter are unimportant at the moment. Let's get them out of here. We can work through the rest later."

She moved to the girl's side. "If you are Gwendolyn's sister, then you must be Arabella."

Arabella offered Rowena a weak smile. "That's right."

Rowena turned to the boy. "And you must be Samuel."

"Aye," he said, straightening. "We want to leave, but what about our sister?"

"I'll send my men to search for her, and I'll have several come to the tower to await Garrick's return." Alastair held a growing ferocity in check. There would be time later to vent his anger over what the MacDonalds had done and continued to do to his family and their allied clans. In that moment, Alastair was suddenly grateful to have been named clan chief. His father's brutality had not stopped the feud between the MacLeods and the MacDonalds. He'd hoped diplomacy would be the answer, but perhaps it was time to take a subtle and more clandestine approach to ending the conflict once and for all. With the help of his own brothers, the four of them might finally succeed in bringing peace to the Isle of Skye.

"As long as you include me in your search, then Arabella and I agree. Set us free." The boy stepped towards them, causing his chain to rattle against the floorboards in an eerie echoing noise.

Rowena drew a tight breath. "That's the sound we've heard coming from the tower for years. Everyone was always so afraid of that eerie rattling. We always assumed it was our mother showing her anger over being trapped in the tower."

"The Grey Lady was never trapped in the tower," Samuel said. "I think she stayed to protect us from Garrick." He stretched out his leg. "Release me first so Arabella can see there is nothing to fear."

Alastair lifted the axe and swung it hard, severing the iron shackle from the chain.

Samuel stumbled to his sister's side and took her hand. "There is nothing to fear. Be brave and let's go find Gwennie."

At Arabella's nod, Alastair repeated the process. Once the prisoners had been set free, they stumbled towards the doorway. Samuel was able to walk with a slight limp on the leg that still held the heavy iron band. Arabella, however, stumbled and fell. She was so frail and weak.

Alastair knelt at her side. "Would you let me carry you down the stairs?"

At her nod, he scooped her into his arms. "Rowena, grab the axe," he said before carrying the girl down the stairs to safety. Rowena and Samuel followed close behind until all four stood outside of the tower. The moon was almost full, and the front courtyard was clearly illuminated. Alastair hurried towards the keep and the warmth it could provide the shivering and coughing girl in his arms.

"Stop," Arabella commanded. "Please, set me down."

"Whatever for?" Alastair stalled his steps.

"Because I want to smell the world for just one moment."

Befuddled by her request, he begrudgingly set the girl on her feet. Her slippers were so worn and threadbare they offered her little protection from the cold, and less support on the rocky ground. "Here, take my arm," Alastair said, lending her something solid to cling to. She placed her hand on his arm and closed her eyes. Her brother did the same, and they each drew a deep breath of the chill night air.

Tears sprang to Arabella's eyes, shimmering in the moonlight. "I don't remember ever smelling anything so wonderful."

"Gwendolyn was right." Samuel's voice filled with awe. "I smell the tangy scent of salt from the sea."

"And the heather smells woody, and mossy, and sweet." Arabella sighed with satisfaction. "I never thought I'd be free from the scent of death and decay." As she drew another breath, she started coughing again, doubling over before she finally stopped. In control once more, she straightened and opened her eyes. "This is truly heaven on earth." She turned to Alastair. "Thank you for coming to our aid. Everything will be perfect once Gwennie is with us."

Alastair wanted nothing more than to find Gwendolyn. He had so many questions for her once he did. The Fairy

Flag went missing the same day Gwendolyn had. He had wondered for the past five years if those two things were somehow connected. If Garrick MacDonald was responsible for imprisoning Gwendolyn and her siblings, could he have also been behind the flag's disappearance?

Rowena doused the torches in a nearby barrel of dirt before rejoining the others in the front courtyard. "If you'll allow us to take you inside, we can start the search for your sister."

Arabella nodded and tightened her grip on Alastair's arm as she attempted to walk to the castle's doorway under her own power. Her skin shimmered in the moonlight as palely as the tombstones in the family graveyard just outside the castle. She took several steps before her legs buckled.

Before Arabella hit the ground, Alastair scooped her up and carried her into the keep, then up the stairs to the family bedchambers.

At the top of the stairs, Mrs Morgan came forward to greet them. She stopped short when she saw the creature in Alastair's arms. "What in heaven's name is this?"

"Mrs Morgan, please send someone to the village to get a healer. They will need to look at both Arabella and Samuel Harris. And send two of my men to stand guard over these two."

"After all these years, the Harris children have been found?" Mrs Morgan's age-weathered hand flew to her lips, stifling her gasp. "Where? How? Is there a threat tae the household? Oh my goodness," she sputtered, waving a hand in the air. "Never ye mind me, there'll be time enough fer questions later." Her skirts rustled against the wooden floor as she disappeared down the stairs.

Samuel kept pace with him and Rowena despite his own lack of strength. Alastair tossed the boy an encouraging smile. The lad had a strong will. They both must, in order to have survived such an ordeal.

"Place Arabella in this room." Rowena brushed past Alastair in the hallway to open the door that was next to her own. "That way I can keep an eye on her."

Alastair set Arabella on the big bed at the center of the chamber then stepped back. "Samuel, you can take the chamber directly across the hall. That way you'll be close as well."

Samuel's gaze lifted to Alastair's. "I know I said I wanted to help with the search for Gwendolyn, but I am needed here. Please let me stay at Arabella's side. I can sleep on a pallet on the floor." When Alastair opened his mouth to object, Samuel added, "We haven't been apart for many years, and a pallet will be a luxury compared with what we've had in the past."

How could he object? If Rowena were in a similar situation, Alastair would not want to leave her side either. "Then it shall be so. In the meanwhile, I will have our cook send up something warm to eat and drink."

"And I will get water for a bath started for you both,

then find some warmer clothing," Rowena said as she turned and headed out the door.

Alastair pulled a thick tartan blanket up over Arabella's body before he stepped back. "Promise me when the healer arrives, you will allow her to examine you both."

"We promise," Samuel said, taking a seat on the bed beside his sister.

Alastair waited until Rowena returned before he left. He hurried below to join his men who had gathered in the front courtyard. Callum was waiting there, along with Graeme, and at least twenty others who were armed and ready for battle.

At Alastair's questioning look, Graeme shook his head. He hadn't managed to overtake Garrick as he'd run from the tower. Alastair frowned. They would find Garrick soon, then he would pay for all he'd done.

"Mrs Morgan said you found two of the Harris children, the younger ones, in the tower?" Graeme asked, bringing Alastair back to the moment.

Alastair nodded. "Chained and trapped."

Callum drew a harsh breath. "They were right under our noses the entire time?" He clenched his fingers together so tightly his knuckles turned white. "I should have—"

"You are not to blame here, Callum," Alastair interrupted. "The MacDonalds are."

"What do you mean?" Graeme's brow furrowed in a frown.

Alastair looked into the distance, seeking his foe in the shadowed darkness. "Garrick MacDonald has been holding them captive for the past five years. If he escaped you, that means he's still here in the castle somewhere." Alastair brought his gaze back to the men gathered. "I need five of you to head to the Fairy Tower. Two of you stay below and three others go up to the tower to wait in case Garrick returns there. The rest of us will fan out around the castle. Be aware, Garrick isn't alone. Gwendolyn Harris is with him."

Callum stepped closer. "As his prisoner or as his accomplice?"

Alastair checked his emotions. "Most likely as a prisoner herself. There was evidence Gwendolyn was chained in the tower as well as her siblings. They claim Garrick is forcing her to impersonate the Grey Lady in order to scare us all. So remember that if you encounter anything ethereal. 'Tis only a trick. Gwendolyn is alive and very real."

Alastair was raw and hurting simply thinking about what Gwendolyn and her siblings had been forced to endure over the past five years. He'd been such a fool to give up his search, to go away for so long. If only he'd come home sooner. . . Alastair balled his fists at his sides. He wanted someone or something to release his anger on, but that would not come until he found Garrick. Until then, there was no one to fight, no one to blame but himself. He could only proceed with the burning ache that compounded with regret and sorrow. "Five years." The words were a whisper that was stolen by the wind.

As the men dispersed in every direction in groups of four or five, Alastair's feet seemed rooted to the ground. "My God, how did they last so long?" He cleared his throat to rid it of its huskiness. "If I had only known. . ."

Graeme remained at Alastair's side. "Stop blaming yourself. You could not have known Gwendolyn was alive. The MacDonalds went to great length to deceive you."

"I left. I could have stayed and fought my father."

Graeme studied him for a long moment before he said, "Nay. You couldn't. Your father was not going to give you or your brothers anything but pain and heartbreak."

Alastair returned his friend's unwavering regard. "All except Callum and Rowena."

Graeme frowned. "Callum was too young at the time to make his way on his own. And your sister's world is different simply because she is a girl."

"As was Gwendolyn's world. As her betrothed, I was supposed to protect her."

"So you feel guilty. We've all failed at things. Stop filling a cup that is already overflowing." Graeme's gaze narrowed. "'Tis time to act. Let us find Gwendolyn and free her from Garrick's control."

Alastair nodded, grimly. "If I were Garrick and wanted to avoid detection, I'd hide in the secret passages that are rumoured to be within the castle walls."

Graeme gave him a puzzled look. "There are secret passages?"

"There were always talk of such things. My brothers and I looked for them for years, but we never found any. But that doesn't mean they aren't there. Perhaps with more mature eyes we might find what we missed as youths in the old kitchen or the old great hall."

Graeme removed a torch from its wall mount in the courtyard. "Then let us go find ourselves a villain."

They headed towards the oldest part of the castle. The old kitchen and great hall had been abandoned years before after the roof had started to fail. Other than the haunted Fairy Tower, it was the least used part of Dunvegan at present. The air in the chamber was cold and still. The soft tread of their footfalls was the only sound in the utter silence as they moved into the abandoned kitchen. Most of the cookware and tools had been moved to the new kitchen. All that remained was an empty spit in the giant hearth, a grinding stone, and a few forgotten kitchen items. Cobwebs lingered in the corners and caught the light of the torch, glistening like gossamer silk in the darkness.

"No one is here," Graeme said, his voice echoing in the emptiness.

The two of them spent several moments searching the old stone walls for signs of a secret passageway. When they found nothing, Alastair said, "Let's head to the great hall." He and Graeme followed the corridor from the kitchen to the great hall. The chamber they emerged into was large. Only a portion could be illuminated at a time with the light of the torch until Graeme made his way along the outer wall and set his flame to the sconces waiting there. Slowly, the center of the chamber came into view, revealing that the furnishings had been moved from the old hall to the new, leaving an empty space filled with only dust and debris.

When Graeme lit yet another sconce, the image of a woman, dressed all in grey, suddenly appeared at the far corner of the chamber. Alastair tensed. *The Grey Lady?*

As the spirit turned towards them, Alastair recognised that halo of blond hair, and the delicate features of a face that was etched in his memory. "Gwendolyn."

Instead of coming to him, she remained still and silent, yet held his gaze, pleading with him to forgive her for some unknown offense.

He raced forward, but when he grew near enough to take her hands in his, his fingers slipped right through her. She was there, and yet she wasn't. He felt the blood drain from his face as he stared at the image before him. He'd told his men to be wary of tricks, but this trick seemed so real. Was she dead then? Her siblings were convinced she was alive.

Graeme reached Alastair's side and held the torch towards the image. It vanished. "How is this possible?" Graeme stepped back, taking the light source with him, and Gwendolyn's image suddenly reappeared.

"This has to be a trick." Alastair turned away from the

illusion of Gwendolyn and peered into the darkness behind them. He grabbed the torch from Graeme's hands and strode towards the back of the chamber. Scrambling noises ensued, then a thump. By the time Alastair reached the area, nothing but emptiness remained. A quick twist behind him confirmed that the image of Gwendolyn had disappeared also.

"What just happened? Is Gwendolyn alive or dead?" Graeme asked as he joined Alastair.

Alastair frowned, trying to keep hope from building inside him that his one-time bride might still be alive. "'Tis a ploy of some sort. It must be. Garrick is playing with us. He has Gwendolyn, and he wants us to know he is in control of what happens to her." Alastair glanced at the panelling on the wall behind them. "It took Garrick and Gwendolyn only seconds to disappear, meaning there must be a secret door in this panelling somewhere." He moved to the panelling and starting from the corner, poked and prodded the elaborately carved wood.

Graeme joined in the search. "You really never found any secret passageways during all the years you've lived here?"

"Now that I think back, my brothers and I did find one behind the chapel in the older portion of the castle. We assumed it was some sort of priest's tunnel that was used during the Reformation. We never found anything else, so we assumed only the chapel had such a secret system of moving about."

"And now?" Graeme moved his fingers slowly over the

woodwork.

"We might have been wrong." Two minutes later Alastair found a catch hidden in the molding. He depressed the catch. Only a few steps away, a piece of the panelling popped free of the rest of the woodwork. He gripped the edge and swung it open.

"There really is a secret passageway." Surprise echoed in Graeme's voice.

Alastair didn't reply as he stepped into the darkness. Gwendolyn was in there somewhere and she needed his help. This time he would not fail her.

CHAPTER FIVE

TOO DISTRAUGHT AT seeing Alastair so close, and weak after years of imprisonment, Gwendolyn was unable to fight Garrick. Instead, she allowed him to force her through the secret passageway hidden in the walls of the old keep merely by his presence behind her. Garrick's progress was slow because of the heavy pane of glass he carried. He'd used the glass to throw her image from one part of the great hall to another. She didn't understand how the illusion had worked, but it had. Alastair had seemed convinced she was a ghost just as Garrick had wanted.

The only thing she'd truly been aware of while Garrick played his cat and mouse game was Alastair himself. In the last five years, his face revealed his character more clearly. The youthful edges of his face had become harder. His cheeks were more clearly defined, and his dark eyes looked at things with more intensity. Those eyes were set under a broad forehead, straight dark brown brows, surprisingly thick lashes, full lips. His square jaw bore witness to his strength and stubbornness which had formerly hid beneath a cloak of heroic charm.

He was, by every measure, the exact opposite of his over-bearing father. Even years ago, she knew that was true. Alastair had proven he was every bit the warrior his father had been, but he was also gentle and kind. In the days they'd spent together between their betrothal and their wedding, she'd become giddy when Alastair drew near. Her breath had caught, and a sensation in her stomach had taken flight.

Those same sensations had swamped her moments ago upon seeing him again. But his eyes had been hard, unrelenting, filled with pain. Her stomach clenched at the thought. She'd done that to him, to them, by disappearing on the most important day in both of their lives thus far.

"Move faster," Garrick prompted from behind, indicating her steps had slowed.

She wanted to stop and challenge Garrick as she'd played out in her mind over the years. She would finally stand up to him and fight back. But how could she do such a thing when he held the lives of her siblings in his hands? With a soft sigh, Gwendolyn pressed forward into the darkness. She had no idea where she was headed, but it didn't really matter. Garrick controlled her life as much now that she was free of her chain as he had while she had been imprisoned in the tower.

Keeping her siblings safe was all that mattered.

"Gwendolyn!" A voice came from behind them in the darkness. The sound of it rocked her. She drew in a tight breath. It had been five years since she'd heard Alastair call her name. His voice was deep and low-toned, with a brogue that carried a certain tension today.

"Keep going," Garrick snarled, pressing her forward.

"Gwendolyn. Your brother and sister are free. They are safe." Alastair's voice was vibrant with urgency.

Her throat tightened as she twisted around. Could it be true? Had they been set free? Would she finally be able to take them away, to make a life for her little family someplace else? Instead of moving forward, she stopped. What did she have to lose? The air in the passageway was cold and dank, making it difficult to catch her breath.

"He's lying. I still have your siblings under my control. Do as I say or they will suffer," Garrick threatened.

Her mind spinning, Gwendolyn simply stared at the man before her. Who should she believe—the man who had hurt her and her family for years, or the man who had never once harmed her?

Garrick's breathing was tight and loud, giving evidence to his displeasure that she continued to remain where she stood. "Turn around and keep moving!"

Hope flared at the same moment she surged forward, hitting both Garrick and the heavy glass panel he clutched in his hands with the full force of her body. Her captor stumbled backwards at the unexpected attack. He would never be able to save the glass and recapture her at the same time. As he struggled to regain his footing, Gwendolyn realised he blocked her path back to Alastair. Too panicked to think of other options, she spun and raced through the tunnel ahead, not knowing where she was going. It didn't matter as long as she was away from Garrick.

Heavy footsteps followed behind and terror closed around her heart until she could scarcely breathe. Dank, smelly darkness closed in on her. The muscles of her legs cramped from the lack of use over the years, but she dared not stop. Clasping her skirt in her hands to keep herself from tripping, she hitched in a shallow breath and followed the corridor until it came to the end. She had to choose: left or right.

Without a hesitation in her step, she moved right, praying it would take her somewhere safe, somewhere she could at least hide. As her feet pounded against the stone floor, her hands clenched convulsively against the fabric in her grasp. She'd lived in fear for so long. She would run and keep on running for as long as she had to in order to find freedom.

A crash came from behind. At the sound, Gwendolyn stumbled, then caught herself and kept going. All that mattered was what lay before her. She ran faster, her breath coming in quick, painful gasps. Though she could not see them through the darkness, she could feel the walls on either side of the passageway were close to her body. Instead of disturbing her, she took comfort in the fact that even though she couldn't see through the darkness, she couldn't go astray in the chiseled-stone passageway.

Suddenly a grey image appeared before her, startling

Gwendolyn to a sudden halt. The Grey Lady's spectral-self floated above the stone floor, making her appear eerie and alarming, yet Gwendolyn knew she was not. The Grey Lady motioned, encouraging Gwendolyn to follow. Her hands were still bound behind her, and she longed to be free, but knew the Grey Lady could not free her. She would have to search for another way to sever the ropes at her wrists.

Gwendolyn stayed close as the Grey Lady's spirit cast a hazy light in the space around them. Gwendolyn raised her chin and made her way through the passageway. She heard the thudding of her heart in her ears and. . .and nothing else.

Her steps faltered. Garrick was no longer chasing her. Had he gone the opposite direction when the passageway had come to two divergent paths? Did that mean she would have time to hide herself? Or would Garrick be waiting for her when she and the Grey Lady exited the passageway?

Her own ragged bursts of breath thundered in the quiet. If Garrick was there, she'd find a way to fight him, to the death if necessary. For she would rather die than be held prisoner again.

Ahead, a tiny pinpoint of light appeared. With each step the light grew larger until Gwendolyn could clearly see stairs leading downwards. At the bottom of the staircase she came out into the old kitchen. It was empty, for which she was grateful.

The Grey Lady signalled for Gwendolyn to follow her from the chamber and into another darkened space. Instantly the smell of fermenting grapes hit her, and she knew they had entered the wine cellar.

Hide here.

The Grey Lady's words filled Gwendolyn's thoughts and sent a shudder of fear down her spine. "I cannot stay here. 'Tis another room that might trap me. Nay, I cannot do it."

Trust me.

"I do trust you. You have been nothing but kind to me and my siblings over the years, but you have to see that this chamber is no safer than the tower."

You will be safe. I will protect you.

"The promise of a ghost."

The promise of a mother.

That motive Gwendolyn understood. It was how she felt about her siblings. She'd do anything to protect them. That thought helped her step forward into the darkened space and behind the barrels of aging wine. Once she was settled in place, the Grey Lady left her in a flash of white light.

Gwendolyn remained where she was as silence settled around her. She sat back and prepared to wait. It was not what she wanted to do, but she had made a promise. Now that she was freed from most of the bonds that had kept her a prisoner for so long, she wanted to do something that would take her small family far away from Dunvegan, the MacDonalds, even Alastair. It would be better to leave and start fresh. Alastair would never want her to stay, not after humiliating him in from of his clan, even though she had not done so intentionally.

Worse than breaking her promise to him, she had done something he might not realise she'd done yet. But if she escaped her current predicament and found her way back to Alastair, she would have to reveal that she had stolen his clan's most prized possession. She'd stolen the Fairy Flag because Garrick had forced her to do so and then he'd handed it over to his clan. She was responsible for its loss, and for that unforgivable sin she might find herself hanging from the end of a rope. At the thought, her breath caught.

She had promised the Grey Lady she would stay. But perhaps it was better to leave now while she was still in control of her own fate. Garrick had not found her. And she knew from her past experience of the castle that there was a doorway from the old kitchen that led to the garden at the back of the castle. She could hide outside and find some way to sever her bonds until she could retrieve her brother and sister. Finally freed from those who would imprison or punish them, they could begin their lives anew.

Mustering her courage, Gwendolyn stood up to leave.

GARRICK RACED THROUGH the darkened passage, cursing himself a fool for allowing Gwendolyn to escape. He'd been making his way through these passageways for the past five years. He knew every inch of them. There was nowhere Gwendolyn could hide in the dark, narrow place. She could only follow the path to the old kitchen or to the old servant's hall.

He should have expected she'd fight back. Even after all these years he hadn't managed to tame her. Carrying the heavy glass panel he'd used to project her image had given her an advantage. He should have abandoned the glass the moment she'd turned towards him. He knew, even in the dark, that wild look in her eyes. She would fight him to the very end, which was why he'd chained her up. And even then, she'd almost bested him once.

She would not best him again. Gwendolyn Harris was a crucial element in exacting his revenge on the MacLeods. Garrick had to find her before Alastair did.

ALASTAIR PAUSED FOR a moment in his search to listen. Graeme stopped behind him and waited. The castle seemed strangely quiet from within its walls.

Several long moments passed when Graeme finally asked, "Did you hear something?"

"Nothing. That is what has me concerned."

"Because you think Gwendolyn truly is a ghost?"

Alastair turned to his friend with a frown. "Don't be ridiculous. She's as alive as you or I. It means she and Garrick may have settled in somewhere to wait us out."

"Where is there to go inside these walls?" Graeme asked.

"There is only one place that truly makes sense. Follow me."

GARRICK ENTERED THE old kitchen. It appeared empty, but then again Gwendolyn would hardly be waiting for him out in the open even though there were few places to hide. He checked the empty hearth, searching the darkened spaces at the corners that were large enough to provide some sort of shelter if someone was desperate enough.

He turned back to the room, and suddenly a grey hazy light appeared before him. The light brightened, became dense, until the image of the Grey Lady hovered above the stone floor. Garrick winced at the look of displeasure upon her face.

Begone.

Her voice filled his thoughts. "You are no barrier to me," Garrick said as a nervous laugh escaped him. He walked through the lady's unsubstantial form.

Begone!

The word seemed to echo all around the mostly empty chamber. The specter backed up, blocking his path once more.

"You don't scare me," he said in an unsteady voice that

belied his words.

He saw the ghost's eyes narrow just as pain erupted at the back of his head. A single candleholder with the stub of a candle crashed to the stone floor and rolled back towards the hearth where it had previously sat.

Garrick brought his hand to the injured spot just as a ladle that had been on a hook near the hearth slammed into the right side of his face. "Argh! Stop that." He ducked, barely avoiding a pewter mug that also came at his head.

Begone!

Garrick rubbed his aching head. All he had to do was race through her. And yet he hesitated. Beside him, the handstone wobbled against a quern that had once been used to grind grain. Slowly it lifted, came towards him. He turned and bolted back up the passageway, away from the specter who seemed intent on killing him.

ALASTAIR HEARD A clattering sound, followed by a second softer thud, then a thunderous crash and footsteps heading away from the kitchen and towards the servants' hall.

"Should I follow the footsteps, while you see what all the racket was about?" Graeme asked.

"Aye," Alastair replied as he moved towards the old kitchen. Heart pounding, he raced through the semi-darkness. At the entrance to the old kitchen, he came to a halt at the image of his mother standing in the doorway. She signalled with her hand that he should follow her inside the wine cellar. A soft iridescent glow coming from his mother's form lit the chamber, enough for him to make out the slim silhouette of another woman standing beside a barrel of wine.

When Gwendolyn saw him, she gasped.

Alastair swallowed thickly. Was she real this time or another illusion? For years he'd imagined her like this, standing so close before him, ready to apologise for abandoning him. But she'd always been a figment of his imagination. The only thing that had been real was his desire to see her again.

He took two steps towards her and hesitantly reached for her face.

She shuddered but did not step away.

Her breath caught as he made contact with her exposed flesh. Gwendolyn's skin was cold beneath the warmth of his touch, but solid. Still needing more proof, he slid his fingers along her jawline towards her neck. Then he felt it: the gentle thudding of her heart against his fingertips. A strange shiver sped through his body. She was alive. She was before him.

"Gwendolyn?"

She looked past him, towards the Grey Lady. "You promised."

I am protecting you. His mother's words filled his mind. Had she promised Gwendolyn something? In a flash of white light, his mother vanished from the chamber, leaving him and Gwendolyn alone.

Gwendolyn brought her gaze back to his. In her eyes Alastair saw an aching, deep-seated despair. He knew that look. He'd experienced the emotions that came with it when his father had forced him and his brothers to leave their mother in the dungeon to die.

He shook off the memory. Gwendolyn was alive and needed his help. Her arms were behind her back instead of settled at her side. Further observation revealed she was bound with ropes. "Turn around so that I might free you of your bonds."

She nodded and turned, holding her arms slightly away from her ill-fitting gown as he reached for his dagger and sliced through the rope. It fell to the ground between them.

She turned around and massaged her abused wrists as her gaze met his once more. "Thank you for freeing me," she said, her voice trembling with emotion.

"It's going to be all right, Gwendolyn. Your brother and sister are safe. You are safe." He started to reach for her hand only to pull it back against his side.

She looked away, pretending not to notice. "Take me to them and we shall leave."

"Leave? Nay. You cannot leave." They weren't going anywhere. Too much still remained unknown, unsaid. But at the sudden look of terror in her eyes, he forced himself to relax and tried to soften his tone. "Garrick MacDonald still hunts you. And your sister has not yet regained her strength. I am sure all of you are weak and in need of nourishment, at the very least."

"Arabella?" Gwendolyn's breath caught. "Is her cough worse?"

"I cannot say for certain, but she is very weak, and I fear she became excessively chilled in the tower. I've sent for the healer in the village to attend both your sister and brother."

"Take me to her."

"Aye. Follow me." Alastair turned and headed back to the old kitchen. He kept looking over his shoulder to make certain Gwendolyn was still there. This time, she was real. This time he wanted to make certain she stayed at Dunvegan, at least for a while. Once they reached the door to the outside, Alastair headed for the new keep.

"What about Garrick?" Gwendolyn asked, her breathing stilted. When Alastair realised she must be every bit as weak as her siblings, he slowed his pace.

"My men and I will search the entire castle once I know you are safely settled with your brother and sister."

At the doorway to the keep, she paused and turned to look about her in the darkness. Her eyes filled with wonder and a satisfied smile came to her lips.

An emotion he'd never felt before came over him as he watched her, her face tipped up in the moonlight. It made his knees weaken and his throat close up. His toes and fingers tingled as though feeling warmth for the first time since he'd left his home many years ago. He could say nothing, do nothing but watch her. She closed her eyes and drew a long, deep breath of the night air.

"I was the lucky one to be chained near the window, but even so, I've dreamed of this moment where I could breathe the air free of everything that has shackled me for years."

Was she talking about her physical shackles, or something more? Perhaps her relationship with him? "I cannot imagine what that was like for you—for your brother and sister. People were so close, and yet no one would come to your aid because of the ghost of my mother." Alastair curled his fingers at his side. "My father's cruelty continues even though he is gone." A soft touch on his arm registered, and he turned to face the woman beside him.

She opened her eyes and turned towards him. Her fingers rested lightly on his right arm. "Consider this. . . I know what your father did to your mother was horrible, but if your mother was not of the spirit world, she would not have been there to protect us. She helped us so many times when we wanted to give up and let the cold take us. . .when we were lonely, she filled our hearts with song. . .when we were weak, she gave us strength. Your mother is the reason we are still alive."

Before he could respond, the door before them crashed open, slamming into the wall. Alastair spun to face Callum who filled the doorway. His brown eyes locked on Alastair. "The healer sent me to find you. You'd better come, and quick."

"What's wrong?"

Callum's gaze slid to the woman beside Alastair. "Is that really you, Gwendolyn?"

She nodded. "What is it? Is something wrong with my sister or brother?"

Callum dropped his gaze. "It's Arabella. She's coughing up blood. The healer says it's Winter Fever."

Alastair watched the colour drain from Gwendolyn's face.

"Nay." Gwendolyn's eyes filled with horror. "Where is she?"

"Second floor. The gold bedchamber," Callum said.

Gwendolyn's fear was palpable as she hitched up her skirts and darted up the stairs and into the castle. Alastair followed with Callum on his heels. "Tragedy seems to cloak Gwendolyn and her family."

"Nay," Callum replied. "Things will turn around for her now that she has you in her life once more."

"She is in my life, aye. But I am not for her."

Callum's brows came together. "How can you say that? You are betrothed."

"We were betrothed five years ago." Alastair threw a look at his brother. "Before I came here, I pledged myself to another."

"But Gwendolyn—"

"—was presumed dead."

Callum frowned. "And now?"

Alastair's gaze returned to the woman racing down the corridor, too far away to hear any of their conversation. "What matters now is the health of her sister. We can sort this out later."

"I don't have much experience with women, but I suspect going back on a betrothal might be something to sort out sooner rather than later."

Alastair watched Gwendolyn pause at the doorway of the bedchamber before she stepped inside. The sound of the forced cheer in her voice reached out to him and twisted his gut. She would be brave for her sister and brother as she probably had every day of the last five years.

At the shadowed doorway, he paused and looked to the bed where Gwendolyn now sat beside her sister, holding her hand while the healer mixed some kind of concoction with her pestle and mortar that would supposedly help ease Arabella's suffering. He turned to Callum. "Say nothing about what we've just talked about. Gwendolyn has enough to worry about at present. Promise me you will."

"I give you my word, but would it be wise for me to send for a solicitor? Perhaps he could advise you about how to handle two brides." Callum raised a brow.

Alastair scowled at his brother. "Your silence is all that is needed."

He would have to speak with Gwendolyn eventually, but for now he would focus on the challenge at hand. Gwendolyn did not need to know about Beatrice Lamont until Arabella's fate was determined. Judging by the pallor of her face and the slight blue colour about her mouth, fate could play an ugly hand at any moment. His standing in the doorway would not change anything. He had a villain to find. Turning away from the scene, he moved down the hallway to the stairs. Coming inside the castle just as Alastair was preparing to return to the old keep was Graeme. "Did you find him?"

"Nay," Graeme replied. "He disappeared into a network of tunnels within these walls."

"He won't escape us for long. Gather all the men. Send two to stand guard outside the gold bedchamber. I'll not leave Gwendolyn or her siblings unguarded again. The rest of us will pursue Garrick."

CHAPTER SIX

G WENDOLYN HELD BACK the tears that threatened as she sat on the bed next to her sister. She must be strong for Arabella. Her sister's eyes were closed, and she struggled to take each breath. Her chest rattled with her efforts. Dark circles appeared below her eyes and a bluish tint came to her lips—the only colour in her otherwise pale face.

How had her sister become so weak and frail in a matter of a few hours? Or was it that now she was in a fully lit chamber, Gwendolyn could see the telltale signs that had been there all along?

Gwendolyn reached out and stroked Arabella's cheek with the back of her hand. Her sister's skin glistened with sweat, and strands of her newly washed hair clung to her face, which was deathly pale. She tossed her head from side to side. "I am here, Sister. We are all safe," Gwendolyn said, brushing away a tendril of hair and wiping Arabella's forehead with the damp cloth from the side table. Arabella released a shallow breath as she settled into her pillow.

Seeking some sense of reassurance, Gwendolyn looked across the bedside to where Samuel sat in a chair, his features tight with worry. "It's going to be all right," she soothed, hoping and praying there was truth behind her words.

On the table next to the window, an older female healer mixed a potion with her mortar and pestle. "What has been done for her?" Gwendolyn asked.

"She was bathed and took a cup of bone broth while warming by the fire. But all that exertion has weakened her even more. I'm mixing her a tonic of hyssop, spurge, and hartshorn. It will help her breath more easily."

"Is there anything I can do?"

"Talk to her. She calms when she hears your voice." When the mixture was smooth, the healer carried it to the bedside. Gently lifting Arabella's head, she placed a spoonful in her mouth. Almost at once, Arabella fell into a paroxysm of coughing as the mixture slipped down her throat.

Not knowing what else to do, Gwendolyn placed her hand on Arabella's chest and hummed one of the songs the Grey Lady had taught them. The soothing actions worked. The fit receded and her sister's breathing came easier. After a few moments, she released a long, slow breath and opened her eyes.

"Gwennie?"

"I'm here, dearest."

"Garrick?"

"You don't need to worry about him any longer. You are safe. There are guards outside your door to protect you." Gwendolyn rinsed out the cloth that lay against her sister's forehead and brought it back to Arabella's face. When Gwendolyn realised her hands were shaking, she left the cloth on her sister's forehead and clutched them together in her lap. "Sleep. It is what you need to get better."

Arabella searched her face, no doubt seeing things Gwendolyn wanted to hide—her own exhaustion, her fear, and the fact that the trauma of this night had taken a toll on her own strength. "I'm sorry I'm being such a bother to you. You should leave me and get some sleep yourself. I can bathe my own face," she said, reaching for the towel.

"Hush." Gwendolyn batted Arabella's hand away from the cloth before removing it herself to rinse it in the cool water once more. "Please don't argue. I don't have the strength to fight you. Let me help you."

The glimmer of a smile came to Arabella's lips. "That's the first time you've ever admitted your weakness to me. I never thought I'd see the day."

"Are you laughing at me?" Gwendolyn asked with a smile touching her lips.

"I would never." A soft giggle erupted from Arabella.

Gwendolyn felt the tension in her shoulders relax as she rinsed the cloth yet again, bringing it across her sister's cheeks and chest. If Arabella could laugh, then things weren't all that bad, were they? "Close your eyes and rest."

"Aye, Gwennie. As long as you promise to do the same eventually."

At Gwendolyn's nod, Arabella shut her eyes and drifted

off to sleep. When Gwendolyn was certain her sister was deep in slumber, she turned to the healer. "Please tell me that she will be well soon."

"There are no guarantees with Winter Fever. I've seen miraculous recoveries and also watched as patients left this world in a fit of coughing." The older woman came forward and took the cloth from Gwendolyn's fingers. "As you told her, she needs sleep. And she must continue to take broth to rebuild her strength so that her lungs can heal. But you and your brother must take care of yourselves if you are to remain strong for Arabella." The healer looked across the bed to where Samuel now slept in the chair. "The both of you need to keep yourselves healthy and strong for your sister."

Gwendolyn nodded as she stood. "I should move him to his pallet."

"I'll have one of the guards do that while you bathe." The healer angled her head towards the hip bath that sat near the hearth. "The water might only be tepid by now."

Gwendolyn released a shattered breath that was part excitement, part relief. "It matters not. It has been so long since we've had such a luxury."

The older woman smiled as she turned back to the bag of medicines she had brought with her. She rooted around in it for a moment before turning back to Gwendolyn. "Take this. It will help you relax." She placed a large shaving of soap in Gwendolyn's hand.

The scents of mint, oats, and rosemary came to her as

Gwendolyn closed her hand around the precious item. "That is very kind of you, Mistress."

"Call me Lottie. Everyone does."

"Then thank you, Lottie. I appreciate your kindness to me and your skill in helping my sister."

A smile brought out the wrinkles around her kind eyes as she shooed Gwendolyn towards the bath. "There is a screen for your privacy. I'll sit with Arabella while you bathe and then sleep. And I promise to wake you if anything changes."

With a nod, Gwendolyn moved to the hearth and set up the panelled screen before she removed the gown Garrick had forced her to put on, then her well-worn chemise before she submerged herself into the hip bath. The water still held some warmth as she put the soap Lottie had given her to work. The fresh, clean scent of rosemary and mint filled the air as she scrubbed at her skin until it flushed pink before washing her hair.

Free of the dirt and grime that had caked on her skin for years, Gwendolyn noted the pinkness of her skin. It no longer held any trace of what had transpired over the past five years, except for the bruising at her ankle from where the shackle had been, and at her wrists where Garrick had bound them together. But those injuries too, would heal with time. And then she would be like everyone else—except for the bruises that would never fade from her memory.

After a final rinse, Gwendolyn stood, her skin tingling with cleanliness, and wrapped herself in one of the drying sheets that had been left for their use. Once she was done, she reluctantly put her soiled clothing back on, then sank down wearily into a chair by the fire, allowing the warmth of the flames to dry her hair and warm her body. Yet even as she relaxed, sleep refused to come. Her thoughts turned to Alastair.

He had seemed surprised to see her in the wine cellar, and almost afraid to believe she was real. Her fantasy of seeing him fall to his knees with remorse the moment he saw she was alive collapsed at her feet. Once his surprise had vanished, he'd watched her through narrowed eyes. She'd thought she'd memorised everything about him. But something more had changed in the time they'd been apart. His dark eyes now held a touch of cynicism, and everything about him exuded raw, brute strength. She had searched his face for some sign of the man who had asked her to marry him, but that man had vanished along with her dreams. Regardless of the changes in him, when he had touched her face, her skin had warmed, and when he moved his fingers to her neck, her heart had leapt in her chest in a way it hadn't ever before.

With a shake of her head, Gwendolyn forced herself to stop thinking of him. There were so many other things to worry about that she hardly knew how to cope. She and her siblings would not be able to leave Dunvegan any time soon, not before Arabella's health improved. Until then, they had no choice but to remain.

It was obvious, even though he had yet to say so, that Alastair had moved on with his life. The fact that he had looked at her with cold aloofness and had not pulled her into an embrace when he'd discovered she was real, told her everything she needed to know. She swallowed against the thickness in her throat.

She and her siblings were not shackled any longer, but they were still trapped. Therefore, she was going to have to find a way to survive the ordeal—without looking back on her past with Alastair—or looking forward into uncertainty. She simply had to live in the moment. Then when Arabella was healthy, they would leave. But whatever happened in the interim, Gwendolyn vowed to be completely composed and imperturbable, no matter what happened. She was no longer an infatuated young girl. Life had matured her, hardened her. When next they were together, she would prove to him that she no longer cared for him. She would move forward as he had.

With all that settled, she closed her eyes when a soft shuffling came from the doorway. A moment later, Rowena appeared followed by the Grey Lady. At the ghost's entrance, Lottie gasped and dropped to her knees behind the bed.

"All is well, Lottie," Gwendolyn said as she stood and headed for Rowena and the Grey Lady.

Lottie peeked over the side of the bed. "But the woman. . .the ghost. . .I've heard stories. . ."

"The Grey Lady is a benevolent ghost and was quite

helpful to me and my brother and sister over the past many years. There is nothing to fear."

Lottie remained behind the bed, using it as a shield. "Let us go out into the hallway," Gwendolyn suggested, "so that we do not wake Arabella or Samuel and give Lottie some peace."

"Agreed," Rowena said, exiting the chamber with her mother. "I came to see how you all were faring? Mother was agitated and seemed to think someone needed help. You were the first person who came to my mind."

Gwendolyn shut the door behind her. "Unless your mother can take the illness from Arabella's lungs, all is as well as can be here."

Rowena looked to her mother's ghostly form. "Can you do such a thing?"

Nay. If not Gwendolyn, then someone else needs our help.

Rowena frowned. "Where is Alastair? I thought he would be here with you?"

"He and the other warriors went to look for Garrick."

Alastair is in danger. The Grey Lady shifted back and forth in agitation.

Gwendolyn reached for her arm to comfort her, but her hand went right through the woman's appendage. Admonishing herself for forgetting the woman wasn't of this world any longer, she pulled her hand back. "Do you know where Alastair is?"

Aye. Come.

Without hesitation, Gwendolyn followed with Rowena at her side as the Grey Lady swept down the stairs and out of the castle, heading back to the old keep. A chill came over her as they entered the place where she had so recently left and had hoped never to enter again. But for Alastair, she could be brave. She owed him this much at least for freeing her from her prison.

———— ✦ ————

"WHAT DO YOU think Garrick seeks to prove by holding the Harris children hostage, and in your own home?" Graeme asked as Alastair led the way through the passageways in the older section of the castle.

"I have a few ideas, and I think you do too." Alastair held his torch high, illuminating the way. So far they'd found no evidence of Garrick or anything other than the usual vermin that seemed ever-present.

Graeme grunted. "It's a powerplay that will not end well for the MacDonalds."

Nay, this would not end well for Garrick MacDonald, especially if the villain had laid a hand on Gwendolyn at any point over the past five years. She was an innocent when they were about to marry. Was she still? At the thought he clutched the torch more tightly in his hand as he made his way through the sheer lacy cobwebs, indicating Garrick hadn't come this far into the labyrinth of tunnels.

Alastair was tempted to turn around, but something inside kept urging him to move forward for Gwendolyn's sake. Even after all the years, the pain, and her betrayal, she held a sort of power over him—a power he had to fortify himself against in any future encounters. He had moved on with his life. She deserved a chance to do the same. And that would only happen when Garrick paid for his ill deeds.

They followed the tunnels until they came out behind a panel in the drawing room located on the second floor of the old keep. The room was as empty and neglected as the rest of this part of the castle. Alastair suddenly wondered why his father had simply abandoned this portion of their home. There was nothing wrong with the building that a new roof and several days' cleaning couldn't fix. Perhaps, once he got more settled into his role as laird, he would see to its restoration.

"Where shall we search next?" Graeme asked, closing the panel behind them.

"While I continue to search, I want you to gather some men to guard each of these exit points in case Garrick decides to utilise them at some future time. The more we block off his access, the sooner he will have to show himself."

"It isn't wise for either of us to be alone," Graeme said with a frown.

"You and I are both far more skilled in the art of warfare than Garrick. I think we can manage ourselves for a few minutes alone."

Graeme still hesitated. "If you're certain."

"I am." He straightened. "The faster you leave, the faster you can return."

"Where will I find you?" Graeme asked.

"I'll head back to the old kitchen and wine cellar in case Garrick looped back around to hide there."

"I'll return shortly. Don't lose your head before then," Graeme's tone was light but the look in his eyes was as serious as Alastair had ever seen.

At Graeme's departure, Alastair headed down the main staircase to the old kitchen in order to save time. He would find his way back into the tunnels there to continue his search. Garrick didn't have many places he could hide. That Alastair or his men had not found the villain yet meant Garrick was somehow keeping one step ahead of them and was constantly on the move, avoiding detection. The trick would be to catch Garrick unaware, which Alastair intended to do. Once in the old kitchen, he set his torch in the hearth, and silently he backed up into the darkness of the tunnel to wait.

He didn't have to wait long. The door of the old kitchen opened, and two shadowed figures moved inside the chamber followed by the slightly illuminated figure of his mother.

"This old part of the castle feels haunted." Instantly, Rowena cringed and turned to their mother. "My apologies, Mother. I do not mean by you. There is an eeriness to this place that is hard to shake."

Alastair left the shadows. "What are you doing here?"

Gwendolyn and Rowena shrieked at his sudden appearance. Rowena's hand flew to cover her mouth, while Gwendolyn's face merely paled. Recovering from her fright, Rowena stepped forward and punched him in the arm. "You fool, you scared us."

He rubbed his assaulted appendage. "That doesn't answer my question. Why are you not in your beds?"

"Mother was worried you were in danger."

His gaze lingered on each of them in turn. "So the three of you thought to come to my rescue?"

Rather than look at him, Gwendolyn stared, as if fascinated, at the flames consuming the torch he'd set in the hearth.

Alastair stood there as well, nervously rubbing the palms of his hands against the sides of his legs. When he realised what he was doing, he clutched his hands before him. "Well, now that you see I am unharmed, you can leave."

Gwendolyn's gaze shot back to his. "Why are you alone?"

Before he could answer, a shuffling sounded in the tunnel behind him. He twisted around, expecting to see Graeme. Instead, Garrick MacDonald advanced on them. He smiled evilly as he came forward, swinging a sword at Alastair's head. "Five years I've waited for the heir to return home. Five long years, you bastard."

"Take cover." Alastair grasped Gwendolyn's arm and pushed her behind him before he did the same to Rowena.

He stepped forward inside the arc of the sword. He grabbed Garrick's arm with one hand and used the man's own momentum to throw him off balance. "You had no right to be here at all."

Garrick did not go down. Instead, he found his balance and continued to scowl at Alastair. "I had every right to violate you as much as you have violated me."

Alastair drew his own sword. "If you had a grievance with me, you should have taken it up with me and not three innocents."

He thrust his sword at Alastair's chest.

Alastair instinctively leapt back. The two men circled each other, looking for an opening to strike.

"I wanted to make certain before I killed you that you knew I could hurt you in ways you never expected. I waited to put a blade through your bride's chest until you could watch me do it—watch me rob you of every joy in your life just as your clan robbed me of mine when they murdered my parents and my siblings."

Garrick swung his blade, but Alastair blocked the strike just as he noticed a shadow shift behind his opponent. Alastair's blood ran cold when he saw Gwendolyn creeping up behind Garrick. He'd told her to hide. Quickly he shifted his gaze back at Garrick just as another swipe came at him.

Gwendolyn rose up behind Garrick and smashed a bottle of wine over his head. A sickening thump sounded as Garrick yelped and lurched forward, totally caught off guard.

Alastair stepped in and seized his opponent's sword, then smashed his boot into the side of Garrick's knee, taking him to the ground. He needed rope to tie the wastrel up but had none. Instead, while Garrick groaned and clutched his leg, Alastair pulled at the hem of his shirt, intending to rip it into long lengths. Gwendolyn stopped him with a touch to his hand.

"Nay, take the hem of my dress instead. 'Tis better to render unusable something that is already defiled." She lifted her skirt and before he could argue, she ripped a length of the hem from the gown and handed it to him.

"My thanks," he said and wondered whether she talked about herself or the gown as defiled? What had this vile man done to Gwendolyn over the past five years? Anger flared as he bent to tie Garrick's hands behind his back. He lifted Garrick to standing and with a strong hand on the prisoner, Alastair forced a limping Garrick forward and out the kitchen door. What Alastair wanted was to throw Gwendolyn's captor in the old dungeon that had taken his mother's life. Instead, Alastair headed towards the courtyard at the front of the castle.

"What will you do to him?" Rowena asked, practically running beside him.

"I should kill him for all he's done."

"Nay!" Rowena jerked on Alastair's arm, forcing him to stop. "Did you not hear him? Our clan killed his parents. He wants to kill you and Gwendolyn. When will the tit-for-tat end?"

Alastair wanted the feud to end as well, but the look in Garrick's eyes said this battle between the MacLeods and the MacDonalds wasn't over. Not by a long shot. He would leave Garrick in the dungeon in the new keep—a dungeon that was far more humane than the one in which his mother had died. Before he interrogated Garrick, he had to speak with Gwendolyn.

Once they entered the keep and headed down the stairs to the depths below the castle, Garrick struggled but Alastair held firm. "You haven't won this battle," Garrick growled. "I still possess something very precious to you. If I do not communicate with my clan by midnight tonight, they have orders to burn the pride of the MacLeods. Its magic will be lost to the world forever."

The Fairy Flag. Alastair hadn't been certain until that moment what had happened to the flag. "And lose the magic of the flag for yourselves?"

Garrick twisted back towards Alastair. Determination reflected in his enemy's eyes. "It would be worthwhile if it meant every MacLeod would mourn its loss."

Alastair locked his jaw. The man wasn't lying. Garrick would do it and that would be Alastair's legacy to his clan— the one who lost the Fairy Flag for all generations to come.

Alastair paused outside the door of the dungeon and turned to Gwendolyn and Rowena. "Rowena, go alert the guards that Garrick has been captured. I want four men here to guard him until I can speak with him." To Gwendolyn he said, "Go to the solar and wait for me there. You and I must talk." Both women left to do his bidding, leaving him alone with his prisoner and the ghost of his mother.

At the doorway, Alastair pulled his dagger from his belt and slashed through the ropes at Garrick's wrists before thrusting him inside the darkened space. "Why steal the Fairy Flag from us? The magic is said to only work for a MacLeod."

Even in the shadowy light, Alastair could see Garrick's wicked smile. "I did not steal the flag, your bride did it for me."

"Because you gave her no choice, I am certain."

Garrick shrugged. "I wanted to take away the source of the MacLeods' power. Just as my clan will destroy that source if I do not report back to them at the appropriate time."

"So the Fairy Flag is with your clan at Monkstadt House? Your clan seat?"

Garrick startled, then forced himself to appear disinterested. "I did not say that."

"You did not have to. Your physical responses told me all I needed to know." Alastair slammed the door shut, engaged the bolt, then secured the lock. He waited in silence with his mother until his men arrived.

"All of you, guard this door and keep constant check on our prisoner through the iron-barred window. I'll not have him slide through my fingers before I can interrogate him."

"Aye, m'laird," they said in unison as Alastair and his mother made their way to the stairs. The two of them walked in silence until Alastair stood outside the solar.

Be kind to her, his mother said as she floated away. *The girl has suffered much in the time you've been apart.*

He was about to ask more of Gwendolyn's suffering, but his mother vanished. If he wanted to know more, he would have to ask her himself.

━━━∿∿∿━━━

ALASTAIR STOOD IN the doorway of the solar, simply watching Gwendolyn as she slowly moved about the chamber. Her back was to him as she ran her hands over the stone lintel above the hearth, then across the ivory keys of the pianoforte. The melodic sound followed her as she moved to the settee, allowing her fingers to brush across the wooden back. She paused before the full-length portrait of Lady Janet MacLeod as she had been when she'd first married their father—young, beautiful, carefree. With a soft sigh she continued her movements to the table where they had spent many nights as a family, playing cards. As she turned towards the door, she startled upon seeing him. Her hands rose to her chest and her cheeks flushed pink. "Were you watching me?"

He shrugged and entered the chamber. "Were you thinking of all the things you'd missed over the past five years?"

The colour in her cheeks fled. "How could you know that?"

He came to her side. "That's what I would be thinking about had I been imprisoned for the past five years." He motioned to the settee. "Come, let us sit down. We have much to discuss."

He sat, intending for her to sit next to him, but she chose her seat at the farthest end of the long furnishing, leaving plenty of space between them. He couldn't blame her for wanting to keep herself apart. And yet, her choice brought a surge of annoyance which he quickly tamped down. If he wanted answers, he shouldn't put her on the defensive before he even started this conversation.

"So it really is you?" he said, his voice soft with amazement. "I am very glad to see you are alive."

She offered him a hesitant smile. "I am no longer a dewy young bride, and I very nearly died several times over the last five years. But aye, I have survived, as have my siblings. In part, thanks to your mother."

The days before all of this happened seemed like a lifetime ago to him. It must seem an eternity to her. Voice gentle, he said, "I am so very sorry for all that you have suffered at Garrick's hand. He will pay for all that he's done. Before I determine his punishment, would you tell me what happened and about your imprisonment?"

She looked away, focusing on something on the opposite side of the chamber as she spoke. "He kidnapped me right outside the chapel while I was waiting for your father to lead me to your side. He wanted to stage my death, so he sliced through my dress, cut a length of my hair and soiled both with a bladder of animal blood he'd brought with him." Her glaze flicked to him then around the chamber once more. "He tossed the soiled garments over the courtyard wall and onto the rocks below."

"But that wasn't the end of his abuse of you that day, was it?"

She stiffened. "Nay. He forced me to steal the Fairy Flag."

Alastair bit off a curse. "He forced you to choose between the lives of your siblings or the Fairy Flag, didn't he?"

She nodded. "He knew only I could get past the guard in the drawing room without raising the alarm. I'm so sorry, Alastair. I had no choice."

"I can see that you didn't." He swallowed roughly as she told him things he'd considered for years. "Garrick handed the flag over to his clan?"

"I assumed so since it was never in the Fairy Tower with us." She studied his face and he wondered if she saw only a stranger looking back.

"I must find the Fairy Flag. It is imperative to my success in gathering the clans."

"You mean to use the flag to help unite the clans?"

He nodded. "They all know about and respect the Fairy Flag's origins. It is the one advantage I have to stop the clans from fighting each other and to unite them against the English instead."

"If only there'd been another option," she said bleakly. "I never would have—"

"I will find a way to get it back." The years they'd been apart had been hard on her. He could see the strain of her suffering around her eyes and in the frailness of her body, and yet she had never looked more lovely. She held the beauty and grace of experience and wisdom. It was a deeper beauty than she'd had as a young girl and far more interesting. He scooted closer to her on the settee.

She stood. "I appreciate your understanding. I must check on my sister. Once she is recovered, we will go."

"Go?" He stood beside her. He fisted his hands to keep from reaching for her.

Her expression hardened. "I do not intend to stay, not for long. Why would you want me here anyway? It is obvious you have moved on with your life."

Until that moment, he'd thought he had. But staring at her now, he wasn't so certain. He was about to marry a beautiful and biddable young woman who wanted him and suited him perfectly. Yet he couldn't seem to pull his gaze away from Gwendolyn's lips. He forced his gaze back to her eyes.

"We were betrothed once."

"Aye, we *were* betrothed. Time has moved on, as must both of us. I might not have a clan anymore, but my family name is not without some status in the Highlands. We will find someone to help us move forward." She turned to leave the chamber.

Anger flared inside Alastair, and something else far more primitive. Before she could step away, he grabbed her hand, turned her towards him, and jerked her hard against his body. Before she could so much as gasp, he covered her lips with his.

CHAPTER SEVEN

G WENDOLYN STARTLED AS she was pulled to a stop, then just as abruptly caught against the masculine strength of Alastair's chest. She felt him draw a quick breath even as his lips descended on hers. She'd dreamed of this moment, played it over and over in her thoughts for the past five years. But everything she'd ever imagined didn't come close to the reality of his kiss.

Heat poured through her as his lips slid over hers, then welled and swelled and spread to every inch of her body, waking her as nothing else had from a long sleep. She could feel it in him, the same helpless reaction, the same long-denied passion finally breaking free as he stole her breath and gave it back.

He wrapped his arms around her and hauled her even closer against his body. They'd never touched each other so intimately until this moment, but for the first time in five years she could honestly say she felt alive, reborn to sensations she'd despaired of ever repeating.

She yielded to the demanding pressure of his lips on hers. He pulled her closer until she could feel the hard ridge that pressed against her belly. Gwendolyn had no difficulty recognizing his desire, and a sizzling response raced through her, hot, instinctive, and dangerous.

She should back away and end this unwise kiss. But she couldn't gather the force within her to pull away as need pounded in her blood. This wasn't a simple kiss but one fueled by anger as much as relief. She had wondered every day she had been locked in the tower what it would be like to kiss him. Had he thought about her as well? Did this kiss signal that he wasn't ready to simply end things with her or allow her to walk away from the promise they had made to each other?

Was that what she wanted? A moment ago, she had wanted nothing more than to leave Dunvegan Castle forever, putting the past behind her. But as desire heated her blood, she wasn't so certain. Her arms stole around his neck, pulling him closer this time, forcing her into vibrant contact with his rigid arousal, and demanding he give more of himself to her. And he responded, splaying his hands across her spine and deepening the kiss.

Through the sensual haze storming her brain she heard the sound of footsteps growing closer. The sound quickly forgotten as Alastair's hands trailed down to her waist then lifted to her breasts. Never had she experienced such a wild, uncontrollable surge of pure emotion as the kiss went on, spun out. She was tempted to forget everything and everyone and simply live in this moment of pure pleasure when a male voice suddenly erupted behind them.

"What in heaven's name is going on here?"

Alastair pulled away with a sharp intake of breath.

Gwendolyn jerked free of his arms in a panic, her gaze flying to an elderly man with an irritated frown on his face who stood framed in the doorway with a redhaired woman at his side. She clutched his arm as though needing it for support as her gaze shifted from Alastair's tousled clothing to Gwendolyn's flushed face.

"You said you were ready to receive us," the redheaded woman stated in a flat voice.

Alastair stared down at Gwendolyn with eyes yet clouded with passion. His gaze lingered on her still-swollen lips before, with an effort, he turned back to the newly arrived woman. "I didn't expect you until tomorrow, but no matter. We are ready for your arrival, Beatrice, Laird Lamont. Welcome to Dunvegan Castle." He pulled away from Gwendolyn's side to offer Beatrice his arm, which she accepted as he guided her to the grouping of chairs before the hearth.

The older man continued to regard Gwendolyn with raised, bushy eyebrows. "Will no one tell me what is going on?"

"I hardly know myself," Gwendolyn admitted as she made her way towards the doorway, suddenly deciding to return to her sister's bedside. Whatever was happening here, and she had imagined all manner of things in the past few moments, she wanted no part of it. She stepped outside the chamber when Alastair's voice halted her footsteps.

"You are needed in here, Gwendolyn."

Without much of a choice, she returned to the solar and regarded Alastair through narrowed eyes as the newly arrived woman continued to hang onto his arm.

"M'laird, milady," Becks and Mrs Morgan greeted with a bow as they entered the chamber. "Ye surprised us arrivin' today. We expected ye on the morrow," Becks said to the older man. "Would ye like me tae take yer luggage upstairs tae yer chambers?"

The grey-haired man's gaze narrowed on Alastair. "Haven't decided if we are staying yet or not. Alastair, would you care to enlighten us about what we just witnessed?"

"There's nothing to explain." Alastair met and held Gwendolyn's gaze. In his eyes she saw both pain and regret before the emotions vanished, replaced with a look that bordered on boredom. "Laird Lamont, Miss Beatrice Lamont, I would like to introduce my ward, Miss Gwendolyn Harris. Gwendolyn is a guest here, as are you until things are fully settled."

Laird Lamont raised his bushy brows. "Your ward, you say? And nothing else? 'Cuz it looked like—"

Callum scrambled into the solar just then. He paused in the doorway, looking to first Alastair, then to Gwendolyn. "Brother, perhaps this isn't the best moment to—"

"Never mind what it looked like," Alastair said, ignoring

his brother. "Gwendolyn, I would like to introduce you to my future wife. Beatrice and I were betrothed two weeks ago."

"Damn," Callum said with a loud sigh. "I had hoped you would be more delicate with this matter for the womenfolk's sake."

"Future wife?" The world suddenly narrowed to a tiny pinhole. She swayed on her feet.

Callum was instantly at her side.

Gwendolyn forced herself to take long, steadying breaths until she finally brought herself under control. She rubbed her arms. They felt cold and numb. "I suppose congratulations are in order," she said hoarsely.

"The Isle Council put forth the match now that I am chief of the Clan MacLeod. It all happened before I returned home to Dunvegan."

Pain and sorrow rolled over her in a relentless tide even as she tried to remind herself of her plans to leave this castle and make a life of her own with her siblings where no one could ever imprison her again. Yet at the first challenge to her independence, she'd fallen victim to her desires. A surge of heat rushed through her veins again at the memory of the passion Alastair had evoked. She blinked, inwardly shook her head, and tried to concentrate on the here and now. Her only purpose for remaining at Dunvegan was because of Arabella. "If you'll excuse me, I would like to return to my sister." Without waiting for permission, she headed for the door.

"It pleases me to see you've at least acknowledged the connection between yourself and my Beatrice." Her father's voice trailed after Gwendolyn. "Say you'll devote yourself to only her and we shall stay."

Alastair gave a reply which she was too far away to hear, but at the redhead's squeal of delight, Gwendolyn could only assume that he'd promised no further interaction with "his ward."

Callum caught up with her in the great hall, matching his steps to hers as she moved out of the chamber then down the hallway and to the stairs that would take her back to Arabella and Samuel. "I'm sorry, Gwendolyn."

"You have nothing to apologise for."

Callum frowned. "It wasn't kind of Alastair to break the news to you in that way."

"He owes me nothing."

"I'm not so certain of that."

Gwendolyn slowed her pace and turned to the man beside her. "He has moved on with his life. I cannot blame him for that. I was missing for five years."

"True, but his betrothal to you might still be valid."

Gwendolyn shook her head. "I do not wish to fight him on this. I must accept what has happened and start my own life anew."

Callum came to a stop, forcing her to do the same. "Where will you go? What will you do to support yourself and your siblings? You have very few options, especially with no clan to return to."

"I don't know. I'll think of something."

"You are entitled to some settlement. In order to determine what that might be, I sent for a friend of mine who is a solicitor. Despite the passage of time, the contract between you and Alastair is still valid in the eyes of the law, if not the church."

"Alastair agreed to this?" Gwendolyn asked.

Callum looked away. "He will see the idea has merit in time."

"Oh, Callum. Please do not put yourself in the middle of all this. I remember in the past, your relationship with your brother was always a little strained."

He turned back to face her. "It still is because he refuses to see Rowena and I are no longer children and are able to make our own decisions."

"He is laird."

"He is my brother, above all. I can go against him and still remain his brother no matter what, so let me do this for you."

She couldn't really stop what he'd already set into motion, but she could force him to interfere no more. "Promise me this will be all you do."

He nodded. "I promise."

"Good, now let us go see how Arabella and Samuel fare."

They continued up the stairs and to the bedchamber

where her siblings resided. Gwendolyn opened the door and stepped inside. Instead of the stale air she expected, the air was fresh and sweet-smelling. The shutter had been opened and a soft breeze circulated about the chamber. The temperature was much warmer than it had ever been in the tower, yet Gwendolyn worried. "Will the air worsen Arabella's condition?"

"Nay," Lottie replied. "The fresh air will help her. Look." The healer tilted her head towards her patient. "Some colour has returned to her cheeks and she's breathing easier now."

Moving to the bed, Gwendolyn stood beside her sister and took her hand in her own. Arabella stirred but fell right back into a deep slumber. Lottie was right. Pink tinged her sister's cheeks, and the sound of her breathing was no longer so labored and rattling. "Thank you," Gwendolyn whispered. "I was so worried."

"Arabella is headed in the right direction; however, she still has a long way to go before she is fully recovered."

Meaning they would not be leaving Dunvegan anytime soon. Gwendolyn turned to her brother. He slept soundly on a pallet near the fire. In that moment, the weight of all that had happened to her, to all of them, hit her. Too weak and too humiliated to keep standing, she sank to the floor. She and her siblings were unwanted guests with nowhere to go and no means to support themselves.

Callum came to her side and knelt on the floor beside her. "Are you well, Gwendolyn? What can I do? How can I help?"

Hunger and exhaustion, combined with a growing sense of despair, brought a hitch to her breath and tears to her eyes. Terrified that the tears burning the backs of her eyes were going to fall, humiliating her even more, Gwendolyn tipped her head back and stared at the ceiling. "I think I simply need to rest. I'll be better in the morning."

Callum stood and offered her his hand. "Then let me help you up and show you to your chamber."

She stared at his hand but did not take it. "I should stay here with Arabella and Samuel."

Before Callum could object, Lottie spoke. "I will be with them all night. If anything changes, I'll come get you. I promise. Right now, the best thing you can do to help your sister is to eat something and go to bed. She'll need your strength come morning."

Lottie moved to the hearth and spooned some of the bone broth she'd made for Arabella into a mug and handed it to Gwendolyn. "Drink this right now. It will give you strength."

Gwendolyn accepted the mug. "Thank you." She remained on the floor as she drank the bone broth. Sip by sip she started to feel her strength return. When she was done, Callum helped her to stand, then guided her from the chamber and across the hall to a beautifully furnished bedchamber in hues of yellow and green. Just stepping into the room brought a sense of peace and comfort, which was so different from the cold stone walls she'd not only stared at but memorised each nook and cranny of for the past five years. "Thank you for being so kind to me, Callum."

His brow creased and his gaze dropped to the floor. "I'm sorry for not knowing. . .for not doing anything. . ."

"Callum, please look at me." Gwendolyn reached out and touched his arm. When he brought his gaze to hers, she said, "You did not imprison us in the tower. None of this is your fault."

"I could have—"

"Nay," she interrupted. "What happened to us happened. It is over now. Let us rejoice in that. Your duty now is to your brother. Garrick MacDonald's plans for the MacLeods started with imprisoning us to torture Alastair, but he will not be satisfied until all the MacLeods are destroyed. You cannot allow that to happen." She pulled her hand back. "Go to Alastair and help him. Help him stop a war between the clans."

"I'll try," he said and after a moment she saw the tension in his shoulders relax. "It's time I show Alastair that I'm not a child. I am his equal."

"Aye, you are," she agreed with a slight smile. "Go show him your worth."

With a nod, he left her, shutting the door softly behind him. When she was alone, she sagged against the wall behind her. Her stomach clenched, and she fought the urge to vomit the broth she had just consumed. The thought of what her life had become through no fault of her own overwhelmed her. The MacDonalds had taken her parents away from her, they'd destroyed her village and everyone in it, except her and her siblings. Then when the three of them had finally found a small sliver of peace, Garrick MacDonald had destroyed that as well.

Leaning her head back, Gwendolyn stifled a moan as she closed her eyes. Alastair taking a new bride had nothing to do with the MacDonalds, but it was because of Garrick that he'd been forced to do so. Gwendolyn was certain Beatrice would not want her or her siblings around much longer to remind Alastair of their past. It was only a matter of time before they once again had no place to rest their heads at night.

It was up to her to find a solution, to find a way for them to move forward. Gwendolyn released a long breath as she straightened, doing everything in her power to keep away the sensation of the floor falling out from beneath her.

Whatever came next for the three of them depended on Arabella's recovery. Gwendolyn made her way to the bed and wearily pulled off her soiled gown, then threw it on the floor before sliding beneath the covers. In the morning she would pick up the threads of her life and move forward. She had proven her courage and strength over the past five years, and she'd overcome huge challenges in her life already. For every problem, there was a solution. She simply had to find one that would work for herself and her siblings.

Challenges were what made life worth living. She had almost convinced herself of that by the time she fell into an exhausted slumber.

CHAPTER EIGHT

ALASTAIR HURRIEDLY SETTLED Beatrice and her father into their bedchambers and then headed to the dungeon. It was time to get some answers from Garrick. Alastair was not one for torture, but as angry as he was right now, if Garrick didn't tell him what he wanted to know about how he breached the castle walls and how he was able to move about Dunvegan without being seen, he might just change his mind about such methods of gaining information.

Alastair moved down the stairs to the dungeon. When no light came from below, his gut tightened. Something was wrong. He raced back up the stairs to grab a torch and continued downwards. Golden light writhed across the cold stone walls, illuminating his way. As he neared the bottom of the stairs, the hairs on the back of his neck stood up. Sensing danger, he drew his sword. At the bottom of the stairs, four bodies were sprawled across the floor and the door to the dungeon was open.

Alastair swore under his breath. Garrick had escaped. He released his fury in a deep-throated growl that bounced around the enclosed space. He had no idea how Garrick had managed such a feat, but Alastair would find out and punish those who had aided the prisoner. For there was no other explanation than that he had help from inside the castle.

Casting the light of the torch around the chamber, Alastair saw no further threat. He sheathed his weapon and knelt beside his men. Bringing his fingers to their necks, he was relieved to feel the thump of their lifeforce pumping through their veins. None of his men had been slain. Instead, they were fast asleep. Ronald still clutched a mug in his hand, while Lindon's, Innis's, and Emery's cups were several inches from their bodies. Alastair brought one of the mugs to his nose. In addition to the yeasty scent of ale, he smelled nutmeg sassafras and myrrh that was indicative of laudanum. Why had his men not detected the scent before they drank from these mugs?

Footsteps sounded on the steps behind him, and for a moment Alastair tensed until he saw Graeme.

"What has happened? We heard you bellow." Fully entering the chamber now, Graeme and the three men behind him came to a stop and stared eyes-wide at the sight of their fellow guards upon the ground.

"Garrick has escaped. Sound the alarm. I want every man posted on the towers, upon the curtain wall, inside the secret passageways, and along the shoreline. If Garrick is still in this castle, I want him recaptured."

Graeme nodded as his gaze shifted to the unresponsive guards. "Are they dead?"

"Asleep. They were somehow tricked into drinking ale that was laced with laudanum," Alastair replied, his voice cold. "We have a traitor in our midst."

"Not for long." Graeme clenched his fists before turning to the men, giving them orders to gather the others and take up their posts until only Graeme and Alastair remained with the unconscious men in the torchlit circle. "You go with the others, Alastair. I'll see to the safety of these men. If they wake, I'll find out who brought them that ale."

Alastair handed the torch to Graeme. "And I will find that bastard no matter what hole he's hiding in now. Upon my life, Garrick will pay for what he's done."

———

BY THE NEXT morning, after every nook and cranny of the old castle had been thoroughly searched, Alastair was forced to conclude that Garrick had escaped. From his position on top of the north tower, Alastair could sense, even though he could not see, that his enemy was not far away.

"What would you have the men do next?" Graeme asked from beside Alastair. "Should we prepare for war?"

A wave of hatred, black and burning like acid, boiled up from the hidden depths of Alastair's soul. He wanted nothing more than to ride out immediately and retaliate against their enemy, but that was not what he'd come to Dunvegan to achieve. He was supposed to be negotiating peace amongst the clans—even with the MacDonalds. "It is much harder to be a peaceful man than to go to war over the slightest provocation," he said through taut white lips.

"That it is. If not war, then what would you have us do?"

Alastair heard the angst in Graeme's voice. He understood it. They were men of action. Doing nothing felt unnatural. "We need to wait. Bide our time. Garrick and the MacDonalds are expecting us to attack, wondering when it will happen. Every moment will stretch out before them as they wait. That anticipation will crawl along their skin, causing an insatiable itch." Alastair allowed himself a grim smile. "In the meanwhile, we will gather the men and train. I know what my men are capable of in battle. I have no idea of the capabilities of those who were here at Dunvegan."

"The men haven't slept during the night."

"And in battle they will not sleep much either. 'Tis good to see them at a disadvantage. It will show us more about their abilities."

Graeme nodded. "I'll assemble the men in the rear courtyard."

"I will find Callum and Samuel Harris and meet you there." He and Graeme descended the tower together but parted ways inside the great hall. While Graeme gathered the men who were just settling down to sleep, Alastair continued on to the solar where he knew he'd find his brother.

Instantly upon entering the chamber, the memories he'd managed to keep at bay while they'd searched for Garrick flooded back to him. It was in this room that he'd taken Gwendolyn in his arms and pressed his lips to hers. He could only attribute his actions to madness. What other reason could he have for pulling her into his arms as he had?

It was a madness beyond anything he had felt before. There was something in the way she looked at him—something that made all reason flee and left instinct to take over. When she was near, he found it difficult to catch his breath, to keep his body relaxed instead of tightening with desire. He shook off the memory and stepped fully into the chamber. Callum sat by the hearth, staring into the dying embers. "I thought I would find you here."

"I couldn't sleep after we called off the search for Garrick. I kept thinking about Gwendolyn, and about how you betrayed her in the most heartless of ways."

Alastair bristled. "She'd been missing for five years. If I had known she was alive, I never would have agreed to betroth myself to Beatrice."

Callum came to stand beside him. "I know. I'm merely frustrated for Gwendolyn. One look into her eyes and you can't help but see the panic she tries so hard to hide."

"What would you have me do?"

"Meet with the solicitor I requested to arrive here later this afternoon."

Alastair frowned. "I asked you not—"

"Do you not want to know for certain the legalities of your past betrothal and how they affect your current betrothal?"

"Do you ever listen to me?" Alastair returned irritably.

"I listen when you make sense, but you cannot avoid the fact that you owe Gwendolyn something now that she's reappeared in your life."

"You want me to come to a financial settlement with her?"

Callum shrugged. "It would be the least of what you owe her. Put yourself in her situation: She has not truly lived a moment of her life since the day she disappeared. She's been locked in isolation, trying to survive each day, trying to keep her siblings' spirits from crumbling, half-starved, and terrified out of her mind every time Garrick MacDonald came near them." Callum narrowed his gaze on his brother. "You on the other hand had the freedom to do whatever you wanted over the past five years. You were fed, clothed, cared for by your servants, and while you might have been angry and a little hurt by what happened to you, you had the world at your fingertips."

Alastair didn't need Callum to remind him that Gwendolyn's suffering had been far greater than his own. He was well aware of that fact. "You're right. I should do something to relieve her fear. I'll meet with the solicitor, but if you don't start doing as I ask, you may need to start worrying about your own welfare."

Callum stood eye to eye with Alastair. A face Alastair remembered as youthful and irresponsible hardened, replaced by that of a grown man who was not only self-assured, but determined and strong.

"Don't threaten me," Callum said in a low tone. "I'm not the scrappy young man you left behind five years ago. I've learned to make my own way in this life. I have my own funds and the means to support myself. I've been here at Dunvegan, holding your position as laird and protecting your castle since Father died. So 'tis you, not me, who needs to wake up and start living up to the role to which you were rightfully born."

They were no longer just talking about his responsibilities towards Gwendolyn. "You're right, Callum." Alastair ran a hand through his hair and released a heavy sigh. "I have failed you and Rowena, Gwendolyn, and the entire clan." He winced at his own words. "I'm here now to stay, and I promise to make up for my lack."

"All any of us wants is for you to take charge and be the laird we need." Callum clapped his brother on the shoulder and smiled. "None of us realised you would have to rise to the challenge of our enemies so soon upon your return."

Alastair returned his brother's smile. "The MacDonalds have been a thorn in our side for decades. I should have expected something."

"What will you do now?"

His smile broadened. "Teach my little brother how to fight if you'll join me in the rear courtyard for warrior's training."

Callum beamed. "You would train me with the rest of the men?"

"Of course. You are a MacLeod and must know how to wield your sword as well as, if not better, than anyone else."

Callum turned towards the door. "Then let's go."

Alastair joined Callum at the door. "Before we join the men who are not already guarding the castle, I'd like to invite young Samuel Harris to join us as well."

"That's a terrific idea." Callum's brow quirked. "Shall we race up the stairs like we used to and see who is now the fastest amongst us?"

Alastair barely nodded when Callum took off, dashing through the great hall, down the hallway, and up the stairs with Alastair at his heels. Alastair slowed his pace as they burst up the staircase, giving his brother the lead and allowing the warmth in his chest to heal a part of himself that had been lifeless for too long. He'd come home. He'd rid himself of Garrick for now. He'd reconnected with his brother. And soon his men would be better trained for conflict in the future. He might say his life was falling back into place if only he didn't have two brides and a traitor amongst them.

A SLIGHT MORNING breeze moved across the open courtyard, carrying with it the pungent scent of the sea as Alastair and Graeme sparred with each other, giving and receiving forceful blows with their swords as they wove themselves through the two sets of men. The sound of steel striking steel rang throughout the courtyard as mock-battles raged all around them.

The warriors from the castle fought with less skill than Alastair would have liked, but after all that was why they were out here practising with his own highly trained men. At the thought, Alastair frowned. He had to stop thinking of them as his men and the men of the castle. After they were all trained in the advanced art of war as he and Graeme had been, these men would be each other's equals and united by the tartan they wore.

Callum and Samuel were the least experienced warriors amongst them, but Alastair was pleased they were both eager for knowledge as they practised basic defensive moves with the others.

"If you do not keep your mind on the battle before you, how can you expect your men to do the same?" Graeme asked with a thrust to Alastair's head.

The clash of steel reverberated through the air as Alastair met the thrust with one of his own, then twisted upwards and sideways, taking Graeme off-balance, then down to the ground. "My thoughts might wonder but my focus is on the battle at hand." Alastair offered Graeme a hand up.

"You spent the last five years perfecting the art of diplomacy," Graeme said as he dusted himself off. "Why not focus on your skills as a negotiator instead of teaching the men to battle?"

"My idea of diplomacy is having the men ready to fight, then negotiating a way to avoid that situation." Alastair assumed his fighting stance, balancing on the balls of his feet, ready to strike. "Shall we go at it again?"

"And if negotiations fail?" Graeme rushed forward, cutting and slashing.

"Then we go to war." Alastair parried his blade.

"And what about the Fairy Flag? How will you retrieve that without going to war against the MacDonalds?" Graeme asked.

Alastair swung his sword. "The same way they took it from us. In secret."

Graeme feinted to the right, avoiding the blow. "Perhaps Rowena's new beau is not such an ill-conceived connection after all."

"Perhaps not," Alastair agreed. When he'd first arrived home, his goal had been to replace the flag with a copy. Was there truly hope of retrieving the original flag from the MacDonalds? Would Marcus help with such a plan? It was worth exploring. In the meanwhile, he and Rowena would continue with their plans to pass off a counterfeit in order to rally the clan members' spirits. Even Graeme did not know of his plans.

Graeme's family had always been the flag bearer when the Fairy Flag had been taken with the clan into battle. Alastair was not certain Graeme would agree with his plans to present the clan with a false rendering of their precious gift from the fairies. For now, the creation of such a flag had to remain between only himself, Rowena, and their laundress, Roberta.

Clearing his thoughts, Alastair went on the attack. His and Graeme's blades clashed again and again, the clink of steel creating rhythmic sounds that reverberated through the morning air. It was a sound he'd heard often as a young boy as he, Tormod, and Orrick had learned to fight. As his sword cut through the air, a pulse entered his blood, bringing a renewed sense of purpose to his soul. He was here to negotiate peace, but never at the expense of defending his clan and all those he loved.

Alastair paused to savour the feeling. In that moment, Graeme advanced. His captain of the guard swiped his sword upwards, catching Alastair's arm and tossing him to the ground.

"Ha!" Graeme exclaimed. "I couldn't let you best me every time." The other men gathered around and applauded while Graeme offered Alastair a hand up.

On his feet once more, Alastair sheathed his sword. "All this practise is for one purpose alone, whether we win or lose while sparring. It is to make sure we have the skills necessary to protect each other when the battle turns serious."

A chorus of "ayes" rang out.

"When will you call for a meeting of the Isle Council?" Graeme asked.

"If all of you continue to improve as much as you have in the past few hours, then I feel safe in calling the clans together on the morrow."

"We'll be ready for battle if that's what it comes to," one warrior said.

"We will make you proud," another warrior shouted from the crowd.

"I am already proud of all of you." Alastair turned to look at his men—all his men. "Keep up your practise, work on your skills, and challenge each other."

"Aye!" They shouted as they returned to their mock battles.

Graeme sheathed his weapon. "If you'll gather on the morrow, then you'll need me and a few of the men to alert the other clan leaders on the isles."

Alastair nodded as he once more observed his men. They all seemed so eager to learn, and yet one of them was working against them. "Thank you, Graeme. I also have another task for you as well that will make certain we will have the advantage when it comes to battling the clans or the English."

Graeme raised a brow. "A secret mission. You know how much I enjoy those."

"Take Crayton and Mathe with you. They have been loyal to you and me in the past. We can trust them. Everyone else is still under suspicion until I can determine who helped Garrick MacDonald escape."

CHAPTER NINE

G WENDOLYN AWOKE TO see late-morning sunshine filtering into her chamber. She sat up abruptly when she realised she'd slept soundly for the first time in ages. Even Lottie had not called upon her. Gwendolyn swung her feet over the bed and stood. Hopefully, she'd not been woken from a sound sleep because her sister was improving, and not out of pity because Gwendolyn had collapsed at Lottie's feet the night before.

Quickly, Gwendolyn bathed with the pitcher of water on the table by the bed before drying herself with the towel that had also been left for her use. She slipped her chemise over her head before she moved to where her gown from last night lay in a pile on the floor. She had no other choice but to wear it. She brushed it off and slipped it over her head just as a knock sounded upon the door.

Gwendolyn hastily pulled the bodice of her gown together before she opened the door wide enough to peek through.

"I'm so glad you are awake," Rowena said with a smile. "May I come in?"

Gwendolyn stepped back, and Rowena brushed past her

into the chamber, carrying a handful of gowns and a basket. "I brought you water and a towel earlier but you were so deep in slumber that I decided not to wake you."

"Thank you for everything. You've all been so kind to us," Gwendolyn said, closing the door and joining the young woman who set the gowns upon the bed and the basket on the table by the bedside.

When she turned back to Gwendolyn, Rowena frowned. "You cannot wear that dress. I brought several others of mine for you to try until we can have more made for you."

"I cannot—"

"I insist." Rowena lifted a clean chemise off the bed and thrust it towards Gwendolyn. "Start with this. Then you can pick which gowns you'd like." The look in Rowena's eyes told Gwendolyn she would not win this battle, so she slipped her old gown over her head and replaced her soiled chemise with the clean one. The scents of heather and sunshine clung to the laundered fabric, and Gwendolyn closed her eyes and drew a deep breath.

At a chuckle from Rowena, Gwendolyn opened her eyes and smiled. "My apologies. It has been so long since I've worn anything unsoiled. I'd forgotten what freshly laundered clothing smelled like."

"Then you'll love the way these dresses smell. Our laundress, Roberta, is a marvel. Not only does she get things cleaned, she dries them in the sun and starches them to perfection." Rowena bent down and picked up a sage-green satin gown with an underskirt of white that was decorated with a scattered flower pattern, featuring pink roses and blue cornflowers. The stomacher was embroidered in flowers that matched the underskirt.

"I brought a corset if you would like to wear it, but I daresay you do not need one," Rowena said after inspecting Gwendolyn's trim waist.

"Nay. I'm sure the stomacher will be constricting enough," Gwendolyn laughed as she slipped into the gown and attached the stomacher over her breasts and stomach. Rowena helped to close then tighten the gown until it fit perfectly. When she was through, Gwendolyn smoothed her hand down the silken fabric. The straight bodice accentuated the roundness of her breasts. She tugged at the bodice but failed to conceal that her figure, though slim, was more curvaceous than Rowena's. Even with a more daring neckline, the dress was preferable to her other gown.

With a shrug, she picked up the brush that Rowena had brought along with the water and towels, and began combing out her long, heavy hair. Now that it wasn't matted and soiled, Gwendolyn could see that all but the section Garrick had clipped had grown well past her knees in the past five years. "Do you have any shears?" she asked Rowena.

Rowena moved to the basket and withdrew a pair of shears. "I came prepared for anything. Would you like to cut it or shall I?"

"Would you? I hardly know the popular lengths of fashion."

Rowena motioned to a chair near the hearth. "Well, you are in luck because I do. Fortunately for us, the styles are no longer teased and piled high. Just simple curls around the face and either a bun at the back of your head or having it gathered in a braid are the trends today."

"A braid will do just fine." Gwendolyn settled in. "Thank you, Rowena, for all your help. I am most grateful."

"You are welcome. I will make certain we cut both Arabella's and Samuel's hair today as well." Rowena wasted no time in snipping off an arm's length of Gwendolyn's golden-blond hair. Instantly her head felt lighter. After only a few minutes more, Rowena proclaimed she was done cutting and proceeded to braid Gwendolyn's hair. Once finished, Rowena brought Gwendolyn a hand looking glass in which to inspect the final results.

Rowena had tied a simple white bow at the end of the braid and then had woven the tails up through the braid in an elegant fashion. Two tendrils of hair had been tugged loose at Gwendolyn's temples to soften the effect, making her eyes seem much wider, and without her hair covering her face, her skin glowed with vitality. Gwendolyn set the looking glass aside, then stood and proceeded to clear the floor of her excess hair while Rowena placed the remaining gowns in the armoire. "When your sister feels better, we can find a new gown for her from these. In the meanwhile, I brought her several chemises to wear as she recovers."

Rowena turned back to Gwendolyn when she had finished. "Are you ready to go belowstairs for a late breakfast?"

Gwendolyn straightened. She wasn't ready to face Beatrice and Alastair together just yet. "Might I go check on Arabella first?"

"Of course," Rowena agreed with a smile. "I will meet you in the great hall when you are done."

At Gwendolyn's nod, Rowena left the chamber. Pausing in the doorway, Gwendolyn thought not about her sister in the opposite room, but about the situation that awaited belowstairs. She and her siblings were in essence trapped at Dunvegan until Arabella's health improved. Therefore, she was going to have to find a way to remain here in relative harmony for however long that took. In order to survive with her heart intact, she vowed to be polite and poised and completely unemotional, no matter what situations presented themselves. She was no longer a naive young girl. Life had tempered her in ways others would never understand.

She would be an excellent guest, and while she waited for her sister's health to improve, she would find some way to support herself and her siblings once they were free to live their lives away from Dunvegan Castle. With all that settled in her mind, Gwendolyn headed for Arabella's chamber.

When she entered the room, it was to see Arabella sitting up in bed. Her face was still pale, but some colour had definitely returned to her cheeks. "How are you feeling this morning?" Gwendolyn moved to sit beside her sister. Lottie stood near the hearth, heating a kettle over the flames.

"Still weak, but I can breathe easier," Arabella said as she reached for her sister's hand. "I'm sorry to cause a fuss."

"You've done nothing of the sort." Gwendolyn turned to gaze at the pallet where Samuel had slept last night. "Where is our brother?"

Lottie returned to the bedside with the steaming kettle and began mixing herbs together with her pestle and mortar. "The laird and his brother, Callum, came to ask Samuel if he would like to train with the other young warriors this morning."

"If you listen, you can hear them in the rear courtyard," Arabella said.

Gwendolyn moved to the window that was still open from last night. She gazed down at the rear of the castle to see several young men with swords practising in the wide-open space. The sound of steel striking steel filled the salt-tinged air. Amongst the young men, she spotted Samuel who sparred with another boy twice his size, and yet her brother seemed to be holding his own. The look on his face was one of total concentration, yet every few moments, a delighted smile appeared. "Our brother looks happy."

"Returning to a normal life will make all of us happy, to be sure," Arabella said in a wheezy voice. A moment later she doubled over, coughing.

Instantly, Lottie was at her side. The healer pressed a mug of the steaming brew she'd been making into Arabella's hands. "Drink this, it will calm your breathing." Then turning towards Gwendolyn she added, "Your sister needs to rest."

Between calming sips, Arabella nodded. "Will you see to me again?"

Gwendolyn came to the bedside and pressed a kiss to her sister's head. "I'll never be that far away, should you need anything."

Gwendolyn left the chamber but paused at the staircase that led up to the drawing room where the MacLeods had once kept their most prized possession. Last night a thought had formed that she needed to right the wrong she had done to the MacLeod family when she'd given Garrick the Fairy Flag. Alastair had been understanding of the situation she'd been forced into. But she hadn't missed the pain in his expression when she'd confessed to handing the flag over to their enemy. Garrick had made it clear over the past few years that a war was brewing between the clans. The MacLeods needed their gift from the fairies to bring them luck in such a situation.

Instead of heading to the great hall, Gwendolyn made her way to the drawing room on the third floor. The chamber was thankfully empty when she stepped inside. Since there was nothing left to protect, the guard was no longer stationed there. Instantly, her gaze moved to the empty frame between the two windows. Had the MacLeods left it up to remind them of what had been lost?

She swallowed to ease the aching tightness in her throat. She'd stood in this place five years ago, but also when she'd first come to the castle. It was on that day that Norman MacLeod had told her his version of how the MacLeods had come to possess the Fairy Flag.

It was in the woods not far from the castle where Iain MacLeod first met a fairy princess. The two fell in love. Her father, Oberon, at first refused to allow the couple to marry. But finally he succumbed to his daughter's pleas and allowed the couple to marry for a year and a day. Nine months later, she gave birth to a son. Eventually, the time came when the fairy had to return to her own world. Before leaving, she made her husband promise never to leave the child alone or let him cry, for that would be too much for her to bear.

In the weeks following his wife's departure, Iain kept his promise and was a devoted father even though he was heartsick at losing his wife. In an attempt to cheer the laird up, his friends and family had a banquet. Iain's spirits began to revive at the merry music and revelry that was so loud it filled the entire castle with noise.

Curious about what was happening belowstairs, his son's nursemaid left the nursery to peek at the excitement. While she was gone, the child started crying, but no one could hear him, except his fairy mother.

She appeared beside him and wrapped him in a fairy shawl. She sang to him a fairy lullaby—a song the Grey Lady had taught Gwendolyn and her siblings—and put the child back to sleep.

When the laird discovered the nursemaid in the great hall, he hurried to the nursery. He could hear the song as it was sung to his child but could not see to whom the voice belonged. It wasn't until the child was older before he told his father that it was his mother who had come to him that night and wrapped him in the Fairy Flag. She'd told him the flag was to be used as a talisman to protect the clan in the future.

Simply having *Am Bratach Sith*, as the Fairy Flag was known to the MacLeods, in their possession, was said to bring them luck. However, if the clan was in distress, and they waved the flag three times, a fairy army would supposedly appear and lead them to victory. The magic was said to only work three times before the Fairy Flag, and the magic it possessed, would return to the fairy world.

Gwendolyn slowly clenched her hands into fists as she turned from the chamber. Self-recrimination would not help her now. At least she knew where the flag had been taken. Garrick had bragged about its location many times over the years. And what was stolen once, could be stolen again. She had to figure out how she could return the flag to its proper resting place, restore the magic to the MacLeods, and clear her conscience.

There had to be a way. And if there was, she would find it. She owed it to the MacLeods and to Alastair.

Having tallied too long already, Gwendolyn hurried to

join Rowena in the great hall. With luck, Alastair might not be there. Perhaps he was practising with the others in the courtyard and she wouldn't have to see him again so soon after the kiss they'd shared. Nervously rubbing her hands together, she entered the chamber to find not only Rowena and Callum, but also Alastair. Yet Beatrice and her father were nowhere in sight. Perhaps they were as worried about dining with her as she was of them.

"Good morning," Callum greeted.

"Good morning, Callum," Gwendolyn answered with what she hoped was a gracious smile. Then, because the situation was as uncomfortable as it was foreign to her, she said the first thing that came to mind. "Something smells good."

"It's rashers." Alastair's gaze drifted over her. It lingered on the tight bodice of her gown before he said, "Something is different about you."

She tried not to squirm at his unsmiling appraisal as she reached up and touched one of the loose tendrils of hair at her cheeks. "Rowena cut my hair and was kind enough to let me borrow one of her gowns."

"Sit down," Callum interrupted in a jovial tone. When she took a seat opposite Alastair at the large table, Callum signalled the servants for a plate to be brought to her. "You slept well, I take it?"

"Very well." The feather mattress had been even softer than she remembered.

Rowena poured a cup of tea from a steaming pot before her and sent it down on the table towards Gwendolyn. She gratefully accepted the cup and held it in her hands. She closed her eyes, savouring the sweet, floral fragrance. Botanical notes mixed with earthy ones reminding her of the joy that tea used to bring her. It had been so long since she'd indulged in such a simple pleasure.

Gwendolyn opened her eyes and took a sip, allowing the heated liquid to bathe her throat. She stopped from taking a second sip when she suddenly realised everyone was staring at her. Quickly, she set the cup down, fearing she had done something wrong.

"Oh my heavens," Rowena said. "It's been five years since you've had a cup of tea hasn't it?"

Gwendolyn nodded. It had been five years since she'd had anything but bread, gruel, or the occasional table scraps. Hot tea in a cup seemed a luxury indeed.

A server set a plate of rashers, eggs, and a broiled tomato before her. The savoury scents almost overwhelmed her. It had been so long since she'd had a hearty breakfast. She wasn't certain she would be able to stomach such rich food.

Rowena must have noticed the way she stared at her plate, because the young woman stood and brought Gwendolyn a slice of toast and a single boiled egg instead. "Why not start with this. It might be easier for you to handle than rashers and eggs."

"I'm so sorry you had to endure such hardship."

Alastair's voice cracked and misery reflected in his dark gaze. "Can you ever forgive us for failing you and your sibling so desperately?"

Gwendolyn looked at the pale faces before her and her heart tightened. "There is nothing to forgive. You did not imprison me. The MacDonalds did." She lifted the toast to her lips and took a small bite, chewing carefully so that it did not turn into a lump in her throat.

Tears came to Callum's eyes. "I failed you most of all, Gwendolyn. And for that I beg your forgiveness. I was here. I could have gone to investigate all the odd noises coming from the Fairy Tower at any time, but I did not because of my father's dictate not to go in there."

Gwendolyn set down her toast. "Please, all of you. I know you realise how much we suffered in that tower. We want nothing more than to put it behind us and move forward with our lives. We have warm beds, clean clothing, delicious food, and you are doing everything possible to bring Arabella back to good health. Even Samuel is thriving. He seems quite happy learning how to battle with the other young men." She lifted her fork and took a small bite of her egg.

"And what about you?" Alastair's voice was gentle, concerned. "What would make you happy?"

Gwendolyn set her fork down, unnerved by the direct question, yet determined to forge ahead with her plans. "I've given it some thought, and I would like to start searching for a position as a lady's maid or a governess somewhere near Glasgow, but only in situations that would take the three of us. In my own time, I will continue to teach Samuel and Arabella what they need to know as they come of age."

"You would work all day and then teach them at night?"

She straightened. "I am not afraid of the task ahead. And I am quite capable of continuing to educate them both as I did in the tower."

"You know Latin? Mathematics? The history of Scotland?" Alastair asked with a frown.

"What. . .are you saying?" She stumbled over her words. "That I am unequal to the task because I was imprisoned for five years? You needn't worry about me. I shall find a way to—"

Alastair surged to his feet and came around the table. "I'll not have you working as a lady's maid. I will find a way for the three of you to survive without you having to find employment." He held out his hand. "Will you come with me to speak to a solicitor? He arrived not long ago and is waiting for us in the library." He looked down at her plate, at the egg and toast with only one bite gone from each. He dropped his hand to his side. "We can wait until you finish your breakfast."

She took a final sip of tea. "That is about all I can stomach for now." She stood. "Callum told me that he'd sent for the man."

Alastair nodded. "It was the right thing to do. 'Tis time to make certain you and your siblings are taken care of."

CHAPTER TEN

A LASTAIR ESCORTED GWENDOLYN to the library. He waved her into a chair beside the desk before addressing the man already in the chamber. "Thank you for coming here so quickly, Mr Buchannan. Gwendolyn Harris will be present for this discussion."

"Of course. Nice to meet you both." The man offered first Alastair, then Gwendolyn, a bow of his head. "Please, call me Geordie."

Alastair took his seat behind the overly large desk that he would forever associate with his father. Instead of looking at Gwendolyn, Alastair turned his gaze to the young man who sat opposite him. He was of medium height with a square, hard jaw. His eyes were an arresting colour of blue that studied Alastair as though contemplating what kind of man he was.

"Callum has already informed me on the specifics of this matter." The solicitor's gaze shifted between them. "As you both know, a betrothal is considered to be a semi-binding contract. I have a few questions to ask both of you. Some of these questions might be uncomfortable, but I need you to answer them honestly." Geordie slipped on a pair of spectacles and glanced down at the papers before him and picked up his quill.

"Was there a negotiation of the match?" Geordie asked matter-of-factly.

"Of a sort. There was a negotiation between Gwendolyn, my father, and myself since she had no other kin to speak for her in these matters," Alastair replied.

Geordie made a notation on his papers. "Was there a bride price paid?"

"Nay," Gwendolyn answered. "There was no one to dower me."

"That is not entirely true," Alastair interrupted with a frown. "You never received it, but my father had a chest of fabric set aside for you." His gaze slid away from Gwendolyn. "I had forgotten about it until this moment."

More notations were made. When he had finished, Geordie looked up once more. "Did you sign a contract?"

"Aye," they both said in unison. Then Alastair continued, "After the signing, the entire castle celebrated that evening with a feast." The memory came to him, sharp and poignant. It was the first time he had touched Gwendolyn. He'd taken her hand in his and had pressed a kiss to her knuckles. A flare of desire had raced through him like nothing he'd experienced before. And he remembered thinking the next few days could not pass quickly enough until they were wed.

Geordie nodded as he scribbled more notes. When he looked up once more, he avoided looking at Gwendolyn. "Was the betrothal ever consummated?"

Gwendolyn's cheeks flamed. She shook her head, yet her gaze shifted to Alastair's lips.

"Nay," Alastair replied with a mirthless smile. It wasn't as if that thought had not entered his mind. He wanted to deny such, but he could not. Scenes from that time paraded through his memory: Gwendolyn looking lovelier than he'd ever seen her sitting in the great hall with Mrs Morgan and Mrs Honey, planning the wedding breakfast. . .Gwendolyn leaning against the courtyard wall, gazing out at the loch with the wind pressing her gown against her exquisite form. . .Gwendolyn dancing in the great hall when she thought no one was watching. Sitting with Gwendolyn along the shores of the loch. . .

He looked at her then to see tears forming in her eyes. Was she remembering the past as well? He'd assumed she'd agreed to the betrothal to ensure her survival and that of her siblings. Could it have been more to her as it had been for him? He'd never thought to ask her then, or even now.

"Excuse me, please. I need—" Her voice filled with anguish, she stood and turned away.

He could not let her go without at least trying to comfort her, and perhaps reveal that he too had memories of that time. He followed her out into the hallway and away from the door. He moved to her, caught her shoulders, and turned her to pull her against his chest, tightening his arms around her.

She struggled. "Nay, you should not. . . We should not."

"'Tis right for us to mourn for what might have been."

At his words, she relaxed into his embrace. With her head bowed, she stood silently in his arms. Alastair tightened his arms more, as if to absorb any of the hurt he might have caused her.

"I have good memories of the times we were together," he admitted. "It is good to mourn for what we both lost."

She looked up at him then. "You remember those times fondly?"

"They were the happiest times of my life thus far."

She stared at him in astonishment until she lowered her gaze.

"Gwendolyn, I must ask you one more question away from the solicitor. Did Garrick ever force himself on you or your sister?"

Gwendolyn's cheeks warmed. "He tried to force himself on me once, but I nearly killed him."

Alastair's breath released in an explosive rush and his shoulders relaxed. "I wish you had."

She shook her head. "Then the three of us would have died as well with no food or water."

"If only I had been here." Profound sadness echoed in his voice.

"It is not you who needs to make amends. Garrick

should pay for what he did to us."

"There will be dire consequences. I promise you that." Alastair straightened. "Are you ready to continue?"

She nodded and glanced at him quickly. It was long enough for him to see that her eyes were still misty, but the pain in those beautiful blue eyes had vanished. She took her seat, keeping her gaze lowered so that he could not read any further emotion reflected there.

"Continuing on," the solicitor announced, turning to Alastair. "Laird MacLeod, did you ever petition the courts to have Gwendolyn Harris declared legally dead after she went missing for five years?"

Alastair tensed. "Nay. It did not occur to me since we found bloody clothing and a swathe of her hair along the shoreline. We all assumed she was. . .dead."

"Yet she was not dead." The solicitor's lips thinned. "I presume you also did not pursue a legal dissolution of marriage?"

"Nay." His jaw tightened.

"Now you are betrothed to another?"

"Aye."

Geordie set his pen down and sat back. His gaze shifted between Gwendolyn and Alastair. "Under Scottish Law, and in the eyes of the courts, you, Laird MacLeod and Gwendolyn Harris are still bound by your original betrothal."

Alastair's first emotion was pure elation. Then he thought of Beatrice and a prick, as sudden as a dagger thrust, pierced through that joy. How many nights had he lain awake in the dark, wondering if he could have done something to avoid Gwendolyn's death? How many times had he walked the shores of the loch, hoping to see her walking along the shoreline as well, returning to him unharmed and alive? And now, Gwendolyn sat beside him, very much alive as he'd always hoped for. They were still legally betrothed, and yet he had betrayed her by committing himself to another woman.

Geordie assumed Alastair's silence was a signal to continue. "There are several ways to move forward from here. Laird MacLeod, if you would like to break the betrothal to Miss Harris, then there will be a financial penalty, such as forfeiting the bride price. Since none was paid, Gwendolyn, you may consider suing Laird MacLeod for breach of promise."

"There will be no need to sue me. I would gladly support Miss Harris with an annual sum whether we stay betrothed or not."

Silence settled over the room as he and Gwendolyn simply looked at each other, neither knowing quite what to say.

Geordie cleared his throat, breaking that silence. "Then the last thing I must inform you of is if you wish to uphold your original betrothal to Gwendolyn Harris, then you will still have to forfeit whatever bride price you paid to Miss Beatrice Lamont." Geordie released a long breath. "How would you like me to proceed?"

A flash of fear shone in Gwendolyn's eyes before it was gone. She stared off into the distance, no longer meeting his gaze. Would she remain silent? Certainly she had an opinion about her own fate. And just when he started to think she was unaffected by the news that they were still betrothed, he saw the flutter of her pulse in the hollow of her throat. He stared at the rhythmic pulse in fascination, warmed by the evidence that she was not unaffected by what had transpired here.

Finally, she straightened and looked at him. "We are both reasonable people, are we not?" Her blue eyes filled with resolve. "Do what you will. If you wish to pursue your relationship with Beatrice, I will not stand in your way."

He reached out blindly to clutch at the arms of his chair as a surge of anger moved through him. Would she not fight for what they could have had together? In the next moment his sanity returned. Some of the tension left his body. Gwendolyn was not trying to hurt him any more than she already had. Quite the opposite. She was allowing him to take the lead and choose the path forward for himself. Except, he did not know what path he preferred: Gwendolyn or Beatrice.

Profound weariness weighed him down as he returned his gaze to Geordie. "Might I have some time to consider what to do? This decision affects others as well as myself. I need time to think things through."

"Of course." Geordie gathered his papers and returned

them to his satchel. "Instead of returning to Kilmuir, I will find a room in Dunvegan village."

Alastair stood. "Nonsense. You will take a room here. There are plenty, and I know Callum will enjoy spending time with a friend."

Geordie smiled. "Thank you, Laird MacLeod. I accept your hospitality."

"Let me summon Becks or Mrs Morgan to take you to your chambers." He moved to the bellpull and tugged it once.

"I can take him to his chamber," Gwendolyn offered.

"Nay. You and I still have much to discuss." He broke off as his steward appeared in the doorway.

"Ye rang, m'laird?"

"Becks, please escort our newest guest to a chamber in the south wing. He'll be staying with us for a few days." At the steward's bow, Alastair turned to Geordie. "Once you are settled, you can find my brother in the great hall. Join him there."

Geordie bowed and followed Becks from the chamber. When they were gone, Alastair turned back to Gwendolyn. She stood by the window now, looking out over the rear courtyard. The strong sunlight streaming through the window highlighted her skin with a burnished glow, making her appear even more ethereal than she had looked when Garrick had thrown her image with the pane of glass. The gown she wore hugged her small waist and fitted snugly over the swell of her breasts. She was of medium height, but she appeared much taller, for despite all she had suffered, she carried herself boldly, proudly, and with grace.

He could feel himself harden just looking at her. She was his if he wanted her. The thought brought a bittersweet smile to his lips.

She turned, and seeing the evidence of his desire, her cheeks flushed. "Thank you for encouraging Samuel to join the others in sword practise."

"Every young man should know how to defend himself and those he cares for."

"And women do not deserve such consideration? Are they not in need of protecting themselves and others as well?"

He lifted a brow and drew closer to her. "Anytime you would like to learn to wield a sword, only say the word and I will teach you."

She lifted her chin in challenge. "You would teach your enemies how to fight?"

"You, dear Gwendolyn, are not my enemy." He wished she looked less challenging and more vulnerable. He was having a difficult time recalling her recent suffering when he was having his own immediate physical response to her presence. Without being conscious of what he was doing, he gently took her chin between his forefinger and thumb, tipping her face up to his. He moved his thumb from her chin to her lower lip, rubbing lightly against its inviting fullness. He realised what he was doing and released her, his hands falling to his sides.

She swallowed roughly and looked away, drew a breath, then turned back to him. "What are you going to do about being betrothed to two women?" In her eyes he saw both fear and uncertainty. She was no doubt thinking of not only her survival, but that of her siblings.

"What would you like to happen?"

Her glance slid away. "I have no opinion in this matter."

"That's not true. I believe you have several opinions and I'd like to hear them."

"I cannot decide your fate."

He arched a brow. "But you'd like me to decide yours?"

Gwendolyn's teeth pressed hard into her lower lip. "It's not just myself I need to consider. I'm afraid for Arabella."

"She'll recover in time. I will spare no expense in seeing her returned to health. Besides, the progress she's made so far proves your sister is a lot like you—strong and determined."

"I thank you for your support of Arabella. As for myself, I've had to be strong my whole life. Which is why I know I can survive losing you if that is what you choose. Can Beatrice do the same?"

She had neatly managed to turn this conversation back on him. "Beatrice has not suffered the way you have. That fact alone is more than enough of a reason to choose you as my bride. You need the security marriage can bring to your life and that of your kin far more than Beatrice does."

Her brow furrowed. "Why did you agree to a marriage that the council set forth?"

He winced at the words. "Is it that obvious that the match between Beatrice and myself is not a love match?"

"Those are your words, not mine, and you still didn't answer the question."

He shrugged. "The entire council seemed to welcome the match in order to facilitate peace amongst the clans."

Her eyes narrowed. "You would sacrifice your own happiness for the council?"

She had laid his decision out before him with simplicity, but the situation was quite complex. He could either have love and marriage with major conflicts amongst the clans, or he could have peace between the clans and a marriage that was lacking. "Peace amongst the clans is vital," he said, his expression grave.

He shook his head, trying to clear his thoughts. "Might we talk of other things?"

"Certainly."

"Would you tell me what it was like for you in the tower?"

"Why would you want to know that?"

He offered her an encouraging smile as he motioned to two chairs near the bookshelves. "I've heard talking about a tragedy, or a time of great emotion, can be very cathartic. Perhaps it will help you move forward with your life, in whatever form that takes."

She pursed her lips, thinking. "It was very dark and very cold."

When she said nothing more, Alastair's anger flared. "That is all? Pray tell, did you like being chained to a wall? Or not knowing if or when someone might come to feed you, or bring you water?"

She tensed and her cheeks flamed. "Nay, I didn't enjoy being chained to the wall like an animal. I hated not knowing when or where Garrick would appear, or wondering if this was the day he would finally kill all of us. I was hungry, thirsty, desperate, and so alone. Even though we had each other, I still felt as though I was in a cocoon, wanting to die, and wanting to live with equal measure. After the first few months, when I'd become more settled into our bizarre reality, the desire to live started to override everything else. I wanted to live to feel the sun shine down upon my face once more, to feel the soft grass slip between my toes. I wanted to live for my brother and sister, to see them grow up and to one day run free as I had done for many more years than they ever had." Gwendolyn drew in a ragged breath. "Is that what you wanted to know? What it's like to be a prisoner?"

Agony coiled in his chest. "I wanted to know what I did to you by not protecting you on our wedding day. I should have walked into the chapel beside you. I've replayed that day over and over in my mind hundreds of times." He looked up at her miserably.

She reached out, took his hands in hers. Her delicate fingers folded around his larger ones.

He held tight as if she were a lifeline. "In every scenario, I failed you. For that I am so terribly sorry."

"Neither of us is at fault. We cannot live backwards. It is how we move forward into the future that matters." At her gentle smile, Alastair felt as though a suffocating weight had been lifted from his chest.

The anxiety that had shadowed her eyes since yesterday vanished, replaced with a glimmer of hope.

"Gwendolyn, I have no right to ask anything more of you, but in this moment, you are the only one I want by my side as I investigate who amongst us might have aided Garrick in his release from our prison."

Gwendolyn released his hand with a light squeeze before settling back into her chair. "I will help you do anything if it means Garrick will pay for what he's done to all of us."

Alastair smiled as the pain of the past faded away. "Good. Here's what I have in mind."

CHAPTER ELEVEN

A LASTAIR AND GWENDOLYN walked down to the ground floor where the four warriors who had been drugged were recovering from the effects of the laudanum. The chamber was in the servants' quarters and had a bed in each corner of the room. Alastair was pleased to find the men sitting up and talking when he and Gwendolyn entered the chamber.

Ronald and Lindon were men who had come to the castle with Alastair. Emery and Innis had lived at Dunvegan all their lives. Their fathers and grandfathers had served the lairds MacLeod for years. And yet, no one was above suspicion.

"M'laird," Ronald greeted as he entered the chamber. He and the others swung their legs over the edge of the bed, intending to rise.

"Remain where you are." Alastair stilled them with a motion of his hand. "We can speak from here." He moved to the corner of the chamber and returned with two chairs, sitting them inside the entrance so that both he and Gwendolyn could see each man in his bed.

Ronald settled back against the headboard. Innis sat on the edge of the bed, his expression grim. Lindon's face was pale as he leaned up on his elbow. Sitting at the edge of the bed, Emery's eyes were faintly red-rimmed, and he fiddled with the edge of the sheet.

Alastair looked to each man, saying nothing. He wasn't certain all these men were victims. It would have been easy for one of them to drug the others then drink the altered ale in order to appear as though they had not helped Garrick escape. Yet none of them looked particularly guilty. "I'd like to know what happened. How did Garrick MacDonald manage to overcome four warriors when he was locked in the dungeon?"

Ronald cleared his throat. "If I may, m'laird." At a nod from Alastair, he continued. "One of the maids brought us the mugs of ale. She said you had ordered the ale be sent to us since we were in for a long shift of guarding the dungeon."

Ronald lowered his eyes. "We should have known something was up, but we were all very thirsty. It wasn't until I started feeling a little strange and couldn't keep my eyes open that I realised the ale had been tampered with. When we were all incapacitated, she must have broken Garrick out of the cell."

"The rest of you, can you remember anything? Was the girl familiar to you?"

They all shook their heads, except for Emery. There was

something in Emery's expression—something that said he knew more than he was saying.

"If you remember even the slightest detail about the girl, please tell us. Do you recall the colour of her hair, her height, the tone of her voice?" Gwendolyn asked sitting forward in her chair.

"She had brown hair that was pulled back in a braid," Lindon offered.

"She was pretty," Innis said as pink tinged his cheeks. "She was of medium height with a narrow waist and," he paused as his cheeks grew red "forgive me, my lady for saying such, but she had a large bosom."

Gwendolyn offered the young man an understanding smile. "The more description, the better. Was she young? Older?"

"Young," they all said in unison.

"And obviously strong," Alastair added. "For not only did she drug all of you, she somehow managed to cleave her way through the lock on the door with an axe. What woman has the strength to do that?"

Alastair's gaze narrowed on Emery as the young man suddenly clutched one hand over his mouth. With the other, he grabbed a pot near his bedside and vomited.

Alastair frowned. Was Emery's body still purging itself of the effects of the laudanum, or was something else at play here? Alastair would have to keep a sharp eye on the lad from this moment forward. "I will gather the serving girls who match that description and bring them here to see if you recognise the one who drugged you."

Alastair met Gwendolyn's gaze, read the hint of excitement there. They knew they were looking for a pretty young woman of medium height with brown hair and an ample bosom. It wasn't a lot to go on, but it was at least a start. "Thank you, gentlemen. We will leave you to rest." Both he and Gwendolyn rose, then left the room.

Once they'd returned to the first floor and out of earshot of anyone else, Alastair turned to Gwendolyn with a grim smile. "I have no right to ask you to help me."

She reached out and placed her hand on his arm. "I want to help. Besides, it would be easier for me to visit the kitchen and ask about such a young woman than the laird of the castle. My query will arouse little suspicion since it would be only natural for me to seek a maid to help both my sister and me."

"Promise you will be careful. Our pretty little nemesis obviously had help from someone else."

"I promise." Gwendolyn drew back her hand. "You think it was Emery who helped the serving maid, don't you? I saw the way you watched him."

"I will keep an eye on him, to be sure." His gaze narrowed on her face. Gwendolyn's cheeks were filled with more colour than they had held earlier today, and her eyes shone with a sense of purpose as they used to in the past. The woman who had suffered unimaginable horrors over the past five years was coming alive once more. His pulse quickened at the thought.

Her lips curved lightly in a genuine smile that was tinged with a hint of challenge. "May we both find the answers we need to hold Garrick and the MacDonalds accountable for their actions."

"Aye." Alastair inclined his head, trying not to focus on the curve of her lips—lips that had so easily molded to his earlier today. He stood with his fists clenched as he watched her move down the corridor and vanish from his sight. While he didn't want to expose her to further harm, he needed her help in finding the maid. To make certain she was not hurt, he would have to stay close, be ready to come to her aid. Which would be easier to accomplish if Beatrice wasn't vying for his time and attention as well.

He would have to find some way to keep that woman distracted and out of his way until he and Gwendolyn could solve the mystery surrounding Garrick's escape.

As GWENDOLYN MADE her way to the kitchen, all the thoughts she'd avoided thinking while she'd been distracted with interviewing the men came back to her full force. She and Alastair were still legally betrothed. What did that mean for her and her siblings? Would it help her in her quest for freedom? Or did that mean she still belonged to him, and that she would remain at Dunvegan? Did that thought make her happy?

Every question she asked brought a fresh rush of blood to pulse through her ears, making her feel a little dizzy. She squared her shoulders and continued on, shifting her thoughts from what was at stake to the past they'd shared. His father had swept her and her siblings away from death and destruction and had given them a new life at Dunvegan. Their world had suddenly been filled with light and possibility and hope. And while she and Alastair had both been young at the time, there had always been an awareness between them.

Over the years, they had exchanged youthful smiles and awkward conversations. Every time he had looked at her, her nerves had jumbled in her stomach. At the sound of his voice, her heart had fluttered madly in her chest. But it was one particular evening they'd shared that came to mind.

They had found themselves at the shore of the loch at dusk. Alastair had invited her to sit with him on one of the large rocks. Side by side, they had stared up at the darkening sky in silence until it had turned from grey to black. When the stars came out overhead, she had known it was time to go. The thought of leaving him, of ending this interlude, had made her feel a moment of panic. "I don't want to leave. . ." she'd said, then realizing she'd said the words aloud, she'd pulled away and stood, terrified by what he must think of her. She held her breath, waiting for him to call her "mad" or "childish."

Instead of deriding her, Alastair had given her a smile that had warmed her clear to her toes and said, "Then don't. Stay with me." He'd patted the surface of the rock once more. "Stay with me. . .always."

Gwendolyn hadn't known what it felt like to love someone until that moment. That emotion had swept through her, filling her soul in a way it had never been filled before. As she sat back down, he had taken her hand in his and had stared down at her.

There was an intensity in his gaze that had stolen her breath. "You are sweet, Gwendolyn Harris. And I like you very much."

She'd given him a trembling smile and had locked that moment away in her heart as her affection for him had turned to love. They had been engaged weeks later, and on her wedding day she'd felt as though she couldn't live without him by her side.

Yet fate, and Garrick MacDonald, had had other plans. And over the course of the last five years, time and circumstance had tempered them and their feelings for each other. She didn't blame him for what had happened. And she didn't blame Alastair for moving on with his life.

But he had moved on.

A prior betrothal could not eradicate that fact. It was time for both of them to face the truth. What they once had was over. Her steps faltered as she entered the kitchen as an overwhelming sense of loss came over her. The bustling activity in the kitchen drew her attention as she regained her footing.

Two serving girls worked around a big table in the center of the chamber. One kneaded bread while the other sliced various vegetables into chunks. A young man stood at the hearth, turning the spit. Mrs Honey's back was to the door upon Gwendolyn's entrance as she set a tray of baked goods upon a table near the oven to cool. She wiped her hands on her apron and turned, then paused.

"Hello, dearie. It is good tae see yer face around here once more," Mrs Honey greeted Gwendolyn with a smile. "Yer just in time tae taste a fresh batch of apple pasties I just pulled from the oven." She scooped a pastry onto a plate.

Gwendolyn started to object until the sweet and savoury scent of the small pies touched her senses. "They smell divine." It had been so long since she'd had such a treat. When Mrs Honey handed her a small plate with a warm, aromatic treat, Gwendolyn could not find the will to object. Instead, she found herself perching on a stool near the oven and popped a small piece of the flaky pastry into her mouth.

Her taste buds erupted, and she groaned her pleasure. "That is the most delicious thing I've ever tasted, Mrs Honey." She took another big bite and tried to keep from groaning again.

The cook's smile brightened her face. "Did ye come here wantin' a morsel tae eat, or can I help ye with somethin' else?"

Gwendolyn finished off the delicacy and set the plate in her lap. She searched the chamber for other young women, but there were only the two at the table in sight. "Is this the entire kitchen staff?" Gwendolyn asked.

"Other than the pantler, butler, and poulterer, it is just me and the scullery maids." She arched a brow. "How can we be of service?"

Neither of the maids matched the description the men had given. "I've been away so long, I was just looking around the castle, trying to remember it all."

"Oh, dearie," she said with understanding. "Take all the time ye need tae reacquaint yerself with this old castle. Feel free tae come visit me anytime. I always have treats fer my favourites."

Gwendolyn was surprised by how at ease she felt with the cook. They'd worked together on occasion before, but only briefly as Gwendolyn had been introduced to the tasks of running the household. The relaxed sensations she felt now went beyond those tasks to a more personal level. It was as if Mrs Honey understood the dangers Gwendolyn had navigated over the past five years. Perhaps the cook had gone through a similar challenge in her life. They were both survivors. "Thank you, Mrs Honey. Would you consider teaching me how to cook?" If she were to leave the castle with her siblings, she needed a few basic skills to see her through.

If the woman was surprised by the request, she did not show it. "Of course. I would be delighted." She took the now empty plate from Gwendolyn. "Come back tomorrow and we will start with making bread."

Gwendolyn stood. "Until tomorrow then." She made her way to the door, feeling a new sense of contentedness. She had not discovered who might have doused the men's ale with laudanum, but she had gained yet another friend amongst the members of this household.

CHAPTER TWELVE

A LASTAIR WAITED FOR Gwendolyn just outside of Arabella's bedchamber. He knew her well enough to know that was where she would head after speaking with the kitchen staff. Her priority was to see her sister returned to full health.

At the sight of Gwendolyn coming down the hallway, Alastair straightened. "Did you discover anything?" he asked when she came closer.

She shook her head. "There are only two serving girls and neither fit the description given to us by the men." Gwendolyn drew an unsteady breath. "What will we do now?"

"You will go inside and visit with your sister. I must think of some way to set a trap for our traitor, or traitors."

The animation in her face vanished. "If you do not need my assistance any longer, then I will go see my sister."

He reached for her chin and tipped her face to his. "I did not say I didn't need your help. In fact, I would dearly appreciate your assistance tomorrow at the council meeting."

"Why would you want me there?"

"The other clan leaders and I will be discussing what to do about the MacDonalds. Your experiences with Garrick MacDonald would be a valuable addition to our discussion. They need to know what he did to you and your siblings during your captivity."

She hesitated a moment before nodding. "If you think I can be of assistance, then aye, I will attend." She opened the door and stepped inside the chamber. "Until tomorrow then."

"Until tomorrow."

Alastair stood in the doorway watching as Gwendolyn and then her brother, who stood by the hearth, joined Arabella on her bed. Their expressions were filled with love, contentment, and ease.

Envy flooded him. They were at peace in each other's company. But then again, he and Gwendolyn had shared a closeness today as well. Despite the passage of time, they'd fallen right back into that same old pattern of trust and companionship. He did trust her, and he liked being near her. She saw him in a way that made him feel solid and reliable—a way others did not. He'd come back to Dunvegan to be the man Gwendolyn saw.

He closed the door and headed down the stairs towards the great hall. He and Gwendolyn could go right back to the place where they'd left off, if that was what they both wanted.

But what did she want? She claimed she wanted to give

him his freedom because he had moved on with his life. And he had. He'd allowed the Isle Council members to arrange his marriage to Beatrice to serve as a bridge between warring clans.

Alastair frowned. Was that enough of a reason to bind himself to the woman for the rest of his days? They were no love match. But peace amongst the clans was vital if they were to avoid the coming clan war and instead consolidate their effort towards fighting the English.

Alastair smothered a groan as he reached the great hall as he realised he was no closer to an answer. What he needed was to spend some time with Beatrice, alone. Perhaps then he might know what was best for all who were caught in this complex situation.

Determined to find some clarity, he entered the solar to find Beatrice and her father. Her father read from a book while Beatrice simply sat in a chair, looking uncomfortable and bored. At his entrance into the chamber, a smile came to her lips. "There you are. I was beginning to despair that I would ever see you today."

"I came to ask you to take a walk with me."

"It would be my pleasure," Beatrice said as she leapt up from her chair. Laird Lamont set his book aside and rose as well.

"Might I have a short time alone with your daughter, Laird Lamont? You have my word I will keep her safe."

Laird Lamont's eyes narrowed as it shifted between

Alastair and Beatrice. "Well, since you are getting married in four days, I suppose I could allow that."

Alastair offered the man a bow as he took Beatrice's hand and placed it on his arm, escorting her towards the door. "Do you have a shawl to cover your shoulders? I thought we might take a walk along the shores of the loch."

She frowned. "Along the water? Won't it be wet and dreary down there?"

"The sky is clear, and the tide is out. Get your shawl and I'll show you." Alastair couldn't keep the excitement he felt from his voice. While the castle held many bad memories for him, the shores of the loch only held pleasant ones.

"If that is what you wish," Beatrice said, releasing her grip on his arm to head upstairs. She returned several minutes later with a brown woolen shawl draped over her shoulders. "Let's go see this loch of yours."

Alastair ignored the irritation in her voice as he led her across the rear courtyard and to the sea gate. "So tell me, Beatrice, what are the things in life that bring you joy?"

At the question, her brown eyes lit up. "I love assemblies where you can socialise with other like-minded people and dance. There is a new assembly room being built on Ingram Street in Glasgow, and I simply adore shopping along Buchanan Street." She frowned as they came to the rocky shoreline. "Must we really walk over that?"

He took her hand in his. "Let me help you." Alastair assisted Beatrice along the rocky shoreline until they were once again on even ground. "Glasgow is far from here. Do you like any activities that are closer to home on the isles?"

"There is nothing remarkable about the Hebrides." She frowned at him as she picked her way along the shore, trying desperately not to touch anything wet. "This is wretched. Why do you like it here?" She moved back to higher ground and glared at him.

Alastair remained where he was. How could he explain what it was about the loch that he cherished? It was the scents of the earth and the sea, the sound of the water lapping against the shore, the feel of the sun warming his skin, the rush of blood moving through his veins as he thought about how many of his ancestors had stood in this very spot, gazing out at the Little Minch in the distance with the wind in their hair.

Dunvegan was an essential part of him. "This is my home," he replied simply. "This is where I will stay. And as my wife, I hope you will stay here with me."

Beatrice's face paled. "Will we ever go to Glasgow or Edinburgh?"

Disappointment flooded him. "Occasionally, I suppose."

Alastair turned back to the water's edge. He drew in a deep breath, taking into himself what he needed from this place. Peace. Connection. Determination.

"Alastair? Why are you ignoring me?" Beatrice's angry voice called out. "I cannot move. There is muck and water everywhere I look. How will I get back to the castle without ruining my boots?"

Alastair drew one last fortifying breath before he turned around, then moving to Beatrice's side, he swept her into his arms and carried her back to the courtyard. At her satisfied smile, he knew she was pleased at the solution.

When he set her down, she clung to his arm. "The next four days cannot pass quickly enough for me, Alastair. I wish you didn't have to hold this council meeting. It's getting in the way of our plans for the wedding. I still haven't talked with your cook about what to serve at our wedding breakfast. And the minister has yet to arrive."

"There is time for all of that," he said absently as he looked back at the shores of the loch then at Dunvegan. The muscles of his stomach clenched as memories of the past came back to him, then suddenly his stomach eased. The horrors of the past were gone. They had vanished along with the afternoon air. Nothing as hideous as his mother's death would ever touch this castle and its people again. And if it did, he would find a way to combat it. He was the laird of the castle, the chief of his people, and now a guardian of all those who lived on the isle. He was committed to finding a peaceful solution to the clan wars, but was marriage to Beatrice the only way to achieve that? He needed more time to consider a path forward. Perhaps tomorrow after the council meeting, he would know for certain the direction his future was supposed to take, and which woman, Beatrice or Gwendolyn, would help him best achieve that goal.

LATER THAT AFTERNOON, Graeme returned to Dunvegan from his secret mission. Alastair met him and the men who had accompanied him at the castle gate. "Success?" Alastair asked his captain of the guard as the men entered the castle along with a wagon that was covered with a tarp, shielding the wagon's contents from onlookers.

"Aye," Graeme replied. "The supplies you sent from France were waiting with your contact in Portree just as you said."

Graeme dismounted and stood alongside Alastair at the side of the wagon. "For a man of peace, I find it interesting that you felt the need for such military force."

Alastair peered beneath the tarp at the one hundred flint-lock pistols and ammunition his contact had secured for him. "You and I both know that it is best to be prepared. It is my hope that the MacLeods never need to use such force, but if we do, we will not be left wanting."

Graeme gave him a sober nod. "To the armory then?"

Alastair secured the tarp then nodded. "I will see to this. You and the men must go once more and invite the isles' clan leaders to the council table. It is time to begin our talks of peace, but to be prepared for war."

AFTER SUPPER THAT evening, Alastair headed upstairs to the drawing room, relishing the moments alone as he stood looking out one of the two windows that overlooked the loch. The moon hung low in the night sky and reflected on the glassy waters below, limning the trees that skirted the shoreline in silver.

A knock sounded behind him and he turned to see Rowena framed in the doorway. "Might I come in for a moment, Brother?"

"Of course," he replied, turning fully to greet her.

She shut the door behind her before making her way to his side. "This is for you," she said, extending a leather hat box out to him.

He accepted the item and waved her towards the settee. She took a seat, and he followed but left enough space between them for him to set the hat box down. "You wished to bring me a hat?" he asked in a sober tone.

"Nay, Brother. Look inside," she said with an eager smile.

He unbuckled the latch and peered at the contents. His breath stilled in his chest at the sight of the unmistakable embroidered red elf dots and crosses upon a sea of faded yellow silk. "Is this what I think it is?"

She nodded. "You asked me to recreate the Fairy Flag, and so I have."

With a careful touch, he lifted the silk from the hat box and held up a perfect replica of their family's prized treasure.

Every detail had been carefully recreated. He met his sister's pleased gaze. "You did this from memory?"

Her smile faded. "You forget that while you were learning what you needed to know to become the heir, and when you and our brothers were busy with war games and other manly accomplishments, I sat in this chamber alone for hours teaching myself how to stitch, or reading the books in Father's library, or pacing the length of the chamber." Rowena swallowed hard, her throat working. "With Mother gone, and then you, Tormod, and Orrick, I was so lonely. I made daily trips to this chamber to talk to the Fairy Flag. It was the one thing that bound all of us together because of its importance to our clan."

Her fingers knotted together in her lap. "I had hoped that a little fairy magic would make its way to you, and somehow let you know how desperately I wanted you to come home."

He returned the flag to the hat box and set it aside, taking her hands in his. "I sent you to Miss Dottie's. I had hoped that you would meet other like-minded young ladies there."

"There were some that made the time away from Dunvegan tolerable, but the head mistress took a special hatred of me because I was a MacLeod. Father and his men had raided her family's village and had killed her one and only child. The woman was vicious to me and made my life there a living hell." Her voice dropped to a raw whisper. "When I finally completed my studies, I could bear no more and finally came home."

He squeezed her fingers. "Rowena, I had no idea." His voice was soft. "I can only guess at your pain, and I am so sorry to have put you through that, alone. You are a very brave young woman, braver than many men I know." He caught her gaze, connected with it in a way he hadn't ever before. "I am very proud to call you my sister."

Determination shone in her gaze. "Does that pride extend to me knowing what is good for me?"

"I trust you to know your own mind, if that's what you mean."

"Good. Then you will have no problem with me marrying Marcus MacDonald."

Alastair laughed. "Let's not jump too far ahead of ourselves. If Marcus MacDonald is of great importance to you, then I promise to get to know him better. Then, and only then, will I consider such a connection." He raised their joined hands and kissed her fingers before releasing her. "You are precious to me, Rowena. And I will not hand you over to just any man."

She smiled. "Marcus is not just any man. You will see."

"I am certain I will."

Rowena's gazed moved to the empty frame between the two windows. "What will you do with the replica of the Fairy Flag now that you have it?"

"Nothing at the moment." Alastair returned the lid to

the hat box and buckled it closed. "I will keep this somewhere safe until after the council meeting, as I had intended to confront the laird of the MacDonalds about stealing the flag from us through Garrick's machinations."

Rowena placed her hand atop the hat box. "Then let us hope this replica will bring our family more luck than the original flag ever seemed to."

Alastair smiled. "How could it not? It was made with love."

"Let's hope that is enough to push the odds in our favour. The outcome of this council meeting affects not only this clan, but all of Scotland."

Rowena was correct. War was coming. This meeting of the Isle Council would help to decide if that war was amongst the clans or if they could somehow put aside their differences with each other to join forces against the English.

The English were a far greater threat. When the time finally came for the Scottish armies to battle the English, they would need every advantage. And that included the MacLeods taking possession of the real Fairy Flag once more.

Only a MacLeod could call upon the fairy magic and turn the tide of battle in their favour when the flag was unfurled for a third and final time.

CHAPTER THIRTEEN

T HE MORNING HAD been a whirlwind of activity as the clan leaders and their entourages arrived at Dunvegan Castle. Gwendolyn had watched from afar until Alastair came to escort her into the great hall. Clusters of men gathered around the long Birnam oak table in the center of the chamber, talking. At her entrance, the conversation stopped and the other men in the chamber took their seats around the council table. Alastair led her to a chair beside him. As she nervously took her seat, she noted that Graeme and Callum stood near the doors of the chamber, ready to assist if needed but not truly part of the assembly.

Then her gaze shifted to the opposite side of the chamber to note that Beatrice and her father had been amongst the clusters of men. They took two seats along the west wall of the chamber. Not participating, but observing the proceedings. It was unusual for any woman to be a part of such discussions, and yet Alastair had invited both her and Beatrice.

For the next half an hour, Gwendolyn sat quietly while the men around the table argued and shouted at one another.

An unbearable tension filled the chamber as talk of war prevailed.

The six main clans occupying the Hebridean Isles were all there: the MacLeods, MacDonalds, MacQueens, Nicolsons, MacKinnons, and MacAskills. The Guardians of the Isles. Laird MacAskill was the oldest of the council members. The seriousness of his expression was only emphasised by his greying hair and beard. The lairds MacDonald, MacQueen, and MacKinnon were in their late forties, probably the same age Alastair's father would have been if he were still alive. Laird Nicolson was in his midthirties, making Alastair the youngest of the six.

Gwendolyn frowned as her gaze moved back to Alastair. Would these men see him as their equal? Or would he have to prove himself to them over and over as he had to his father?

At a shout from Laird MacDonald, her thoughts focused once more on the matter at hand—her kidnapping and imprisonment at the hands of Garrick MacDonald.

"Lies, nothing but lies. Garrick has been amongst us for the past five years. How is a man supposed to be in two places at once? And if he had stolen the Fairy Flag, would we have not already used it? Clan Donald is fractured across Scotland. In small segments, we are far less powerful than if we joined together once more. But have we done such a thing? Nay!" He pounded his fist on the table.

"If Garrick has been amongst you, then why did you not

bring him here today as proof?" Alastair's tone was laced with accusation.

Alexander MacDonald responded with a blistering glare. "He did not wish to come to this den of vipers."

Alastair did not react. Instead he continued to survey the laird over his steepled fingers. "You did not bring him here today, because he is not with you or your clan. He escaped my dungeon with help from someone to whom I will show no mercy once I find them. And I have it on excellent authority that Garrick did steal the Fairy Flag. He gave it to you, Laird MacDonald, and I have a witness who will testify to that fact."

"Then bring this witness forward so that we can dispute this lie," Laird MacDonald clipped angrily.

Alastair turned to the woman beside him. "Gentlemen, I give you Gwendolyn Harris."

"Gwendolyn Harris?" Laird MacAskill's face paled at the sight of her. "You're alive?"

"Alive, but with a tale to tell," Alastair said.

Tension seemed to scream through the large chamber. The other five men at the table leaned forward in their seats. Gwendolyn looked around the table at the grim-faced men.

"In your own words, Gwendolyn, tell these men what has happened to you during the past five years," Alastair said in an encouraging tone.

Clutching the wooden edge of the table for support, Gwendolyn explained to the council what had transpired from the time of her abduction until she had been freed two days ago. The only time she faltered was when she had to confess to stealing the Fairy Flag and giving it to Garrick MacDonald.

"That's a lie." Laird MacDonald surged to his feet. "The girl has concocted the entire story." Despite his protest, Laird MacDonald's expression held a hint of satisfaction. "Why have you wasted our time with this outrageous tale that was no doubt invented by the MacLeod himself in order to push the clans to the brink of war?"

A deafening silence followed Laird MacDonald's statement as the men at the table all stared at her, as though waiting for some type of proof. But what proof did she have? She dropped her gaze to her hands as icy fear started to quake through her. It was then that she saw the bruises that still remained.

She lifted her hands and bared her wrists for those gathered around the table. "'Tis no tale I have spun, but the truth as evidenced by the deep bruises around my wrists from being bound with a rope. Similar wounds exist around my ankle from the shackle I wore for five years. If you demand to see my ankle, I will reveal that to you, in spite of my modesty."

"You could have injured yourself." Laird MacDonald narrowed his gaze, his face now filled with disgust.

"I did no such thing. I promise you." Gwendolyn's gaze raced over the male faces around the table. She could see not one that looked anything but either dubious or contemptuous of the truths she had told. For Alastair and his clan's safety, she had to convince them, but how?

Madly, she tried to think of something, anything that might help his cause when all of a sudden the door to the chamber flew open and an icy breeze swept through. Gwendolyn stiffened knowing what was to come. A heartbeat later, the Grey Lady drifted into the great hall in a sea of mist.

As though moving in unison, the men at the table leapt to their feet. Beatrice screamed as she sank to the floor in a dead faint. Her father did nothing to assist her as he stood frozen with fear. His words were slurred as he exclaimed, "Good God, what kind of horror is this?"

Laird MacQueen's face drained of all colour. "I've heard tales of the Grey Lady."

"'Tis a ghost!" Laird Nicolson took shelter behind his chair.

"An evil spirit!" Laird MacAskill drew his sword, as did Laird MacKinnon.

"The lady is my mother." Alastair left Gwendolyn's side to approach the apparition. "Thank you for your support, Mother. But 'tis best if you leave this matter to Gwendolyn and me."

I'll not let anyone else hurt her.

At the lady's words, the fear clutching Gwendolyn subsided. Once again, the Grey Lady, sensing her distress, had come to her aid. Despite the seriousness of the situation,

Gwendolyn allowed herself a small smile. "The Grey Lady was with my siblings and me while we were imprisoned in the tower. She knows what I say is the truth."

Garrick MacDonald is as vile a man as there ever was. He not only kidnapped Gwendolyn, but he also falsified her death, then forced her to steal the Fairy Flag. I watched him as he handed the Fairy Flag over to his kin along the shore of Loch Dunvegan under the cloak of darkness. For five years he has terrorised this castle with one mishap or another, destroyed the happiness of a young couple on their wedding day, and might be responsible for the death of Arabella Harris if her health does not improve.

The Grey Lady's voice boomed inside their minds, leaving the men with their mouths slack and eyes wide. When she had finished speaking, the grey mist shifted to a bright white. The light lifted towards the ceiling, then disappeared as quickly as it had come.

"We are supposed to take the word of a ghost as the truth?" Laird MacDonald was the first to recover from the Grey Lady's presence and disappearance.

"Why would a spirit lie about such things?" Laird Nicolson left the shelter of his chair and stood beside the table. "She has nothing in this life to lose, but perhaps she still has something to protect."

The lairds MacQueen, Nicolson, MacKinnon, and MacAskill exchanged glances before turning their narrowed gazes on Alexander MacDonald. Laird MacKinnon stepped forward. "A ghost has no reason to lie, but you on the other hand have much to gain from causing distrust and disorder amongst the clans on the isles and on the mainland."

Laird MacAskill's gaze shifted to Beatrice who was just now regaining her senses. Her father helped her from the floor and into her chair. Then his gaze shifted to Laird MacDonald. "You were the one to push for Laird MacLeod to be wed before he took his role as a guardian on the council, claiming 'by having a wife it would temper his need for war.'"

MacAskill's dark gaze narrowed on the man before him. "It was you who put forth Beatrice Lamont as a potential bride. You are allied with the Lamont clan, are you not?"

"We are all allied with many mainland clans." MacDonald's lips set grimly. "What are you implying?"

"That you sent a spy into Dunvegan under the pretext of marriage." Laird MacAskill's face reddened.

Alastair bolted out of his chair. He had his hand wrapped around the MacDonald's neck, effortlessly raising the man out of his chair until he drove him back, slamming him hard against the wall. "Your clan nearly destroyed my fiancée and her family, you stole the Fairy Flag, and now you dare to place a spy in our midst?"

"I. . .did. . .none of. . .those things," the MacDonald choked out as his face reddened.

"Can you say as much for your clan?"

"Nay."

Laird Nicholson came forward. "Let him go, Alastair.

This kind of violence isn't helping anyone's cause."

At a blazing glance from Alastair, Laird Nicolson backed away. Returning his attention to the man caught in his grasp, Alastair said, "Return the Fairy Flag to the MacLeods and this council might be able to move forward in talking about peace."

The Fairy Flag had never brought his family much luck, but he knew its magical influence when unfurled in battle to be true especially when they'd used it against the MacDonald clan in 1490. During a desperate battle between the two clans, the flag was unfurled and immediately the tide of the battle turned. Then again in 1520 at Waternish, the MacLeods were hopelessly outnumbered when the MacDonalds and clan Ranald joined forces against them. The flag was unfurled and the MacDonalds were defeated.

"I shall. . .consider it," the MacDonald leader choked out, his face turning purple.

Alastair loosened his grip slightly, allowing the man to draw a breath. "This is also your last warning not to meddle in my affairs or with anyone in this house and under my protection," he said in a lethal voice as he stood eye to eye with the MacDonald. "If you do, I will not hesitate to kill you, regardless of my desire for peace amongst the clans. Am I clear?"

The MacDonald's gaze was murderous, but he managed to mumble something that sounded like assent.

"See that you remember that promise." Alastair released

his hold on the man's neck and the laird collapsed to the floor, choking. Alastair's gaze slid to Beatrice. Her face held a look of innocence, or feigned innocence. He did not have the time right now to determine which. But she and he would have a serious discussion before the night was through.

Alastair shifted his attention back to the lairds as the chamber erupted in a cacophony of sound. The lairds shouted at one another, hurling past accusations for injustices done to them by the clans who were present and those who were not.

Gwendolyn blocked out the noise. Instead, her gaze shifted to Beatrice. After the accusation made by Laird MacAskill, another had occurred to Gwendolyn: Was Beatrice responsible for freeing Garrick MacDonald? Their gazes connected. Instead of paling as someone who had just fainted at the sight of a ghost might suggest she would, a bloom of colour came to Beatrice's cheeks and her lips lifted in a faint smile. A challenge reflected there.

Gwendolyn drew a sharp breath. What these men accused Beatrice of was true. She had betrothed herself to Alastair to become a spy for the MacDonalds; it wasn't a stretch to imagine she had disguised herself and dosed the guards in the dungeon with laudanum in order to set Garrick free. At first fear crept in, leaving a sour taste in Gwendolyn's mouth. Then anger took over. While the MacLeods had their failings, they had also been nothing but kind to her and her siblings. No one took advantage of Alastair MacLeod or his kin if she could do something about it. While she couldn't fight in the more conventional ways, she had one weapon in her arsenal that Beatrice and her father had not known about.

She was still legally betrothed to Alastair.

Gwendolyn might have earlier considered ending her relationship with Alastair, but now she had a reason to at least pretend to fight for what they'd once had as long as it protected him from the MacDonalds and their allies.

Beatrice's gaze connected with Gwendolyn's. Neither woman turned away. A war was coming. It might not be the war Alastair had expected. But a battle had begun right here in this chamber to win the heart of a man who deserved more than trickery and manipulation from those who lived within his castle's walls.

CHAPTER FOURTEEN

A LASTAIR HAD ENDED the council meeting abruptly, sending the men in different directions to calm down after an hour of arguing and accusing each other of villainy. The men left the chamber, including Beatrice's father, Callum, and Graeme. Yet Beatrice and Gwendolyn remained in the big, empty room.

Beatrice came forward—undulated was a more apt description of the way her hips swayed beneath her cinnamon-coloured gown as she crossed the planked floor. "So you're the dead girl."

Gwendolyn bristled. "I'm neither dead nor a girl."

Beatrice's gaze scanned the tight bodice of Gwendolyn's gown, her narrow waist, and the worn slippers that had yet to be replaced. "You aren't much to look at, are you? Captivity must have stunted your growth."

Gwendolyn had no response for the insult. With a twinge of envy, she couldn't help but notice that her rival was both tall and curvaceous. Her skin was pale, and yet a smattering of freckles brought a hint of colour to her cheeks. Her long, fiery-red hair was lush, with natural waves that cascaded across her shoulders. Her eyes were large and brown, with flecks of gold. She stopped before Gwendolyn and put a hand on her hips, a stance she had apparently perfected to best display the fullness of her breasts.

"Alastair and I are to be married soon. And when we are, you will no longer be a member of this household."

Gwendolyn was tempted to divulge the information the solicitor had shared with Alastair earlier, but that was a blow that would be best dealt by Alastair himself. At least the thought of that meeting brought a sense of peace to Gwendolyn. Beatrice might not know it, but they were battling upon equal ground. "That is Alastair's decision, not yours."

Beatrice's eyes flared. "A wife has ways of making her husband see what is in the best interest of their relationship. And that means sending you and your little family away. Far away."

"From what I know of Alastair, he always goes against what others expect of him," Gwendolyn countered as she brushed past Beatrice, heading for the door. "Though I've enjoyed your company, I must excuse myself. I have duties that must be attended to. Since you cannot say the same until you are made mistress of this castle, I can have a light repast sent up to your chamber for you and your father."

Beatrice's eyes sparked. "You'll do no such thing. I shall do it myself. Is it Mrs Morgan or Mrs Honey who is the cook? Oh, never mind. I'll figure it out myself."

GWENDOLYN SAT AT her sister's bedside, watching Arabella's chest rising and falling with ease while she slept. It warmed her spirit seeing her sister looking healthier, peaceful, calm. Gwendolyn shifted her gaze to Lottie who quietly rocked in a chair by the hearth, to the window, then back again to her sister. Gwendolyn's own nerves were anything but calm as idea after idea flitted through her mind about how she could wrest Alastair away from Beatrice. Manipulation and lies were not for her, which left Gwendolyn with nothing but brutal honesty to make her case against his marrying Beatrice.

But even that might not work in Gwendolyn's favour since only hours before Gwendolyn had claimed to want nothing more than to venture out on her own and somehow provide for herself and her family. She released her breath in a rush as despair overtook her. Would Alastair see her change of heart as a lie? Would he decide she was no better for him than Beatrice? Would the MacDonalds win this battle no matter what Gwendolyn tried to do? They did have the Fairy Flag after all. Garrick had told her he'd sent the flag back to the seat of their clan at Monkstadt House. She could only imagine he'd told her such because he hadn't expected them to live long enough to convey that information to anyone else. But since she had lived, could she retrieve the Fairy Flag and return it to its proper place at Dunvegan? Laird Mac-

Donald had indicated that he would return the stolen item. Yet she doubted he would. Five years of lies from Garrick MacDonald had taught her not to believe any of them.

Alastair was more than capable of going after the flag himself, but to do so with a full company of men would be seen as an act of war. She, on the other hand, could use stealth to recover the MacLeods' most treasured possession. In spite of the fact that she'd had no choice but to steal the flag and hand it over to the MacDonalds, Gwendolyn still felt a deep-seated guilt over what she had done. With her guilt assuaged and his resentment of what she'd done no longer a factor between them, they might actually have a change to start anew.

Gwendolyn pressed her lips together, giving the idea serious consideration when the door to the chamber opened and the steward, Becks, stepped inside. She hastened to the door, to prevent any conversation that might wake her sister. In a whisper she asked, "Is there something you need?"

He understood the wish for quiet and stepped back outside the door, signalling for her to follow.

In the hallway, Gwendolyn shut the door behind her, suddenly noticing the worry etched into the lines of the steward's face. "What is it, Becks? What's wrong?"

He opened and closed his hands nervously before him. "I didn't know where else to turn, milady. M'laird asked that no one disturb him while he returned to the council meeting. Master Callum is with him, as is his Captain of the

Guard. I do not feel right in discussing the matter with Miss Lamont, and Lady Rowena is out of the question," he hesitated, "so I came to you."

Gwendolyn reached out and placed her hand atop his, stilling his movements. "I will help with whatever I can. Please explain the situation more fully."

"Can we walk belowstairs while we talk, milady?"

"Of course." They walked quickly down the hallway and to the stairs, making their way towards the front of the castle.

"It's Marcus MacDonald," Becks said. "He's outside the castle gate and refusing to leave, especially now that Lady Rowena is on the opposite side of the gate, begging for someone to let him in."

"That is a problem," Gwendolyn agreed as they stepped outside and into the front courtyard. They continued towards the gate where a small crowd of the household staff and some of the castle's warriors had gathered to watch the unfolding drama.

When they drew nearer, Gwendolyn saw Rowena pressed against the gate with Marcus's arms wrapped around her. "I will take care of the situation, but you must convince the gatekeeper to open the portcullis."

Becks released a heavy sigh. "Thank you, milady. I know m'laird will be grateful to have your assistance in this matter."

Gwendolyn frowned. She wasn't so certain Alastair would be glad of her help when it came to Rowena, but someone had to do something before the situation got further out of hand. Making her way to Rowena's side, Gwendolyn looked past the love-stricken girl to the man on the other side of the gate. "If you ever want to see each other again, the two of you need to release each other this moment."

They shared a look, then stepped apart. As they separated, the gatekeeper raised the portcullis. When it was halfway raised, Marcus stepped through. Becks immediately signalled for the barrier to be dropped once more.

Before Rowena and Marcus could come together, Gwendolyn stepped between them, and linking Rowena's arm through her own, headed back towards the castle. Marcus trailed behind them. "Whatever else you have to say to each other would be best discussed in private. Understood?"

They both agreed as the three of them headed into the castle. They needed somewhere public to talk, yet without an audience. The two lovebirds had already overstepped the bounds of propriety. They needed a public room, but most of the chambers were either filled with people going about their daily routines, or with the clan leaders and their entourage.

Suddenly an idea came to Gwendolyn as she headed back out of the main keep and towards the old keep. The chapel in the older section of the castle would serve them well.

Once they were in the chapel, Gwendolyn released Rowena's arm and studied the two young people before her.

Marcus had obviously taken great care in dressing for his visit today. His dark brown hair was drawn back from his face and fastened with a black tie, and his dark blue coat fitted his shoulders impeccably. "All right, make your case as to why the two of you should be together despite the friction between your clans."

An expression of surprise crossed Marcus's face. "Rowena and I care for each other."

Gwendolyn's frown increased. Surely, if their affections were engaged, their feelings would be stronger than that. "Have you any idea the kind of scrutiny your relationship will be under if it is allowed to move forward? Your affections will have to be stronger than 'caring' for each other in order to survive the ordeal ahead of you."

Rowena glanced at Gwendolyn impatiently. "He meant to say we love each other."

"Then prove that to me. Rowena, what do you love about Marcus?"

Rowena remained silent as her brow furrowed in thought. "He is kind and gentle, yet strong and ready to fight against his own clan if necessary in order for us to be together. He does not look at me as his enemy. He sees me as I am."

Gwendolyn turned to Marcus. "And you, what do you love about Rowena?"

"Rowena is like a burst of sunlight on a misty day. Simply being near her soothes the rawness of my soul." He turned his gaze to Rowena. "I want to turn away from the violence that has fallen between our two clans. A union between Rowena and myself might be the first tentative link in forging that bond."

Gwendolyn released a pent-up breath. They truly did care for each other. "Well, before a link can be forged, a fire must be built." Her gaze narrowed on Marcus's face. "A man like Alastair MacLeod will require proof of your devotion, and your willingness to turn away from your clan if an accord cannot be reached."

Marcus smiled mockingly. "How am I supposed to do that when I am not even permitted to see Rowena?"

Gwendolyn stared at the man thoughtfully. "There is something. . . I have an idea that is a bit devious, but once executed, it would prove beyond a shadow of doubt where your loyalties lie."

"I'm listening."

"The MacDonalds stole something from the MacLeods."

Rowena gave a startled gasp, but then remained silent.

Marcus's gaze shifted from Rowena to Gwendolyn as a frown came to his lips. "The Fairy Flag."

Gwendolyn nodded. "The Fairy Flag's return will right a wrong. You helping me do this would be an incontestable show of loyalty."

"If I help you, and I am discovered, I will be forever banished from the clan." His face remained expressionless and for a heartbeat, Gwendolyn feared she might have revealed her plan to the wrong person.

"No one has to know you were involved. I will remove the flag from the premises once you help me gain access. Will you do it?"

Marcus was silent.

"I cannot do this without you, Marcus. If you help me, I will be an advocate for you and Rowena. The two of you need someone on your side if you truly wish to be together."

When he still didn't answer, Gwendolyn's heart pounded in her chest. What had she done? If Marcus refused to help her, any chance of retrieving the artifact might be lost. "We can devise a plan that has the least amount of risk to you. If caught, I will never reveal your part in this scheme." She opened her mouth to further bargain with him.

He held up his hand. "Enough. I will help you."

"You will?" Gwendolyn breathed a sigh of relief.

"How can I resist if it means winning the hand of the woman I love?"

A silence fell between them until Marcus asked, "When?"

"Tonight. Our best chance of success is to strike while Alexander MacDonald is still here at Dunvegan, along with several of his most trusted guards. And before Alastair can gather his army to march against your clan. Such an attack will not go well for either side, I fear."

Marcus nodded.

"I am going with you," Rowena said.

"You will do no such thing," Marcus countered. "I'll not

have you involved in this in any way."

"But what if—"

"Nay." Marcus gathered her hands in his. "I could not bear it if something happened to you. Please, stay here." The look in his eyes spoke more of the emotions he had for Rowena than his words had.

"Aye," Gwendolyn agreed. "I need you to help cover for my absence. You can tell everyone that after supper, I came to your chamber to talk and fell asleep, should anyone come looking."

Rowena's eyes were wide in her suddenly white face. "If anything happens to either of you, I will never forgive you."

Marcus pulled Rowena into an embrace. This time Gwendolyn did not try to stop them. They deserved these few precious moments together in case something went horribly wrong later this evening. Gwendolyn gave the two of them their privacy as she stepped up to the altar and gazed at the stained glass window behind it. The reflection of light upon the glass told her it was late afternoon. It would only be a few more hours until they could put their plan into action.

Before they did, however, since there had been many witnesses to Marcus's arrival, they would need just as many to see that he left. After several minutes, Gwendolyn rejoined the couple. "As much as it pains me to break the two of you apart for another day, it must be done. Until Alastair approves of this match, which he will not do until we succeed in bringing the Fairy Flag home, I am afraid you will have to leave Dunvegan, Marcus."

"Agreed. For your safety and mine."

Gwendolyn nodded. "The two of you say your goodbyes now, then I shall escort Marcus to the gate, making sure there are several witnesses to his departure."

"Where shall I meet you when it is time to go to Monkstadt House?"

"Ready your horse and meet me in the woodlands to the south. I will join you as soon as I can safely slip away from tonight's festivities."

Gwendolyn and Marcus left Rowena in the chapel as they headed for the gate. At the sound of the grinding portcullis, several people came out to watch as Marcus retrieved the horse he'd left tied outside the gate and made his way across the land bridge that separated Dunvegan from the rest of the Isle of Skye.

Once Marcus was out of view, Gwendolyn turned and headed inside the castle. With each step, anxiety and unease coiled inside her. Alastair's future, her own livelihood, and the fate of a young couple all rested upon their success tonight. Nothing could go wrong, or they would all suffer the consequences of their actions.

AS SOON AS the council meeting ended. Alastair made his

way to Beatrice's chamber. He wouldn't wait another moment to confront her about not only coming to Dunvegan to spy on him for his enemy, but also about her role in freeing Garrick from the dungeon. It made perfect sense that she had been the one to free him.

He'd watched the way Beatrice swayed her hips at his men as she passed them in the hallways. She used her feminine assets to turn heads, and then turn his seasoned warriors into malleable clay. The guards in the dungeon had not stood a chance against her—not when they thought with a different part of their anatomy than their heads.

He knocked on the door. "Beatrice. Open the door. We need to talk."

She must have been expecting him because the door opened immediately. "Alastair. How nice of you to come to check on me after my fainting spell this morning." She stepped back, allowing him to enter, then shut the door behind him.

"That is not why I am here, and you know it. I need to know. Did you agree to come here as my fiancée or as a spy for the MacDonalds?"

Her cheeks flamed red. "How could you think I would betray you in such a way? The accusations against me are false." Beatrice reached out and stroked the length of his arm, lingering where it rested against his thigh.

Alastair straightened and stepped back, refusing to let her manipulate him as she might have in the past. "I don't believe you. In fact, I believe you were the one who released Garrick MacDonald from the dungeon."

"I. . . I. . ." She staggered on her feet. "I'm not feeling well." She collapsed on the floor.

Alastair crossed his arms instead of falling to her side with an offer of help. "Are you quite done?"

She released a soft groan and put a hand to her head. "I'm so dizzy."

He remained where he was for several long moments before he finally bent down and helped her to her feet. Then in the next moment he lifted her up and tossed her over his shoulder like a sack of wheat.

"Put me down!"

He strode across the chamber and tossed her on the bed. "If you are so dizzy, then I expect you to stay here all night to regain your strength so that you and your father can leave on the morrow."

She brushed her hair out of her eyes and straightened her skirts before turning an indignant gaze upon him. "What about tonight's banquet? I am supposed to act as hostess."

"I'm sure Mrs Morgan can handle that task," Alastair said, backing towards the door.

"You cannot imprison me here." Beatrice pressed her lips into a thin line.

"Why? Because it befouls your plans?"

Her eyes narrowed to flinty shards. "We are betrothed. We are set to marry in three days."

Despite his anger, Alastair could not hold back a satisfied smile. "Yesterday I discovered that Gwendolyn and I are still legally betrothed. Which means I cannot engage in a similar contract with you."

Beatrice gasped. "What trickery is this?"

"No trickery. Just the truth, which is more than you are willing to give me." He reached the door and stood in the doorframe. "I will return the bride price to your father, and that will invalidate our arrangement."

"You cannot do this."

"Be packed and ready to depart on the morrow. I will inform your father of the change in plans." He stepped outside and closed the door, leaving Beatrice with her mouth gaping wide.

CHAPTER FIFTEEN

G WENDOLYN DRESSED CAREFULLY for supper in another of Rowena's borrowed dresses. She'd chosen a simple silk gown in a beautiful shade of sapphire blue with only one petticoat beneath. She'd gathered her hair into a bun at her nape and had threaded a strand of freshwater pearls, which Rowena had also lent her, into the mass. Finally, she slipped her feet into a new pair of shoes Mrs Morgan had brought to her, saying Alastair had had them made specifically for her.

After a quick appraisal in her handheld looking glass, Gwendolyn had deemed her appearance plain and practical and was completely oblivious to the way her dress reflected the colour of her eyes, or how the simplicity only accentuated her natural beauty. Without anything further to delay her, she made her way to the great hall and the feast Mrs Honey had devised to celebrate their guests.

The sound of laughter and the clinking of glasses came to Gwendolyn as she approached the doorway. For a moment, she stopped, hanging back as her nerves suddenly faltered. It had been a very long time since she'd had to converse in such a situation. She knew nothing witty or clever to say, and she had no knowledge of any of the politics of the day or any social conventions. She was about to turn around and head back to her chamber when Laird MacAskill and his wife came up behind her.

"Come, lassie," Laird MacAskill said, "all the festivities are inside the doorway. Not out here." He and his wife did not step around her, instead waiting until she entered the chamber before they joined her.

The room was full of glittering candlelight and splashes of brightly hued tartan. At her appearance, it seemed as though all the conversation in the chamber ground to a halt, and all eyes turned to the doorway. Gwendolyn felt a blush heat her cheeks. Ignoring their stares, she crossed the room to the huge hearth where Rowena, a man she recognised as Laird MacKinnon, and a woman who must have been his wife stood, their heads bent in conversation.

At Gwendolyn's approach, Rowena turned to greet her. "You look splendid." She offered Gwendolyn her arm and pulled her close to her side. Leaning in so that no one else could hear, she said, "I knew that dress would look better on you than it did me. You look quite enchanting tonight."

"Miss Harris," Laird MacKinnon said. "I was quite moved today by all you have suffered at the hands of the MacDonalds."

"Thank you, m'laird. The MacDonalds are not only a continuing threat to the MacLeods, but to all the clans who oppose them."

"Aye," he agreed as he took a sip of the whisky in his hand, then launched into a discussion about how the water on Skye made the whisky produced there finer than all the other whisky in Scotland.

Gwendolyn paid little attention as she caught sight of Alastair across the chamber. He stood with Laird Nicolson and his wife. Trying to cast her gaze elsewhere, Gwendolyn looked around the entire chamber until, compelled by a force she couldn't control, her gaze returned to Alastair once more.

He wore a richly shaded coat that was such a dark colour of blue it was almost black. The sleeves were turned back, almost to the elbow and trimmed with gold braid. The coat was left open, revealing a gold damask waistcoat beneath, buttoned high to the throat. Over this he wore a white, multitiered lace jabot that matched the lace at his shirt-sleeves. Beneath the waistcoat he wore a pleated and belted blue and green tartan with accents of red, gold, and black. The end of the tartan was brought up and draped across one shoulder and fastened to his coat with a large silver brooch studded with four small sapphires and a large sapphire at the center. His face had been shaved clean and his ebony hair had been neatly barbered, but his natural curl refused to be tamed and yet curled at his temples and nape.

He looked magnificent. She had thought she appraised him unknowingly, until suddenly his gaze was upon her, sending her nerves skittering. An appreciative smile pulled up the corner of his mouth as his gaze moved over her like a lover's caress.

Gwendolyn welcomed the unfamiliar sensation that warmed her core. For so many years she'd felt only partially alive—Survival had been her one and only goal. Yet, tonight, she could feel her pulse thrumming as Alastair's heated gaze slid long and lingeringly over her body, over the blue silk that clung to her form.

Without breaking his gaze, he made his way across the room. The beat of her heart punctuated his steps until he stood before her. "Good evening, Gwendolyn." His voice was silken soft.

Rowena and the others, sensing he wished to speak to her alone, moved away, until it was just the two of them standing before the roaring fire. The pop and hiss of the wood as it was devoured by the flame receded as he stared down at her. "You were magnificent today in the council meeting."

"I only told the truth."

"You convinced the lairds to censure the MacDonalds. On the morrow we will discuss penalties against the clan for imprisoning you and your siblings. I'm almost certain there will be a financial settlement. You will not have to work as a governess in order to support yourself and your family."

The news should have made her happy. Instead, she shivered as a chill slithered down her spine and she looked away.

"That is what you still desire, is it not? Your freedom?"

Her throat tightened. She wanted to say nay, but found the word caught in her throat. Instead of offering a reply, she lifted her skirts and raced out the door, down the hallway, and to a private nook she'd discovered in her early days at the castle. She was running away when she should stay and fight. Beatrice was still here at Dunvegan and she and Alastair were still engaged. Could she fight the conniving woman and win the battle between them?

Gwendolyn leaned against the wall for support, as she tried to dredge up that fighting spirit from earlier today. Her plan had been to retrieve the flag, offer it in reconciliation to Alastair, and to tell him she wanted to start fresh. Instead of moving straight to marriage, she had wanted time for the two of them to get to know each other again.

It was a great plan except for the part where Alastair would marry Beatrice in three more days. She clenched her fists, trying to hold back her frustration.

"Why did you run away again?" All of a sudden, Alastair stood before her.

She startled and pitched forward straight into his arms. Her breath caught in her throat as she landed flush against his body. "I had to."

"Are you running from yourself or me?"

"Both." Her hands gripped his arms as she braced herself to pull away when his arms encircled her waist, locking her against his hardness.

"'Tis time to stop running, Gwendolyn." In his dark eyes

she saw not anger, but desire. Before she could reply, his lips descended on hers.

He kissed her, not gently as he had the night before, but with a passion that spoke of longing. His kiss said what his words did not—that he still cared for her.

She found herself reeling, sinking into her own primitive response. Too urgent to be denied, too powerful to resist. She plunged into the temptation of his hot, demanding mouth, into the whirling vortex of desire that beat in her veins. Free of all restraints, she gave herself over to the passion of the moment, feeling the beat of his heart against her chest, the warmth of his touch as it caressed her back and neck, until he plunged his hand into her hair, freeing the length and sending the strand of pearls falling to their feet.

Through the sensual storm hazing her brain, the sound of bagpipes registered, reminding her they were not alone. No matter how much her body wanted this moment, it was the wrong time and the wrong place. Yet, she couldn't seem to pull away.

***

ALASTAIR HEARD THE call of the piper and forced himself to end the kiss—a kiss that had been fueled by something he hadn't understood when first his lips touched hers. But when her lips had parted, every instinct in him told him to bring her close and never let her go. It was a kiss that left him hungry and aching for more. It was a kiss that had been brewing, unfulfilled, for five long years. And yet it was not the time to fulfill the need they had for each other.

Lifting his head, he looked down into her face, at her magnificent blue eyes now clouded with passion. Her lips were slightly swollen from his kiss. Stepping away, trying to rein in the clawing need her kiss had evoked was harder than he ever imagined. He withdrew his hands from her hair and waist and stepped back. Some distant spark of sanity returned as the sound of the pipes pressed further into his thoughts. "That is the call for supper."

Gwendolyn nodded, then bent to retrieve the strand of pearls at her feet. Quickly, she coiled her hair and simply wound the pearls around it. The effect was even more enchanting than before.

"After supper, I would like to talk with you. It is important."

Her face paled. "I promised Rowena we would talk after supper. Might the matter wait until morning?"

He tried to hide his disappointment. Now that he had made the decision to send Beatrice away, he wanted nothing more than to spend each moment with Gwendolyn. "Of course. If that is what you wish." He took her arm and led her back into the great hall.

Inside the chamber, the guests all seated themselves at the long table. Something had changed between them in those stolen moments in the nook, something they could no longer deny or discredit. Their passion had been mutual, potent and powerful. He doubted he would sleep much this night, not until he could finally tell Gwendolyn he had broken his betrothal to Beatrice. And more importantly, to admit to Gwendolyn that he still had feelings for her.

Alastair pulled Gwendolyn infinitesimally closer as they neared the table at the far end of the great hall. At his arrival, the sound of the pipes faded. Alastair seated Gwendolyn in a chair next to his before he took his own seat at the head of the table and looked out at his guests and family.

The peace he'd experienced in Gwendolyn's arms faded and a sudden restlessness took hold. Today's council meeting had been successful as far as getting the clans to see that the MacDonalds were manipulating the lot of them for their own purposes. The discussions would continue on the morrow when he intended to press the six clans to work together, while the rest of Scotland splintered into factions of those who supported the return of the Stuarts to the throne and those who opposed it.

Thoughts of war fled his mind when the piper heralded the first course. Mrs Honey served him first. "I made this dish just fer ye, *brochan buidh*."

"Thank you," he replied with a grateful smile as the savoury aroma of the ham and lentils filled his senses. Immediately following the first course were platters of monkfish smothered in a rich butter sauce, mutton with garlic and rosemary, kidney pies smothered in gravy, baked apples, and sausages. To finish the meal, Mrs Honey brought out castle cake with a sweet lemon scent and served it with a dollop of syllabub.

Throughout the meal, the conversation stayed light for which Alastair was grateful. Finally, when all had been satisfied with the meal, the lairds sat back, enjoying yet another glass of claret.

"Yer father might have been a difficult man, Alastair, but he knew how tae keep his cellar well stocked." Laird Nicolson raised his glass. "Tae the Wicked Man MacLeod. May he rest in peace."

"Rest in peace," those gathered responded and one by one raised their glasses then tilted them back, except for Alexander MacDonald.

"That man was never peaceful a day in his life. Why would he deserve such a reward on the other side? Rotting in hell is more like it for all the chaos he created."

Laird Nicolson's lips thinned. "The man is dead. Leave him be. The younger MacLeod is laird now. He's already proven to be more of a diplomat than his father. He'll bring peace to the isles."

Alexander MacDonald scoffed. "Nothing and no one will bring peace to the isles now that the Old Pretender is in France, obtaining renewed support from the French government to invade England." The laird drained his glass. "War is coming whether we want it or not."

"Agreed." Laird MacQueen stroked his chin. "'Tis time

to stop fighting each other and pick a side."

"The Young Pretender is ready to fight for his rightful place on the throne. He's called for an army, and when he gets it, he'll clear our lands of the English vermin and send them back home." Laird MacAskill searched the faces of those gathered. "Will we support his cause when the time comes?"

"Gentlemen," Alastair interrupted, concerned how quickly the conversation had turned from wine to war. "Let's not hold a war council around the supper table. I'm certain the ladies would rather talk of more pleasant things."

"Shall I ask the piper to return and entertain us?" Callum interjected, trying to help Alastair steer the conversation in a different direction. "Or I could play the mandolin for you. I've a new ballad I could share."

Ignoring Callum, Lady MacQueen gave an inelegant snort. "You men like to think we are all delicate as bluebells during a spring rain." She leaned forward, her gaze narrowing on Alastair. "You're forgetting we are Scottish women. We're as hale and hearty as our men."

Rowena nodded and cast Alastair a meaningful glance. "We are stronger than the men would like to believe."

"We will all have to be strong. Whether we want to acknowledge it or not, war is on our doorsteps," Lady MacAskill said. "As a mother who lost her only son in the last rebellion, I cannot allow his death to have been in vain. I'll encourage my husband to go to battle for the rightful king, and I intend to fight alongside him."

Laird MacKinnon pushed away from the table. "The Pretender should go back to France before more of our sons die. We have neither the men nor the weapons necessary to fight and win. Even with France's support, the English army's numbers will overwhelm us in no time at all. If we fight for the prince, we die."

"I'd rather die a Scot who honours a rightful king, than a man who runs with his tail between his legs where his manhood should be," Alexander MacDonald spat.

Alastair pressed his lips into a thin line. Since the conversation had started and built, they might as well see it through. If he didn't want these men to compare him to his father, he needed to at least appear neutral despite his own feeling about the matter. "The young prince came to us, wanting our support even though he knew there could be no uprising without strong support from the French. And yet he came to us anyway. He came without men, or guns, or powder. He broke his promise to us, therefore we do not have to honour our promise to support him."

"By all that is holy, I am honour-bound to protect King Jaime." Laird MacQueen pounded his beefy fist on the table. "He wants war."

"He only wants what is rightfully his and his father's," Lady MacQueen chimed in to support her husband.

"God's blood," Laird Nicolson erupted. "Not one army has invaded England in six hundred years for good reason.

The Royal Navy has more ships than the Scots do. English soldiers are highly trained. They have cannons and muskets, and plenty of powder. You'd have us go up against them with our claymores and targes? You think we'd win such a conflict?"

Laird MacDonald stood. "Our Scottish pride will see us to victory."

Laird Nicolson glared at the man. "We'll choke on our pride and our own blood if we take up the sword for the prince."

Alastair stood as well. He'd let this conversation run longer than it should have. If it kept on going, they'd all soon be drawing their swords. Before he could speak Gwendolyn also stood.

"Ho-ro-veel-a-vok, bone and flesh of me. Ho-ro-veel-a-vok, blood and pith of me," she sang softly. "Skin like falling snow, green thy mail coat. Live thy steeds be, dauntless thy following." At the sound of her melodic voice, all conversation in the room halted as they listened to the story of a fairy in a green kirtle who came to Dunvegan to quiet the laird's half-fae child.

Letting Gwendolyn's voice wash over him, Alastair concentrated on her mouth. But that was a mistake. For it made him remember the sweetness of her kiss. He closed his eyes, and the sound of her voice moved across his mind, until suddenly he remembered it all—every second they'd been together, every touch they'd shared. The memories sent his pulse racing even as they evoked a bittersweet sense of loss. He kept his eyes closed, listening to the fairy lore of Dunvegan. His mother must have taught her the tune while Gwendolyn had been imprisoned in the tower.

When she finished, Alastair opened his eyes and clapped his appreciation along with the others. Thanks to Gwendolyn, the volatile mood in the chamber had softened, and conversation turned to safer subjects. How had he allowed himself to forget how incredible she was? Even as an orphaned girl, she'd shown a strength of spirit that was unusual in a woman.

Was that why the MacDonalds had left her and her siblings alive when they'd taken the lives of everyone else in the village? Had Alexander MacDonald unknowingly recognised that strength? Or had he left them alive so that they could tell the tale about who had claimed the lives of the Harris clan?

Alastair did not really care why they were spared. He was simply grateful that they were. He drew a satisfied breath. Their lives had been filled with turmoil, and much suffering on Gwendolyn's part, but they had survived it all to get them to this moment. There was still much to resolve between them, so many things to discuss, but he was no longer afraid of doing whatever he had to in order to demonstrate to Gwendolyn that he was a different man, a better man than the one who had failed her so terribly before. He was older and wiser and would be everything she and her siblings needed in the days, months, and years ahead. He flexed his hand, wanting nothing more than to go to her side, to touch her, but he was pulled from his thoughts when Laird MacQueen tapped him on the shoulder.

"The supper was delicious, Laird MacLeod, but isn't it time to send the women away and get back to our discussion? We have yet to decide whether to join forces to support Bonnie Prince Charlie or if we should forgo him in favour of preparing for the inevitable attack by the English."

"Supporting the prince will help us to cleanse our lands of the English," Laird MacAskill said, setting his whisky glass down with a thump.

Before the arguments started up again, Alastair stood and addressed the ladies present. "Excuse us for being such boorish supper companions. As you can see, we still have much to discuss. If you will excuse us, I promise to return your husbands to you before the hour grows too late."

Taking the hint that he wanted the chamber cleared, Gwendolyn and Rowena stood, forcing the other ladies to do the same.

"See that you do," Lady MacQueen said, turning a sour gaze on Alastair before she left the chamber in a flurry of ruffled skirts.

Gwendolyn waited at the door, and when the others were past her, she moved to close the chamber doors. Before she did, she cast him a look he did not understand. He had the feeling she was steeling herself for something.

But what?

He moved to go to her, when Laird Nicolson's voice pierced his thoughts, pulling him back to the conversation buzzing around him. In the next moment she was gone, and he had no choice but to turn his attention to the matter at hand.

CHAPTER SIXTEEN

A S SOON AS the other women were back in their respective bedchambers, Gwendolyn and Rowena headed for her bedchamber. Rowena shut the door behind them. "Are you certain about this?"

"It is the only option we have—both of us." Gwendolyn wasted no time in stripping off her petticoat and placing it on the bed. She didn't need the extra volume slowing her down. She removed the pearls from her hair and gave them to Rowena before retrieving the grey cloak Garrick had forced her to wear. She'd kept the garment because she had no other. She slipped it over her shoulders. The dark colour would suit her purposes tonight.

"How will you leave here unseen?" Rowena worried her lip between her teeth.

"The window is too far from the ground and there are no trees to aid me, so I have no choice but to go through the hallway to the servants' staircase. From there, it should be easy enough to disappear through the sea gate and into the night."

"You make it sound simple enough."

"It won't be since the sea gate is guarded, but I have a plan." Gwendolyn fastened the cloak, then headed for the door, but Rowena gripped her arm, stopping her.

Rowena shifted away and lifted the pillow on the bed to reveal a slim dagger no bigger than her hand. She slid it out of its sheath. The candlelight in the chamber glittered off the wickedly sharp blade. She returned it to its sheath then held it out. "Take this. Tuck it into the bodice of your gown. If you are discovered. . . If someone attacks you, do not hesitate to aim it right between their legs. You don't have to be accurate in your aim, striking anything in that region will render them helpless."

"How do you know this?" Gwendolyn accepted the weapon, and pushing her cloak aside, carefully fitted the short blade between her breasts. The tight bodice would hold it in place.

"Callum is a good brother, who at times has been concerned for my safety. He taught me several ways to defend myself."

Gwendolyn studied Rowena's solemn features. The young woman had been nothing but kind to her in the past few days despite the fact she truly owed Gwendolyn nothing. She took Rowena's hands in her own. "Thank you, Rowena. You are a special young woman. And Marcus is very lucky to have fallen in love with you."

Rowena flushed as she moved to the door, opened it, and scanned the hallway. "It's all clear. You'd better go now, before someone comes along."

"If all goes well, I'll be back before dawn." She lifted the cloak's hood over her head and slipped from the chamber. Her heart pounded and her hands shook as she slipped silently down the hallway and stairs, until she came to the door outside the kitchen. The staff were still cleaning up after the evening's meal. Fortunately for her, they were so busy, no one paid any heed to the door softly opening then closing once more.

The full moon sat high in the night sky, hanging like a shimmering pearl against a canvas of black velvet. Keeping to the shadows, Gwendolyn crept across the rear courtyard to the pathway that led to the sea gate. She paused and tossed a rock to the right and another to the left. Then two more. The guards went to investigate, leaving the gate clear. Quickly before they returned, she unlocked the iron gate, then partially closed it behind her. She needed the gate open for when she returned.

Forced to go slowly along the shoreline of the loch, Gwendolyn stepped carefully along the rocky shoreline below the castle. The next hurdle was a creek that fed into the loch. It was too wide to jump, and the ground surrounding it was too boggy to wade through without getting her shoes and feet soaking wet. There used to be a section closer to the castle where large rocks provided stepstones across the stream. It had been five years since she'd last navigated those rocks. With luck they were still there.

Her heart leapt when she saw that they were. Carefully leaping from one slick rock to another, she made her way across the water until she was once again on solid ground. From there, the path to the forest was easy to navigate. She only slowed as she passed the opening of a cave hidden amongst the trees. While living at Dunvegan she'd been told that cave was a portal to the fairy world.

Leaving the fairy story behind, Gwendolyn continued deeper into the woodland. As the night settled its ebon shroud around her, she took comfort in the steady rhythm of the water lapping against the shore in the distance. An eerie white mist formed close to the ground, forcing her to slow her steps so as not to trip over the exposed roots and rocks that riddled the forest floor. Now and again the moon pierced the tree branches overhead with its silvered light, creating an unearthly landscape of dark shapes rising from the mist. She kept going, deeper into the trees until one shape stood out amongst the rest—that of a man astride a horse. "Marcus?"

"Aye," he confirmed.

Her madly beating heart settled into a steady rhythm at the knowledge that she'd made it this far without being detected. When she approached the horse, Marcus held down his hand and lifted her onto the saddle behind him.

"Hold on to me," he said. "There is no time to waste. Let's be on our way."

Gwendolyn wrapped her arms around his waist as he set

the horse in motion. The rushing wind snatched the woolen hood from her head, freeing her golden hair of its confining coil until her hair streamed out behind her. As they raced deeper into the trees, she threw a glance back over her shoulder. Her eyes swept along the trail as if expecting to find someone following in pursuit. Seeing no one, she finally relaxed. Very soon, she would retrieve the Fairy Flag and return its magic to the MacLeods.

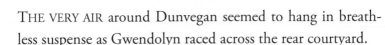

THE VERY AIR around Dunvegan seemed to hang in breathless suspense as Gwendolyn raced across the rear courtyard.

From the top of the prison tower he'd made for her and her siblings, a pair of watchful eyes followed her progress as she moved towards the tree line. Hurrying down the spiral staircase so as not to lose sight of her, he erupted into the night and made his way to the sea gate. He was not so kind to the guards as he struck one with an arrow to the shoulder and the other in the back. He'd been waiting and watching for the past few days, keeping himself hidden, knowing that it was only a matter of time before he caught her alone once more. This time he would have his revenge.

Unbeknownst to the first observer, a second pair of eyes watched as both Gwendolyn and then a male figure moved along the castle wall. She concealed herself in the shadows as Gwendolyn stepped lightly across the creek. The foolish girl had left the safety of Dunvegan Castle and Alastair Mac-Leod.

A smile of satisfaction came to the woman's lips. How perfect. She couldn't have planned this any better. She clutched a dagger in her hands as a sense of satisfaction raced through her blood. No one could blame her if Gwendolyn met her demise at the hands of thugs while she'd slipped away from the castle to do who knows what. Gwendolyn's purpose for leaving was unimportant. All that mattered was that she never return.

The second observer was unaware that she, too, was being followed. This pursuer had both a sword and a pistol on his person, and was more than capable of defending Gwendolyn.

Finally, following all of those who chased after Gwendolyn was something not of this world. Her ethereal body glided across the shoreline and over the creek without ever touching the ground. But at the trees, the often-seen specter stopped as a force beyond herself seemed to hold her back.

She struggled against its hold but could not break free. She was tethered to the castle, the place where she had died. She could not help the one she'd been protecting for years except from the safety of the castle. But there was someone else who could protect the girl.

She had to go find him, and fast.

CHAPTER SEVENTEEN

THE SIGHT OF Monkstadt House, the new seat of the MacDonald clan, surprised Gwendolyn as they approached. Instead of the well-protected castle they had abandoned, their new home was merely a fortified country home. Its whitewashed walls stood out like a beacon in the silvery moonlight.

Still shielded from view by the tree line at the edge of the estate, Marcus guided his horse to a nearby rowan tree and dismounted before assisting her to the ground. Gwendolyn tensed as one of the guards patrolling the outside of the stone wall drew closer.

Marcus pulled her deeper into the shadow of the trees as the guard passed the two of them, his steps crisp with military precision. Once he was out of sight, Marcus waved her forward towards a door in the stone wall at the rear of the house. Gwendolyn drew her woolen cloak more closely about her as a chill of apprehension ran through her.

At the door Marcus paused and withdrew a skeleton key from his sporran. Placing it in the iron padlock, he turned it and the shackle disengaged. "Once we are through this door, we will have to move very quickly across the open area to the cellar door. Can you do that?" His expression was grim.

She nodded. "Go as quickly as you must. I assure you I can keep pace."

Once the door was open, Marcus sprinted across the open grounds. She pushed herself to keep up. They were almost at a doorway when Gwendolyn heard a sound. She glanced over her shoulder across the grassy area they had just traversed. Dots of light punctuated the darkness. "Lanterns," she whispered.

"Come with me." Marcus yanked her sideways towards a wooden shed. He opened the shed door, pulled her inside and shut the door. The scents of burning wood and smoky meat filled her senses. They'd found refuge in the smokehouse. Marcus peered through a crack in the wood. "More guards."

Gwendolyn's heart skipped a beat. "Are they looking for us?"

"Possibly." Marcus watched for a moment longer then shook his head. "There is no urgency in their steps. Probably a patrol making rounds. We were lucky we avoided them as we ran here."

Gwendolyn leaned back against the wooden wall, trying to steady her breathing. "Thank you for taking this risk, Marcus."

"If it helps me win Rowena's hand, then it is worth everything." As the men disappeared around the side of the house, Marcus opened the shed door and they made their way into the cellar. "We'll have to be quick. We don't want to run into them again on our way back to the gate."

Inside the cellar, it was dark. And the icy cold air seemed to pierce right through her garments, straight to her bones. She shivered as she kept pace with Marcus for fear of losing him in a sea of black. She was frightened, but she wouldn't give in to fear. "Where is the Fairy Flag?" Did the MacDonalds display it like a spoil of war in their hall? Or did they hide it away in fear that it might be taken away from them by another clan?

Marcus came to a stop. Once more he fiddled with a key, trying to slide it into the lock in the darkness, and a heartbeat later she heard a familiar click. "The Fairy Flag is kept inside a secret compartment carved into the hearth in the main hall. Fortunately for us, the household is all abed, except for the guards. With luck, we can slip in and out without incident."

As Marcus moved to open the door, Gwendolyn stalled him with a hand on his arm. "I said I would not involve you. There's too much—"

"I am already involved. The two of us can work faster than one." He cracked the door open and peered first left, then right, before he waved her to follow.

Silently they made their way down a long hallway before entering a room on their right. The flame from two sconces near the hearth still burned, casting the chamber in golden light. The hearth was the largest she'd ever seen, spanning one third of the room's length and extending all the way to the ceiling. If the secret chamber was behind one of those rocks, there would be hundreds for them to search.

Marcus moved to the right-hand side of the wall of stone. "I'm not certain exactly where the chamber is, but it is in this vicinity," he whispered. "Start running your hands over the stone, looking for irregularities that might serve as a latch of sorts."

Using both her hands, Gwendolyn ran her fingers over the surface of the large rocks, finding them smooth. Marcus did the same to a section to the left of her.

When feeling for a lever failed, Gwendolyn pushed against each rock in frustration. Suddenly one rock moved. Her hands trembling, she pushed again, harder. The rock swung in at a right angle, revealing a deep cavity. She thrust her hand into the opening, but was too short to reach what might be hidden deeper inside.

Instantly, Marcus was beside her. "Allow me." He reached into the depth and withdrew a small wooden chest that was a foot long and a half a foot wide. He handed the chest to her as he once again reached inside and pulled the rock back into place.

Holding her breath, Gwendolyn released the latch on the lid and opened the chest. The Fairy Flag rested inside. Relief washed over her at the sight. The burden of guilt she'd been carrying with her for the past five years lightened. Now if they could only make it back to Dunvegan without being discovered.

"Is that the flag?"

Gwendolyn shut the lid and nodded.

"Then let's go," Marcus whispered, already heading in the direction they had come.

Gwendolyn followed closely behind. Her heart thundered in her ears, and her body continued to quake until they were safely outside the gate in the stone wall. Once there, she released her pent-up breath. It was over. They had succeeded in righting a wrong.

They hurried towards where they'd left the horse when a dark shape separated itself from the shadows. "What have we here?"

Gwendolyn's stomach twisted at the sound of a familiar voice.

Garrick.

"You followed me?" The words were only a whisper of sound. He appeared as she'd last seen him. His clothes, his anger, nothing had changed. Except for the dagger in his hand and the murderous look on his face.

"I knew if I waited long enough, I would finally have a chance to finish what I started. This time it will not end well for you, I'm afraid. Now that MacLeod knows you're alive, I'll have to kill you to torment him even more." Garrick moved slowly towards her, his blade raised to strike.

Marcus stepped before her, shielding Gwendolyn from

his own kin. "If you want to harm her, you'll have to go through me."

"You're a traitor, Marcus MacDonald. Consorting with the enemy."

Marcus's features hardened. "The MacLeods are not our enemy. Alastair MacLeod is not his father. He wants what we all want. Peace between the clans."

"The son bears the stains of his father. Or have you forgotten that the Wicked Man killed my mother and murdered our people when he raided Duntulm village six years ago."

"And the MacDonalds raided the village that killed Gwendolyn Harris's parents and her entire clan. They've attacked the Campbells countless times, and more recently, they raided the MacLeans of Coll and not only stole their cattle, but raped the laird's sister. Need I go on? Both the MacDonalds and the MacLeods have done things that neither clan is proud of. Again, I say to you, let the past rest for the sake of the future."

A rustle of the bushes sounded behind Garrick, catching him off guard. He turned to the sound just as Marcus leapt forward. He kicked Garrick in the chest, the blow knocking the dagger from his hand.

"Intruders! Help! Intruders," Garrick yelled, trying to alert the guards not far away.

Her heart pounding in her ears, Gwendolyn set the wooden chest beneath a shrub then lunged for the dagger.

Instead of gripping the weapon, she was hauled backwards by an arm at her throat.

"Let me go!" Her stomach clenched with a terrible mix of sudden dread and absolute determination to never again be someone's prisoner. Gwendolyn kicked backwards, hitting something. But instead of breaking free, the deadly edge of a knife pressed against her throat. "You'll never have Alastair as long as I still draw breath."

Beatrice.

Marcus snatched the blade Garrick had dropped from the ground and spun towards Beatrice. "Release her. You are no match for me with a weapon."

"Drop your blade or I will slit her throat." Beatrice pressed the knife's edge deeper against Gwendolyn's flesh. A warm trickle of blood raced down her neck.

It didn't matter. All that mattered was breaking free. She could not grasp the hidden dagger between her breasts fast enough and use it while Beatrice held her this way. Instead, Gwendolyn doubled her fists and thrust them backwards, aiming blindly at whatever she could strike. She hit soft flesh.

Beatrice grunted in pain, loosening her grip enough for Gwendolyn to draw a breath and wrench away. Marcus moved in, taking Beatrice to the ground.

Gwendolyn backed away. She had to reach the horse, free it and then she and Marcus could escape. She took two steps and Garrick blocked her way. He grabbed her arm, his fingers biting into her tender flesh and yanked her towards him. "You will pay for this, I promise."

He caught her around the waist with his other arm, holding her so tightly she could not breathe. Marcus and Beatrice were still struggling in the dirt when the sound of footsteps sounded in the direction of Monkstadt House. The wall gate opened and ten men spilled into the darkness. Four carried pistols, the rest were armed with swords.

"Marcus!" Gwendolyn managed enough breath to warn him. Garrick jerked her head back so roughly she saw stars.

"Let her go, Garrick." A voice came from behind them.

Graeme.

Graeme pressed a pistol to Garrick's throat, but Garrick didn't release his hold on Gwendolyn. "If you harm me, the guards will shoot all of you. None of us will survive, but it might almost be worth dying, knowing I took down not only the MacLeod's two women, but also the great Graeme Duff."

Four of the guards from Monkstadt House continued forward, their pistols aimed.

Gwendolyn's fingers were like ice. She felt tears just behind her eyes and she fought them, forcing them back, blinking in an effort not to cry. The world had not been kind to her, but despite the harshness of her life, she'd been able to find the one thing that eluded most people. Love. She had the love of her siblings, and she'd experienced kindness at the hands of Alastair MacLeod. She only wished she could see him one more time, tell him how she felt.

"Ready." A shout called out. The sound of several pistols cocking filled the air.

Her heart raced in her chest, so loud it almost sounded like hoofbeats in the distance.

"Aim."

"Stop." A new voice from behind her was harsh and commanding. "Release them now and lower your weapons."

Alastair.

No one moved. "Let her go."

Gwendolyn's breath hitched. The air stilled as both sides weighed the odds of proceeding. Marcus gained his feet and stepped away from Beatrice, leaving her to struggle up by herself.

"I would rather die than surrender to you," Garrick hissed.

The crack of a gun cut through the darkness. Garrick howled in pain, the sound an animalistic mixture of rage, fury, and frustration. He released his grip on her waist. Gwendolyn twisted away to see Alastair astride a big grey horse with twenty men all armed with pistols.

Garrick staggered backwards but didn't get far as Graeme took him to the ground. Gwendolyn looked from the MacLeods to the MacDonalds, then back again. Both sides were armed and ready to fire upon each other.

"Graeme, take Gwendolyn. Get her out of here." Alastair's voice was hard.

Graeme got to his feet. "Come, Gwendolyn." He waved

her back towards the depths of the woodlands.

"Not without Marcus." An image of what would happen once she left this scene pierced Gwendolyn's brain. She would not return to Dunvegan without Marcus, not after all he and Rowena had done to help her.

"What about me?" Beatrice cried. "I am the true victim here. Dragged from my sleep by this horrid woman so she could murder me and make it appear as if the MacDonalds had done me in."

"Spare us your lies, Beatrice," Alastair said as ten more guards joined the others on the MacDonalds' side. He turned to Gwendolyn, and she could see the intensity of his gaze even in the moonlight. "If you won't leave any other way, then take Marcus and get out of here."

"And Beatrice?"

"I will take care of her. Go now."

Gwendolyn nodded. She turned and followed Graeme for a moment before she stepped back to the bush under which she'd hidden the wooden chest. She cast one more glance at Alastair before turning away. "He has to survive this conflict. Tell me he will survive, Graeme." Her throat was thick with emotion.

"Alastair knows better than most how to defuse a conflict without it coming to war. Trust that he will do so now." He lifted her up onto his horse and swung into the saddle behind her. Gwendolyn was grateful Graeme didn't ask her about the wooden chest. She clung to it, praying that the magic of the Fairy Flag would remain with Alastair even as they rode back towards Dunvegan with Marcus following close behind.

———∼∼∼———

THE VERY AIR around them hung in breathless anticipation as the sound of the horses carrying Gwendolyn, Graeme, and Marcus faded behind them. Alastair did not want to battle this out—not here, not now. But he would if given no other option. Before that happened he had one more female to contend with.

He shifted his gaze from the men aiming their pistols at him to Beatrice. "It's time to pick a side, Beatrice. I know you've been spying on me for the MacDonalds. Despite that fact, you would still be welcome in my castle until things are settled between your father and myself. Only say the word and one of my men will escort you back to Dunvegan."

Her face was colourless in the moonlight as she staggered towards him. "We could have had a nice life together. We could have had it all—wealth, power, prestige. Instead, you chose her." Beatrice's gaze shifted to the darkness into which Gwendolyn had vanished. "She is no one. She has nothing. So why choose her?"

"She will never betray me. I cannot say the same about you. It was you who set Garrick free from the dungeon, wasn't it?"

"I had help from one of your own guards." Her eyes narrowed and a smile of satisfaction came to her lips. "How does that make you feel, MacLeod? To know there is someone willing to betray you amongst your men. The lad has more guts than I originally anticipated."

An alarm went off in his brain. Of the guards who were doused with laudanum, only Emery Howden could be considered young enough to be called a 'lad.' Alastair frowned. "How long has Emery been spying for you?"

Beatrice stared at him in surprise. "I named no one."

"You didn't have to. I know my men, but I also know you do not have to continue down this path the MacDonalds have laid for you. Come back to Dunvegan with me. Return to your father. I could forgive you for releasing Garrick if that is where this madness ends."

"I do not need, nor do I want your forgiveness." Beatrice took a step back, then another until she stood beside Garrick. She reached up and grasped him by both cheeks, bringing his lips to hers in a kiss that was at first a surprise, and then exuberantly returned. The MacDonald men behind them chuckled at the sight. When she broke the kiss, she turned back to Alastair. "I've chosen my bed. As you will have when you feel the wrath of the MacDonalds."

Alastair held up his hand and sent a signal to his men to come forward. The twenty lined up beside Alastair, then beside him came twenty more, and behind them another twenty. Their weapons all shimmered in the moonlight.

A low murmur started amongst the MacDonalds, no doubt weighing their odds of prevailing in this conflict with their twenty men against his mounted sixty. Most of his men carried both a pistol and a sword, whereas the MacDonalds had only four powdered weapons. It wasn't much of a match, and clearly the MacDonalds sensed that and started moving back towards their gate, until Beatrice and Garrick stood alone.

"This isn't over," Garrick growled, his eyes sparking for a moment before he slipped his arm around Beatrice's waist and led her back behind the protective walls.

Nay. Alastair very much regretted that this conflict between the MacDonalds and the MacLeods wasn't over. When Laird Lamont discovered his daughter had left Alastair's care to consort with Garrick MacDonald, the MacLeods would have a new enemy in the Lamonts. All of Alastair's efforts to establish peace amongst the clans of the isle were falling down around him. He hadn't made anything better. He'd only made things worse.

There would be hell to pay when the lairds of the council found out what had happened this night. Even so, Alastair would have done nothing different. When his mother had come to him and told him Gwendolyn was in danger, he hadn't hesitated in gathering his men for battle. Still, a feeling of anxiety and unease chased him all the way back to the castle.

The battle between the MacDonalds and the MacLeods was not over. Perhaps it never would be.

CHAPTER EIGHTEEN

THE FLAME ON the candle by Gwendolyn's bedside shifted from yellowish orange, to red, then blue, and back again as she waited in the silence of her chamber for news of Alastair. When she'd returned to her chamber, she'd removed the dagger from between her breasts, grateful she hadn't had to use it, and set it near the candle. Her gaze shifted from the dagger back to the candle. She stared at the light as if in a trance for what seemed like hours, willing her nerves to settle.

"Are you well?"

A deep masculine voice, taut, hard, issued from somewhere beyond the flame.

Gwendolyn jerked her gaze from the flame to the face beyond the candle. *Alastair. He was here.* Wild joy soared through her at the sight of him. He'd shed most of his finery from tonight's festivities, wearing only his tartan and the shirt beneath, but to her he appeared even more breathtaking as his presence filled the doorway.

"Answer me. Did Garrick harm you in any way?" He entered her chamber and shut the door behind him.

"Nay." She threw back the covers, but before she could go to him he came to her bedside.

He sat on the bed and reached out, touching her chin, lifting it to better view the damage to her neck that was now bandaged with a thin strip of linen. "You were bleeding."

"'Twas but a cut. Nothing serious. When I returned, Lottie washed then dressed the wound. She also helped treat the two guards that Garrick had injured."

His breath released in a rush and he dropped his hand to his lap. "Three blessings then. I have enough to worry about without adding your assault by Garrick or injuries to my men to the list."

"I did not mean to cause you more trouble." Gwendolyn could feel her eyes filling with tears and determinedly blinked them back. "I was only trying to help."

"What were you and Marcus doing at the MacDonalds in the first place?"

She reached for the small wooden chest on the bed beside her and with it atop her palms, held it out to him. "Even though I had no choice but to take this from you, I wanted to right that wrong." This time she could not stop the tears that fell from her lashes onto her cheeks. "Forgive me?"

He accepted the wooden chest and with great care opened the latch. His eyes widened in surprise. Inside lay the Fairy Flag. The small golden crosses on the yellowed silk had faded over the years, leaving only the telltale red "elf dots" upon the fabric's surface. "You are more important to me than any flag. If anything had happened to you. . ."

"It was important for me to do this."

Alastair set the flag on the floor beside the bed before turning back to her. "Promise me you will never go near the MacDonald clan again." He took her hand in his. "Now that I have you back, I could not bear to lose you again."

The words swept over her, sank into her. She heard the care in them and the warmth, and she felt shaky inside. "I promise."

His arms moved to her arms, slid down to her elbows, over her bare arms. His touch sent shivers through her body, sent longing stabbing straight into her heart. "I was only successful because of Marcus." She paused, took a breath. "He truly does love Rowena, regardless of his surname. He risked everything for me, for this flag, in an attempt to prove that his loyalty to Rowena was more important than his own clan."

"I will speak to them both soon. And Marcus can convince me of his affection then." Alastair reached up and dried the tears from her cheeks. He did not pull his hand away. Instead, he wound his forefinger in one of the curls at her left temple. "You never needed my forgiveness, Gwendolyn. I know you did what you had to do to survive." The words were thick. "It is I who needs to beg your forgiveness for so many years of neglect. Had I not left Dunvegan, I might have discovered you sooner."

"Neither of us can change the past."

"Nay, we cannot. But we must both start thinking about the future." The tip of his finger rested lightly against her cheekbone while he ran the silky texture of the curl between his forefinger and thumb. The action brought a catch to her breath.

"What about Beatrice?"

"Our betrothal is broken, which leaves just you and me." She remembered that strange huskiness that came to his voice from when they'd been together on the shore of the loch so long ago. The sound of it worked its same magic over her now. The back of his hand feathered lightly across her bandaged neck and to her left shoulder, while his other hand rested on her right arm.

"How did you know I needed help? I thought no one saw me leave Dunvegan, though I was wrong about that."

"My mother came to me. She warned me that Garrick and Beatrice had followed you."

"The Grey Lady followed me?"

"She tried but could not go past the edge of the castle wall, so she alerted me to the danger." He gave Gwendolyn a half-smile. "I believe my mother has a fondness for you."

"And I for her." Gwendolyn paused as her throat went thick. "And her son."

Their gazes caught and held as Alastair's hands tightened imperceptibly on her arm and shoulder, slowly drawing her closer until he bent his head. He brushed his lips over hers, rubbing lightly. This time his kiss was an invitation, a challenge for her to accept or deny.

She answered the challenge slowly, leaning into his arms. Her hand slid softly up his shirt. His hands came down to her waist and pulled her closer against his hard chest. Gwendolyn's heartbeat thundered in her chest as his tongue flicked against her lips, teasing, inviting. And she answered his challenge in the only way she could. She slid her hands around his shoulders and kissed him back with a fierceness she didn't know she possessed. She allowed him to part her lips and, when his tongue probed, she welcomed the invasion with equal fervor and need.

Their wills met and matched in a clash of fire and passion. The sorrow she had experienced moments before converted in a heartbeat to something more potent, to a compulsion that thrummed in her blood, and filled her with dizzying desire. That desire burgeoned, erupted, and swept her up in an all-consuming need. She gave in to the powerful emotions that overwhelmed her until she felt Alastair stiffen.

He wrenched his mouth from hers. His dark eyes stared at her, drowning in the same passion that had fired her blood. "If we continue, there will be no turning back. Is that what you wish?"

A queer sensation fluttered in the pit of her stomach— part pain and part pleasure. He was giving her an opportunity to refuse him and the life he offered her. If they continued, they would eventually come together in the most intimate of ways. They both knew it would not be just for that moment, it would be forever. Their betrothal would be unbreakable, and she would never have the life she thought she wanted.

Did she truly want that life anymore? Or did she want a life with him more? His gaze caressed the bare flesh of her shoulders, and her body trembled in response, wanting him to own her, claim her, devour her. Something flowered in her depths, a part of her that was suddenly free, reborn. She was no longer trapped by anyone, not even herself. She wanted to feel sensations like those he had evoked, every day. To live the full life she had always been denied.

Gwendolyn could not keep a smile from her lips. Alastair's eyes widened as she bent forward. She took his still-smooth cheeks between her hands and hauled his head down to hers. She captured his lips with her own. At the sharp intake of his breath, mutual desire flared once more.

His hands came up to her shoulders. Slowly, he pushed the neckline of her nightrail down to her waist, exposing her pink-tipped breasts which rose and fell with her quickened breathing. His lips left hers, slid lower. His mouth fastened over her left nipple, and she made a low sound and involuntarily arched upwards. "Alastair. . ."

"Soon enough, my dear." His warm, wet tongue moved over her left breast into the valley between, then shifted to caress her right breast. "I used to wonder how you would taste." His voice was thick. "How you would feel."

His mouth closed fully over her right nipple. *Fire. Hun-*

ger. Need. She gasped as hot pleasure rippled through her. He stimulated her other breast as he continued to suckle, drawing each nipple up until they were both pointed and throbbing. She could see the pulse beating wildly in his temple, and his breath was coming faster, harsher.

He lifted his head to reveal eyes that were glazed with passion. He pushed her back onto the bed and slipped her nightrail past her hips and tossed it to the floor before he stripped himself of his clothing, all while his gaze roved over her swollen breasts, then on the curls surrounding her womanhood. "You are as beautiful as God could make you."

He was more than beautiful. He was magnificent as he stood before her, sculpted with muscle and strength, and powerfully aroused. His dark eyes were wild in his flushed face, his mouth heavy with sensuality. He brought his hands down to stroke her thighs—down the long length of the outside then up to the apex of her womanhood, his touch feather-light. Heat erupted inside her, followed by an ache between her thighs.

He spread her legs with one hand and stood there staring at her. She burned, and yet suddenly self-conscious, she started to close her legs when he joined her on the bed. He positioned himself, kneeling between her legs, and began stroking her curls in wide circles that grew more and more narrow until one long, hard finger slipped between the folds. He moved in and out of her body in a rhythm that was as maddening as it was exhilarating.

"I can feel you expanding, preparing for me. Can you feel it too?" Another finger joined the first, and she released a fractured breath. The tension inside her was building but to what she did not know.

He plunged his fingers deeply, rotating, exploring. With his other hand he continued circling at the very heart of her. He bent down and pressed kisses from her shoulder to her neck, avoiding the injured and bandaged areas. He drew in a deep breath and smiled. "You smell exactly how I imagined you would. Like sunshine and heather on a spring morning." His lips found hers and he kissed her deeply, his tongue moving wildly as his fingers pursued their own rhythm.

Needing to explore him, her hands travelled over the expanse of his chest, his muscled arms and shoulders, before shifting to the expanse of his back. He was a study in texture—firm and soft, corded and smooth.

She was breathing hard, and her muscles were locked with tension when he broke the kiss. He pulled his fingers out of her, then shifted his body forward until his manhood pressed against her core. Slowly he thrust forward, allowing her to accept his invasion inch by inch until he met with resistance.

"Kiss me," he demanded softly.

She lifted and brought her lips to his, wanting to absorb the tension she could feel inside him. Lost once again in the sweetness of his mouth, she felt him pull back then plunge forward. She gasped as pain, sharp and lightning-quick, pierced her. Then, with her next heartbeat, it was gone, replaced with fullness. "It only hurts the first time. There will be only pleasure from here on out, I promise."

Alastair remained still for a moment, allowing her to catch her breath and grow accustomed to his presence inside her, filling her, stretching her until slowly he started to move.

He reached down and lifted her buttocks, thrusting into her with long, hard strokes. His body claimed hers. He plunged deeper and deeper into her core, and just when she grew accustomed to his rhythm, he changed it. Keeping her guessing, making her want more and more of what he offered. She arched up, meeting each thrust.

She moaned her pleasure as she curled her fingers into the coverlet beneath her. She thrashed her head back and forth as the tension inside her built, tightening, tightening as he pushed into her, hot and hard. Desire swamped her. Her breath came in panting gasps as he withdrew and thrust anew. Her nerves sizzled and stretched, until she erupted in a glorious, rippling cascade. It was unlike anything she could have ever imagined.

As her pleasure peaked, he continued to thrust, harder and faster, until his body tensed. She tightened around him. Deep inside her she felt him shudder as his release swept through him. She clung to him, as she too was swept once more into a vortex of sensation, erupting, bright and hot, enfolding them both in a sea of shared pleasure.

He put his hands on either side of her head and bent

down to kiss her, despite his harsh and laboured breathing, before he shifted to the side and slumped upon the bed. He pulled her back against him, curling his body protectively against hers. He pressed another kiss to her shoulder before he nestled his head against hers. She could feel the evocative beat of his heart against her back, felt that beat match her own. Her womb clenched, and where he had entered her throbbed, but it was not pain. It was a continuing reminder of what they had shared, of all they had become in these moments.

She was his, and he was hers.

As their heartbeats settled, Alastair pulled the coverlet up and over their bodies. Slowly the world around them faded as they drifted off to sleep.

Sometime later, when a faint light seeped into the chamber, Gwendolyn startled to wakefulness at the sound of screeching.

"Where is she. Where is my daughter!" Beatrice's father bellowed.

"MacLeod!" Another deeper voice cried. "Where are you? You attacked the MacDonalds. Explain your actions."

"He attacked the MacDonalds?" A third voice joined the others. "Of all the brazen, underhanded things to do. His father would not have attacked under the cover of night. He was decent enough to do so in the daylight. Where is the bastard?"

Gwendolyn rolled over to see Alastair, propped on his

elbow, gazing down at her. Despite the anger in the voices outside in the hallway, a smile pulled up the corners of his lips. "Good morrow, my dear." He bent over and kissed her.

"How can you be so at ease?" she asked. "Do you not hear them?"

"How can anyone not hear them is more the question."

She frowned. "Does it not concern you?"

"I knew this moment would come. I expected it last night." He shrugged one shoulder. "That the lot of them allowed me last night with you, I will be forever grateful for."

Gwendolyn felt heat rise to her cheeks at the memory of all they had done last night, of what they now were to each other.

He bent down and kissed her as he slid his hand beneath the covers and found her breast. "You were every bit as delightful last night as I always dreamed you would be."

"You dreamed about us?" She sucked in a breath as his fingers grazed her nipple.

"Aye. I admit you were never far from my thoughts."

"MacLeod!" Alexander MacDonald's voice came from right outside the door. They had found him.

His hand left her, and his smile slipped. "I want more than anything to stay and show you what a splendid thing lovemaking in the morning can be, but duty calls." He sat up fully.

"Step back, sir. Give the laird his privacy. He'll be with ye shortly." Becks's voice was as strong and demanding as any laird's. A moment later, footsteps sounded in the hallway, fading into the distance.

A knock came upon the door. "M'laird, I have the chest ye requested. May I enter?"

Alastair pulled the bedsheets up over Gwendolyn's body. "You may enter."

Becks opened the door, then carried a large wooden chest into the chamber, setting it before the hearth. He kept his eyes averted. "Breakfast is waitin' belowstairs as are several of the lairds. They're in high spirits this mornin'."

"After the events of last night, no doubt. Thank you for hindering their pursuit of me so far."

Becks bowed and left the room, closing the door behind him.

Alastair stood and pulled his shirt over his head before quickly refolding his tartan and belting it about him.

"What's in the chest?" Gwendolyn asked.

"It is the bride price you were given for our betrothal." He angled his head towards the chest while he slipped on his boots. "Go ahead. Have a look."

Gwendolyn slipped her nightrail over her head before she moved from the bed to the chest. She opened the latch and lifted the lid to reveal what must have been over twenty lengths of richly hued fabrics in silk, brocades, damask, wool, and linen.

He finished with his boots and came to join her. "My father gifted these to you so that you could have dresses made that were befitting of your station as a laird's wife." He bent and kissed her cheek. "I've sent for a dressmaker to come to the castle today. I'd like to see you wear something that isn't my baby sister's cast-off."

Gwendolyn didn't know what to say as she ran her fingers over the lush fabrics inside the chest. The gift was overwhelmingly generous, and that it had been considered so long ago, especially by a man who wasn't known for his little kindnesses, surprised her. "Was your mother behind this?"

"My mother was long-dead by the time we were betrothed, but perhaps her ghost had a hand in making my father see to the matter."

Gwendolyn stood. "About Rowena. You know she is no longer your 'baby sister.' She is a woman fully grown, and she knows her own mind and her own heart."

He smiled. "I can only agree."

"Will you meet with Rowena and Marcus today and help them come to an arrangement?"

His expression turned grim. "As soon as I leave this chamber, I will be trying to stop a war. That has to take precedence over my sister's needs, I fear."

She touched his arm. "You are going to war with the MacDonalds?"

"I do not see a way around it."

She swallowed. "Then I am glad I retrieved the Fairy Flag. It will bring you good luck and can be used to help win the day if things turn for the worst."

"Alastair. The screeching lairds belowstairs are dissolving into chaos," Graeme called from behind the door. "I would make haste."

Alastair reached down and lifted the wooden box containing the Fairy Flag into his hands. "I accept the luck this flag brings to my family, but I will not be the laird who uses its magic to turn the tide of this war with the MacDonalds. There are much bigger conflicts ahead for Scotland, and that is when we will need the magic to spur us to victory." Alastair's arms closed around her, holding her tightly, molding his body into hers while he pressed a kiss to her forehead. "The MacDonalds will not succeed. It is time for me as clan leader to take a stand against them. Every person in this castle and in the adjoining village is under my care. I shall rise to this challenge and be the man I am destined to become as heir of the MacLeods." Reluctantly, he released her and stepped back and made his way to the door.

He was nearly out the door when she called after him. "Have a care that you are not hurt."

He stopped and turned back, grinning. "It's been a long time since someone cared about my well-being." His dark eyes seemed to devour her where she stood. "There is not a man more blessed in Christendom than I am. What we shared last night will carry me through the conflict ahead."

"Godspeed."

"And may he and the army I leave behind here at Dunvegan keep you safe while I am gone." He opened the door and walked through, greeting Graeme, whose dire look brought a twist of fear to her stomach.

Gwendolyn stared after them as they disappeared down the stairs. It wasn't until she heard the shouting from the great hall that she returned to her bed and sank down upon it. Her hand crept up to her lips—lips he had so recently kissed—as she wondered if he would ever kiss her again.

War made many a widow. She had retrieved the Fairy Flag and returned it to Alastair. She closed her eyes and willed whatever fairy magic the artifact possessed to keep those she loved from harm. At the thought she trembled as the revelation came over her. There was no other word to describe how she felt. She loved Alastair MacLeod.

Last night, she and Alastair had shared something beautiful, something excruciatingly intimate. He'd made himself vulnerable to her and given her his trust, repairing any damage Garrick had inflicted upon them, and any damage they had done to each other.

She'd finally been gifted with everything she'd ever wanted, and now the man she loved was headed off to war.

CHAPTER NINETEEN

ANGRY SHOUTS GREW louder as Alastair, Graeme, and a company of guards from the castle entered the great hall. It was time for Alastair to put his diplomacy skills to the test. He did not want to go to war, but he would if the MacDonalds left him no other choice.

His men filled the chamber, lining the walls, each armed with a sword and a pistol. The bellowing in the chamber ceased as the angry lairds took in the show of arms.

"What is the meaning of this, MacLeod?" Alexander MacDonald drew his own sword.

Paying no heed to the tense situation, Laird Lamont rushed Alastair. The older man's face was flushed red, his eyes were bloodshot, and rings of worry bracketed his mouth. "Where is Beatrice? What have you done to her?"

Did the man truly have no idea of the scheme she had played a role in? "Beatrice left the castle last night of her own free will and made her way to the seat of the MacDonalds."

Laird Lamont lurched back. "Why would she do that? Something must have happened."

"I broke off our engagement when I learned our betrothal was orchestrated by the MacDonalds in order for Beatrice to spy on me for them."

Beatrice's father froze. "That's a lie."

Alastair lifted his gaze to the two men gathered behind Lamont—Lairds MacDonald and MacQueen.

Laird MacDonald's lips thinned. "That accusation is entirely false."

"It is the truth," Alastair said. "Garrick MacDonald admitted everything to me last night."

Alexander MacDonald remained silent, gazing at Alastair with no expression.

"But Garrick and Beatrice were not the ones who came up with this game that has been playing out in my life for the past five years." Alastair tapped a finger to his temple. "Neither Garrick nor Beatrice are devious enough to carry out such an elaborate plan. And Garrick hardly had the means to sustain himself in secret within the walls of Dunvegan for five years. He had help from his clan, and from someone else within this castle. Someone we all trusted."

After a quick glance at Graeme, Alastair turned to face one of his own castle guards. Emery Howden flinched beneath Alastair's accusing gaze. In the next heartbeat he bolted for the door, but Graeme stepped forward and with a well-placed punch to Emery's gut, succeeded in not only stopping his escape, but disarming him as well. The pistol and sword went flying. Two guards nearby retrieved the weapons while two others moved in to grab his arms.

"Let me go. You don't understand. They threatened to hurt my ma and pa. My little sister and brother. I had no choice."

To four of his guards, Alastair said, "Go to Howden's home. Bring his family here under our protection. I'll not have the MacDonalds take their revenge out on Emery's family now." The guards nodded, then left the chamber.

Alastair had suspected Emery had been manipulated to help the MacDonalds. He would most likely let the young man off with a warning if he cooperated, but at this moment, Alastair needed the fear of possible confinement in the dungeon to get Emery to divulge the rest of the details Alastair and Graeme had yet to figure out. "You brought food to Garrick? To the Harris children?"

Emery shook his head. "Once a month I was paid to bring supplies to Garrick MacDonald only. It was his task to feed the others. And I had to make certain the sea gate was unlocked every evening after sunset so that Garrick could come and go as he needed."

"What about any strange supplies. Were you ever asked to bring Garrick anything like that?"

Emery nodded. "The first items were a woman's dress, and some blood from a lamb. The strangest thing by far was a large sheet of glass."

Two memories came to mind: the blood smeared on Gwendolyn's wedding gown, and the glass used to throw Gwendolyn's image. "Do you know who paid you every month for the past five years?"

Emery cast a quick glance at Alexander MacDonald before looking away. "Laird MacDonald himself."

Alastair shifted his gaze to the man who had just been accused of orchestrating the entire plan to kidnap Gwendolyn and sustaining the efforts to keep her imprisoned. "Why would you do something so cruel to an innocent girl and her family?"

"I did nothing."

"Aye, Garrick did it for you. He informed me of all the reasons why he hates my clan last night."

MacDonald's eyes narrowed. "Aye. The night you attacked my clan."

Alastair gestured about the chamber. "I have sixty guards who will attest to the fact there was no engagement. Your men retreated when they realised they were at a disadvantage."

"Is that true?" Laird Nicolson asked.

Laird MacKinnon frowned. "Laird MacDonald led us to believe there had been a massacre, led by you."

"Why would he want you to believe that?" Alastair asked, already knowing the answer.

"To take us to the brink of war," Laird MacAskill said contemptuously as his gaze burned into Alexander MacDonald. "You did all this to shift the balance of power from the council to yourself and your clan."

The MacDonald pulled his sword. "So what if I did?

Someone had to rise up before we are all overridden by the bloody English. They have already taken over the rule of this country. Shall we stand by and let them devour everything else we have and leave naught for us—our castles, our women, our very lives—if we do not stop them?" Ten guards rushed forward and seized him and his weapon before he could strike.

"Throw him in the dungeon," Alastair ordered his men.

Fighting against those who held him, Alexander Mac-Donald called back over his shoulder, "You can rid yourself of me, but you canna rid yourself of all of us. The MacDonalds will have their revenge."

As he disappeared from view and his shouting became nothing but muffled noise, Laird MacQueen turned on Alastair. "The MacDonald is still part of this council whether he attacked your clan or not. You cannot silence his voice."

"Silence his voice? The man just declared war on the rest of us."

"How long will you imprison him?" Laird Nicolson asked with a frown.

"For a few hours. Then my men will escort him back to his lands—long enough for him to have a taste of what awaits if he keeps trying to manipulate this council."

Laird MacKinnon frowned. "He would not release you if your situations were reversed."

Alastair lifted his chin. "I can be the better man here because his clan will still come after all of us, with or without their laird." Alastair cast his gaze over the remaining lairds. "Prepare your men. For the sake of the isle, we ride against the MacDonald clan at midday."

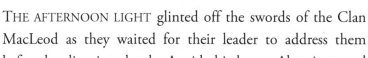

THE AFTERNOON LIGHT glinted off the swords of the Clan MacLeod as they waited for their leader to address them before heading into battle. Astride his horse, Alastair turned to his men. His hand tightened around the hilt of his sword, feeling the grooves of the intricate detailing fit themselves to the calluses of his palm.

"Today we go to battle. There are things worth fighting for, and dying for. All a man can do is choose his causes carefully, then follow that path. Our path takes us to Monkstadt House where we will hopefully put this centuries-old feud with the MacDonalds to rest. We do not go into this battle unprepared. You've worked hard to improve your fighting skills over the last several days. You are armed and ready for whatever comes our way."

"But will we be protected as we have been in the past?" one of the warriors amongst the foot soldiers shouted.

"Without the Fairy Flag, how can we guarantee our success?" another warrior called out from the middle of the columns of men on horseback.

"Thanks to Gwendolyn Harris and Marcus MacDonald." Alastair paused to look at the man beside him. Marcus would ride with them into battle against his own clan. "Gwendolyn and Marcus risked their lives for all of us last night. The Fairy Flag has been returned to the MacLeods." Alastair sent Graeme a signal to come alongside him.

Graeme untied the small wooden box from his saddle and opened it. From inside he drew out the original Fairy Flag. At the sight of it, the men let out shouts of joy.

"Praise the heavens!" Ronald exclaimed from atop his horse.

"The fairy magic that protected us once, protects us again." Alastair looked at the celebration amongst his men and wished Gwendolyn was there to see how her efforts made a difference for these men on their way to war. "Graeme Duff, your family has been the flag bearer for centuries. Will you continue to accept this honour, even knowing if we use the flag's magic one more time, you could be taken to Fairyland along with the flag?"

"I bear that burden with honour, m'laird." Voice firming, Graeme continued, "For the Clan MacLeod."

"For the Clan MacLeod," the others echoed in high spirits.

Graeme attached the Fairy Flag to the standard pole before he tied a silk ribbon around the flag. It would be unfurled in a time of need, but it would come into battle with them.

Alastair's gaze travelled over his men. "Today we will settle this feud with the MacDonalds, but we fight a battle on two fronts. I will need forty men to stay here at Dunvegan to protect our home and those we leave inside. The rest will travel with me and the flag to Monkstadt House. Ronald, I ask that you take the lead on those men who will remain here."

Ronald nodded and broke formation. "Those who will stay at Dunvegan with me, come forward." Moments later forty of the foot soldiers stood behind Ronald while the others rode off towards the MacDonald lands.

———— ❧ ————

AT THE HEAD of the column of men, Alastair thought back to a past battle in the late fifteenth century between the MacDonalds and the MacLeods that had started the feud between them. The Battle of Bloody Bay or *Blàr Bàgh na Fala* in their Gaelic tongue, was a conflict between the old laird, John MacDonald, and Angus MacDonald, his son, over the lands of the isles. The MacLeods joined the old laird in protecting his claim.

The fighting had been fierce, and ultimately cost the laird of the MacLeods his life along with many of his men. The keeper of the Fairy Flag had unfurled his banner and helped turn the tide of battle in favour of the old laird.

After the battle, James IV stripped the MacDonalds of the claim to the Lordship of the Isles, and only the Mac-Leods of Dunvegan and Harris rose up to meet the vacuum of political power in the Highlands that was created by that decision. The MacDonalds had hated the MacLeods for claiming the leadership role of the isles ever since. Alastair remained in his thoughts until he and his men finally arrived atop a rise in the landscape where they could see the Mac-Donalds' clan seat below. Monkstadt House. Yet the battle would not be fought at the fortified country house. Instead, the MacDonald clan gathered for battle in the grassland below. Judging by the pennants flapping in the wind, the MacDonalds had been joined by the MacQueens and the Lamonts. The MacKinnons, the Nicolsons, and the MacAskills had joined the ranks of the MacLeods. Alastair turned to Marcus on his left.

"Are you certain you want to proceed?" Alastair asked Marcus one last time. "If you fight against your clan, you will be lost to them forever."

Marcus's gaze fixed soberly on Alastair's face. "I am already lost. The moment I set eyes on Rowena, I knew the course of my destiny. I am a man with no clan."

So far, Marcus's words had proven true. He had helped Gwendolyn reclaim the Fairy Flag, and for today's conflict he had not worn his clan tartan. Instead he'd chosen black breeches and a black muslin shirt. With his dark hair and dark eyes, he looked the part of a rogue warrior, beholden to none. Which was why Alastair had positioned him next to both him and Graeme. The two of them would keep an eye on him—to keep him safe as Rowena had begged and to keep him from turning on them at some unexpected moment.

Alastair turned his thoughts back to the battlefield when the thundering sound of horses filled the air. He tensed and drew his sword. A quick glance at the MacDonalds confirmed that they held their position below. It was then that the sound coalesced, and Alastair realised it came from behind his men. "Hold the line," he barked at Graeme as he kicked his horse into motion, moving out and down the line of his warriors to see what was coming their way. Had the MacDonald set a trap? Did they mean to attack from both sides?

Alastair's heart thundered in his chest as he came around the back of his men to see a hundred men on horses advancing towards him. "Half of you, about-turn," he ordered his men, splitting his unit into half facing forward, half facing back.

Instead of attacking, the riders coming at them slowed their approach until Alastair could see two familiar faces at the front of the others.

Could it be? Alastair could hardly believe the sight before him as he released the iron grip on his sword and returned the blade to its scabbard.

Tormod and Orrick? His brothers had come to fight?

They pulled their horses to a stop before him. "We heard you were having a battle with the MacDonalds," Orrick, the youngest of the three triplets, said with a note of seriousness in his tone.

"And you didn't invite us to the party," Tormod quipped.

Alastair tried to hold back a smile and failed. Nothing had changed with his brothers in the five years they'd been apart. One still took the world too seriously, the other not seriously enough. "How did you know we were going to war?"

"Word travels fast in these parts when the great MacLeod is off to punish his enemies." Tormod's eager smile made him appear to Alastair as though he were twelve years old again and battling over who could convince Mrs Honey to give them a sweet treat.

Orrick frowned at his brother. "We heard nothing of war until we arrived at Dunvegan. We came because we learned Gwendolyn Harris had been found. Is it true?"

"Aye," Alastair acknowledged. "She was kidnapped and held hostage by the MacDonalds in our own castle. They also sent a spy into our midst disguised as my newest betrothed, and turned one of our own against us, hence the reason we go to war."

Orrick and Tormod shared a wide-eyed look before Tormod turned back to his brother. "Sounds like there is more to all of that, but it can wait until we are finished here."

"What would you have us do, Brother?" Orrick asked.

"Have your men join the ranks, and prepare yourselves

for battle. The two of you, come to the front with me. Let the MacDonalds see that the three of us are a force to be reckoned with."

"Our first big battle together," Tormod said as they rode to the front. "How exciting."

Orrick frowned. "I can think of better ways to spend our time."

Tormod rolled his eyes. "Your books are waiting for you back at Dunvegan."

At the front, the two brothers greeted Graeme. "This is Marcus MacDonald." Alastair tilted his head towards the young man in black.

"A MacDonald fights for us?" Tormod asked in a leery voice.

"'Tis a long story. One we will discuss later."

Orrick's frowned deepened. "How many stories can there be? You've only been back at Dunvegan for four days?"

"Too many," Alastair and Graeme said in unison.

Alastair drew a breath he hoped would settle him as he turned his thoughts and his gaze back to the battlefield. He still hoped this would not become an all-out war. "I'm going to meet with the MacDonald one last time."

He would ride halfway between the two battalions and try to negotiate peace. Peace amongst the clans was the only way they would be able to outmaneuver the English when that moment finally came. . .and it was coming faster than any of them wanted to acknowledge. With a nod at Graeme,

Alastair made his way down the hill as the MacDonald came forward.

"We do not have to fight this out," Alastair said when they met, mounted horse to mounted horse. "The MacLeods have three men to your one."

"The numbers do not matter. The MacDonald fighting spirit will carry the day."

Alastair was not so sure of that. Since his return he had trained the MacLeod men to use many new battle techniques. They were also well-armed with targes, swords, and the pistols Graeme had secured. And the Fairy Flag was once again in their possession. "I am willing to let bygones be bygones if you promise never to place spies in my castle or steal the Fairy Flag from us again."

At the mention of the Fairy Flag, Alexander MacDonald startled and his gaze searched the men before him until it rested on Graeme and the standard pole he held in his hands. "I should have known your little foray here last night was more than simply a tactic to capture Garrick or to punish me, however temporarily."

Alastair ignored the barb. "Will you agree to a truce between our clans? And will you allow the Isle Council to move forward in seeking to unify the clans against the English?"

"Why would I agree to any such thing?"

"There is no honour lost in backing away from a fight. Saving our men is honourable enough. The days of the MacDonalds lording over the isles are gone. The political power must now be shared amongst the clans for the good of all."

"My men would rather die than run home with the promise of peace from a MacLeod."

Alastair straightened, his patience stretching thin. Was there no reasoning with this man? "You know as well as I do that we need to save all our men and all our resources for when the English make their move against us."

"Why would they fight those of us on the isles? We have no resources they can extort. The land is no good for farming."

"It is not the land they want. It is the dominance over our people, our way of life, and our possible loyalty to a different king to which they take exception." Alastair forced himself to relax, to continue offering another option besides war. "Our kin do not deserve to die this day. My clan has suffered abuse at the hands of your clan, yet I am willing to entertain a peaceful resolution. Can you do the same? Can you be the leader your clan needs you to be?"

Anger flashed in the older man's eyes, and his hands clenched around the reins in his hands. Sensing unease, his horse pranced beneath him before the MacDonald released a fractured breath. "You think we can achieve peace? That by avoiding a conflict today, that we will not end up in the same place at a later date?"

"No one can predict the future. But the two of us can at least try to see reason when it comes to putting our kin at risk."

As suddenly as it had come, all signs of anger vanished, and a slow, sly grin pulled up the corners of Alexander MacDonald's mouth. "Very well. I agree to preserving the peace this day. What we had hoped to accomplish has already been achieved."

A chill snaked down Alastair's spine. At the satisfied gleam in the MacDonald's eyes, Alastair suddenly realised something darker was at play here. His heart faltered. "You bastard!" Alastair jerked the reins of his horse, guiding the animal back up the hill at a full gallop. He reined to a stop before his brothers, Graeme, and Marcus. "The battle is a ploy. The MacDonalds wanted us here, leaving Dunvegan only minimally guarded."

Graeme's face mirrored Alastair's dread. "You don't think they waited for us to leave before they breached the castle?"

Bile rose in Alastair's throat. "Aye, I do. They are after Gwendolyn." For the past five years, Alastair had been learning the ways of peace, but in that moment all he wanted to do was fight. "Graeme, Orrick, Tormod," Alastair said. "I'll leave this battle against the MacDonalds to you. It is time to put an end to their machinations against us."

"We will lead the men with pride," Tormod said as he donned his battle helm.

"I'm going back to Dunvegan." Alastair turned his horse around.

"I'm going too," Marcus said, joining him. "Rowena is there, unprotected. If anything happens to the women. . ."

Alastair didn't argue. He spurred his horse towards Dunvegan. He knew in the depth of his soul that the MacDonalds had attacked Dunvegan while he and his men were gone. Alastair's heart pounded as fear took root inside him. He'd failed to keep Gwendolyn safe before. Had he done so again? Fear, anxiety, and rage all coiled together inside his gut as his horse raced over the rocky terrain.

Unable to hold the emotions inside him a moment longer, he released an inhuman sound that was part howl, part cry. He had to get back to Gwendolyn before it was too late.

CHAPTER TWENTY

AFTER THE DRESSMAKER had left, Gwendolyn sat at Arabella's bedside, trying not to think about all the things that could happen to Alastair upon the field of battle. He had promised he would come home to her, and she had to trust that he would. Pushing her thoughts aside, she smiled at her sister. "You look so much stronger today. Are you feeling better?"

Arabella nodded and reached for another biscuit from the plate that Gwendolyn had brought her from the kitchen. "I must be because I am suddenly starving."

"Mrs Morgan made these biscuits especially for you. She is eager to fatten the three of us up," Gwendolyn said with a smile. "She looks forward to when you are well enough to join us at the table."

Arabella laughed. "That day is coming soon, for I was able to sit at the bedside for my meal this afternoon. My strength is returning."

Gwendolyn sent Lottie a grateful smile. "No one is more pleased than I am to hear that news."

Arabella finished her biscuit, then dusted the crumbs off

the bedcovers. She leaned towards her sister. "And how are things with you and Alastair?" She narrowed her gaze on Gwendolyn's face. "There is a glow about you today that is different."

Gwendolyn's cheeks flamed. "He is. . . We are. . ."

A loud crash sounded from outside in the front courtyard, followed by shouting. Samuel who had been practising his reading by the fire near Lottie, stood. "What was that?"

More shouting and loud crashes. It sounded as if the castle were under attack.

Gwendolyn stood as her heart thundered in her chest. "All of you stay here. I will go investigate. Samuel, I'm leaving you in charge."

He stood rigid, and nodded, sensing as did Gwendolyn that something was terribly wrong.

Gwendolyn raced down the staircase and to the door. She threw the door open and stepped outside to find Callum and several other armed warriors there. The acrid scent of war filled the air as she searched through the smoke to see a row of MacLeod archers fire one volley after another, trying to fend off the enemy climbing through a gap they must have blown through the curtain wall with a catapult.

"Who is attacking?" Gwendolyn moved to Callum's side. He clutched a sword in one hand and a dagger in the other, and balanced on the balls of his feet, ready to attack.

"The MacDonalds must have split their army into two— one part that went to greet Alastair and another led by the laird's son, Alex MacDonald, who came to Dunvegan."

Gwendolyn's heart clenched as the MacDonald men continued over the breach in the curtain wall. "What can I do? How can I help?"

All around them the shouts of their enemy clashed with those of the clan. "Go back inside and pray." Callum charged forward, flinging himself at the men who were not taken down by the arrows. The screech of metal upon metal filled the once quiet courtyard.

Her heartbeat in her throat, Gwendolyn lifted her skirts and raced back towards the door.

"Where are you going?" A rough hand clamped around her arm and jerked her backwards, then lifted her off her feet.

Gwendolyn fought against Garrick's grasp. She screamed, hoping the men fighting in the distance would hear her, or see her struggling and come to help her, but her scream barely rose above the din of battle. "Release me," she cried as the thug with Garrick wrestled with her, trying to subdue her.

"The new laird made it almost impossible to get back inside these walls, but I prevailed." Garrick laughed.

Gwendolyn writhed, making it difficult for her captors to hold on to her. "You might have entered, but you shall never exit again. Not once Alastair discovers what you've done."

The thug's grip loosened enough for Gwendolyn to kick out wildly, connecting with the brute's body. She heard his grunt of pain as her feet once again touched the floor. She barely regained her balance before Garrick lashed out, slapping her so viciously that her head snapped to one side.

"You're the one whose minutes on this earth are numbered, not mine." He knocked her to the floor. Before she could fight back, the man helping Garrick grabbed her ankles and tied them together.

Fear rose up fast and thick inside her. Her mind raced and her heart beat so wildly she was certain it would pop out of her chest. *Nay. She would never be a prisoner again.* Gwendolyn bucked and writhed against her restraints. She wrenched her hands free and dug her nails into Garrick's arm, squeezing as tightly as she could.

"God's bones." Garrick slapped her again.

Her vision blurred and tiny explosions of light appeared before her.

"Do that again and I'll kill you right here and now." He grabbed her wrists, digging painfully into her skin as he forced her arms together. The other man came forward and lashed her wrists tight.

Gwendolyn pulled in a deep, terrified breath as the two men lifted her, like a slaughtered pig, and carried her through the keep. They moved down the hallway to the rear stairs. At the landing a flash of black bombazine appeared as Mrs Morgan rushed towards the men with a frying pan held above her head. The iron pan came down hard against Garrick's head with a resounding thump. He dropped his grip on Gwendolyn. A heartbeat later the thug released her as he charged towards Mrs Morgan.

Mrs Morgan shrieked and swung her pan, missing the man.

Gwendolyn tried to roll into the path of the thug as he advanced towards Mrs Morgan. "Watch out!" she tried to warn the chatelaine, but too late.

Mrs Morgan cried out as he slashed her shoulder with his dagger. Gwendolyn reached the thug's feet and slammed her body into his legs, knocking him off-balance. He tripped, stumbled, but then caught himself.

He growled his anger and prepared to attack once more when Garrick suddenly stood, regaining his senses. "We are here for Gwendolyn," he barked as he ruthlessly picked her up by her hair instead of the ropes that bound her hands. "We must hurry." The thug grabbed Gwendolyn's feet and together they carried her down the stairs.

At the exit to the rear courtyard, the men found their way blocked by Becks. The aged servant gripped his sword with white-knuckled force. "Release her now."

"Or what?" Garrick taunted.

Becks charged. He swung his sword at Garrick's head and connected with his cheek before Garrick threw Gwendolyn's body at the older man, knocking him to the ground. His sword clattered to the ground beside him.

The thug picked it up and poised it to strike Becks's chest.

"No! Do not hurt him." Gwendolyn cried.

"Leave the bastard to wallow in his failure," Garrick said, clutching a hand to his cheek, trying to staunch the bleeding.

With a grunt, the thug palmed the sword and instead, whacked Becks on the side of the head with the flat of the blade, knocking him senseless.

"I hope there will be no more interruptions by devoted servants," Garrick growled as he picked Gwendolyn up by the ropes at her hands once more. "Your next saviour, I'll have no choice but to kill."

The rear courtyard was empty, allowing them an easy escape down the path to the sea gate. The guards were not there, having moved to the front of the castle to help with the attack. Trying to make their task as difficult as possible, Gwendolyn squirmed against her restraints. She wiggled and lashed out with her bound hands and legs. "Let me go!"

Garrick dropped her to the ground once again. He bent down until his face was close to hers. "You stupid, stupid girl." He slapped her again, this time so hard her vision narrowed to a pinpoint, then everything went black.

—❧—

FOR THE FIRST time since his mother had died, Alastair prayed. He breathed every prayer he remembered as he urged his horse to faster and faster speeds. Those prayers caught in his throat as he neared Dunvegan and saw the ensuing battle.

He slowed his horse and took in the scene. Fifteen or so MacDonalds lay upon the ground while ten more fought his men in the front courtyard. The fighting was fierce, and Alastair was filled with pride at their skill and resilience. "Come, Marcus. We can fend off any aggressors as we make our way inside the breach."

"Agreed."

Drawing their swords, Alastair and Marcus forged ahead, riding swiftly towards the castle. They met with little resistance as they guided their horses through the crumbled remains of the curtain wall and into the courtyard. Alastair inhaled the damp smell of sea air mixed with the tang of blood.

As he and Marcus entered the fray, one man raced towards them on horseback. Alastair charged, engaging the man in an explosive clash of swords.

The MacDonald warrior came around for another attack. "I'll have your head for all you've done to our people!" Alex MacDonald's sword hacked down in an arc.

"Why does your clan always forget it was you who started this feud?" Alastair deflected the blow, then pulled his dagger free and charged forward. He wasn't close enough to strike the blow himself, so he palmed the dagger and sent it flying through the air, straight into Alex's shoulder. The chief's son tumbled from his horse and hit the ground.

All around Alastair, his men, his kin, wielded lethal blows, sending the MacDonalds to the ground, moaning their defeat as the battle turned in their favour. Alastair slid from his horse to kneel beside the fallen heir to the Mac-Donald clan. He pulled his dagger from the man's shoulder.

"Come to finish me off?" Alex hissed.

"Nay." Alastair met his pain-filled gaze as he pressed a strip of cloth from his own shirt against the man's wound. "I intend to send you back to your father in defeat."

Alex rolled to his side, then tried to sit up. "You have already lost."

Alastair's stomach clenched. "What do you mean?"

Alex smiled. "Garrick has taken what you treasure most."

Alastair shook his head. "The Fairy Flag has been returned to us."

Satisfaction shone in his eyes. "That is not what you treasure most."

Gwendolyn. What had they done to her now?

Alastair knocked the smug smile from Alex's face with a well-placed blow to the head that sent him to the ground once more.

Marcus came to Alastair's side as the enemy retreated. "Alex deserves a serious punishment for what he's done here. Shall I take him to the dungeon?"

"Nay. Come with me. We must find Gwendolyn. Alex's men will eventually find him and haul him home," Alastair said as he raced for the keep.

Upon seeing Alastair, Callum headed him off at the stairs to the keep with Ronald at his side. There were gashes at his brother's shoulder and temple. His face was smeared with blood.

"You're wounded."

"'Tis nothing serious, I promise," Callum said. "But I do think I need a few more fighting lessons."

Alastair held Callum's gaze, making certain his brother was not more seriously hurt before he turned to Ronald. "How many casualties were there amongst the men?"

"No one was killed. There are a few men with serious wounds. Lottie is attending them now."

Alastair nodded. "Your first command was a success, Ronald. Congratulations."

"On the contrary, m'laird." His lips tightened. "Garrick came with the first wave of men to breach the wall. He slipped past us and took Gwendolyn."

"Where?"

"To the loch where Garrick forced her into one of the fishing vessels. She was bound at the hands and feet." Callum paused before adding, "I think he means to dump Gwendolyn into the loch. Mother tried to stop him. I've never witnessed anything like it. She threw everything she could at him—rocks, stones from the castle, shells upon the beach, even a fish, and several big waves—but nothing slowed him down."

"I'm going after Garrick." Alastair started for the sea gate when Marcus stopped him with a jerk on his arm.

Marcus's eyes filled with a plea. "Not to the sea gate. To

the horses. You must trust me. I know how to overtake Garrick quickly."

Indecision tore Alastair in two. Could he trust Marcus? A MacDonald?

As though reading his thoughts, Marcus added, "We are on the same side, Alastair. Trust me."

Alastair nodded. "To the horses then."

"First, I must know, is Rowena well?" He turned to Callum.

Callum nodded. "She hid in the castle with Arabella, Samuel, and Lottie. They are all safe."

Marcus breathed a relieved sigh. "Then let's ride out, and quickly."

Ronald and Callum stayed behind to see that the MacDonalds left peacefully with their dead.

Alastair and Marcus rode out of the castle and were about to turn north when the rest of Alastair's men could be seen returning to the castle with Orrick and Tormod at the front.

Despite his desire to hurry to put into play whatever scheme Marcus had in mind, he waited for Orrick and Tormod to reach them.

"I am eager to hear what happened with the MacDonalds, but at this moment I need Orrick to head back to the castle and oversee whatever is happening there. Tormod, I need you to come with us." His brothers asked no questions, simply followed his orders.

Alastair, Marcus, and Tormod rode north for a couple of miles until Marcus turned towards the cliffs. It wasn't until they were closer that Alastair spotted a lee in the rocks and a trail down to the shores of the loch. As they descended the pathway to the beach, a double-masted ship came into view. The wind tugged at their clothes, their hair, as they emerged on the sandy shore.

"Tie the horses here and follow me," Marcus called over his shoulder as he hurried towards a dock that Alastair had not known was there. Marcus ran down the planked wood and to the ship. "Drop a ladder," he called to a man leaning over the railing, watching their approach.

"Aye, Captain."

A rope ladder appeared and the three of them scrambled up. Once on deck, Marcus signalled for the ladder to come up and shouted, "Quickly. Set sail, heading south towards Dunvegan."

His orders were executed with swift precision, and the boat lurched forward, catching the wind in her hastily raised sails. Men dressed in blue and white striped shirts with red handkerchiefs tied loosely about their necks hurried across the deck in response to Marcus's commands, unfurling sails and tightening ropes. The ship picked up speed as the white canvas caught the wind, propelling them forward.

Alastair could hardly believe the scene unfolding before him. "Do you want to explain how you happen to have a ship, just when one is needed?"

"Luck, I suppose." Marcus handed a spyglass to Alastair. "Start scanning the water for them. I'm going to the crow's nest." He climbed the mast and searched from above.

The wind was stiff, allowing the ship to move quickly towards the waters beyond Dunvegan. Alastair and Tormod leaned against the railings as they looked over the open water for any signs of a boat. It was too late in the day for many fishermen to be out, so any vessels that remained would be possible options to explore.

"There," Marcus called down, pointing at a small boat with two passengers inside. "To the left of the bow."

His heart leapt as Alastair fixed on the location with his spyglass. Only to feel his heart sink to his stomach again. "'Tis two fishermen."

Moments passed as the ship sliced through the water and wind tugged at their bodies, sending Alastair's hair to dance about his face.

Hair. Gwendolyn's hair would do the same. He stopped searching the boats on the water for anything other than long, flowing golden locks.

"There. To the starboard side. I see her. Hurry!" Alastair watched as Garrick forced Gwendolyn to stand. Her hands were bound before her. To her feet, he'd tied a large rock. Her golden hair tangled wildly about her face. Even so, he could clearly read the look of desperation in her eyes.

Garrick shouted something.

Gwendolyn's face hardened.

Alastair's breath caught as Garrick advanced on her, no doubt finding it harder to get her to leap to her death than he expected. The thought should have made Alastair smile, knowing Gwendolyn was a fighter to the end. Instead, Alastair looked on as panic snaked through him. They wouldn't make it to her in time.

GWENDOLYN WATCHED AS Garrick inched forward in the boat. She might be able to stall him for a few moments, but eventually he would force her overboard. Her head pounded where he had struck her, but the sensation was slowly ebbing and her faculties were returning. She only hoped that would happen before he forced her into the loch.

"No one will come to save you this time," Garrick taunted. "Alastair MacLeod is a fool if he thought I could not get to him, get to you, anytime I wanted. I will have my revenge against the MacLeods for all they've done to me."

Garrick might not think it possible, yet she knew Alastair would come for her. It surprised her how confident she was about that fact. He might not have come to save her on their wedding day, but then he hadn't known she needed saving. This time he would know. This time he would come.

"Murdering me will serve that purpose?" Gwendolyn asked. She had to keep Garrick talking, with his eyes on her face, while she tried desperately to loosen the bonds at her feet. She had to rid herself of the rock before he forced her overboard.

"Losing you will cut the MacLeod to his core. I've watched the two of you together from within the castle walls. Never have I seen the MacLeod look at anyone the way he looks at you." Garrick crept forward.

She inched back, sending the small vessel rocking back and forth. The motion gave her a crazy idea. She wasn't about to let him kill her without a fight.

Tamping down her fear, she allowed Garrick to get closer, then closer still before she lurched to the left and again to the right, sending the tiny boat rocking wildly back and forth. The boat dipped, then pitched to the left just as she caught sight of a sailing vessel, heading in their direction.

Her heart leapt. *Alastair.* It had to be him. Yet it was too late to stop what she'd set in motion.

"Nay!" Garrick cried as they both plunged over the side and into the ice-cold water.

Everything around Gwendolyn was a chaos of motion and water. She tried to concentrate as the rock pulled her farther from the light, from air, from life. She brought hands to her feet, pulling and twisting the rope. Her fingers started to tingle, going numb from the cold. Her lungs ached. Still she fought the urge to take a breath, until finally the rope gave way. The rock continued to fall while her descent slowed.

Desperate for air, she thrashed her bound arms and

kicked her feet, trying to make her way back to the surface, but the water pressed in on her. Her gown tangled about her legs, weighing her down further.

Nay! She wasn't ready to die, not when Alastair had come for her. Instinctively, Gwendolyn kicked her feet and pumped her arms, fighting her way towards the light. Pain seared her chest and panic exploded inside her. She wanted to cry out as the need to breathe overwhelmed her.

Gathering what was left of her strength, Gwendolyn forced herself up. In a surge of effort she broke through the surface and hitched in a convulsive breath, taking in water instead. As she choked and coughed, she felt herself sinking once more.

Garrick's hands were on her shoulders. A jolt of fear shot through her, paralyzing her limbs. A cry of defeat echoed inside her. Yet she refused to give up. Mustering the remnants of her strength, she struggled against his iron grip. He might drown her, but she would not make the task easy for him. But instead of pushing her beneath the water, he reared back as an explosion rent the air.

Despite Garrick's release of her, her head dipped below the water and she was too tired, too cold to fight it. A heartbeat later, another pair of hands propelled her towards the light. Air touched her face and for a shocked moment, she forgot to breathe.

She looked into Alastair's familiar dark gaze. Anxiety, pain, helplessness stared back at her.

"Gwendolyn, for God's sake, breathe!"

Alastair's plea jolted her back to her senses. She dragged in a shallow breath. Her lungs clenched, then spasmed, and she coughed up the water she had inhaled.

As she continued to sputter and cough, Alastair pulled her tight against his chest as he swam back to the ship. He grabbed hold of a rope and tied it around them, and slowly the two of them were hauled aboard.

Alastair set her on the deck and slashed through the rope at her wrists before cradling her against his chest. "Take a deep breath," he ordered.

She obeyed and precious air filled her lungs. Unable to resist her body's response to the trauma, her muscles went limp and she leaned against the solid wall of Alastair's chest. "You came for me."

"Nothing and no one could keep me away." He smiled down at her. "Though we must thank Marcus for the use of his fine ship."

Gwendolyn looked beyond Alastair to see Marcus and another man who startlingly resembled the man who held her.

"Gwendolyn, you remember my brother, Tormod."

He came forward and placed a blanket over her. "I'm pleased I am that you are not dead from our current adventure, and from past events which I still need explained."

"In time," Alastair said, returning his gaze to hers.

Tears stung her eyes. "You came for me."

"I will always come for you." A smile pulled up the corners of his mouth. "But from this moment forward, I doubt I will ever let you out of my sight."

Wrapped in the warmth of his gaze, she returned his smile with one of her own. "Then I will have to reward you appropriately for your efforts later."

He grinned, then a heartbeat later his expression hardened. "Where is Garrick? Did anyone see what happened to him after I shot him?"

Tormod frowned. "He dipped below the surface of the water, and we've seen nothing of him since."

"Do you think you killed him?" Marcus asked.

Alastair nodded. "The ball hit his chest. I doubt he could survive a wound like that on land, let alone in the chill water. Still, I want that fishing boat destroyed. I'll leave no way for him to get back to shore. Then all the secrets he has about Dunvegan will die with him."

Marcus shouted to his crew to load a cannon. One single shot was fired, hitting the vessel and splintering it into hundreds of pieces.

"Thank you, Marcus."

"Garrick had to die for what he's done. Both the Mac-Leods and the MacDonalds are better off without him. Hopefully, we will find his body along the shore in the next few days and can help his spirit find the peace he never found on this earth," Marcus said before ordering his crew to take the boat back to shore.

"Back to Dunvegan?" Gwendolyn asked.

Alastair nodded. "Now we must deal with the aftermath of Garrick and the MacDonalds' plans."

CHAPTER TWENTY-ONE

N EVER IN HER life had Gwendolyn been more excited to see the golden-brown stones of Dunvegan Castle and all the warriors in the courtyards and on the towers. It seemed as if men dotted the entire landscape. They were here to make certain what happened only a short time ago never happened again.

They hadn't even made it inside the keep when Alastair commanded four men to barricade the sea gate with stone, making it impossible to use it as a way to enter the castle, at least temporarily, until a more permanent fix could be found. Another dozen men were sent to guard the breach in the curtain wall. Repairs would take months, but until they were complete, guards would be on rotation both day and night.

Somberly, Gwendolyn, Alastair, Marcus, and Tormod entered the castle and made their way to the great hall. At the sight of Mrs Morgan, sitting by the hearth, Gwendolyn's heart filled with joy. "I am so happy to see you are well. I was so afraid. . ."

The chatelaine's cheeks tinged pink. "Oh, deary, it

would take more than a wound to my shoulder tae take this old Scottish curmudgeon out."

"And Becks?" Gwendolyn moved to warm herself by the fire. She'd dried herself on the ship, but parts of her were still damp.

Mrs Morgan sent her a reassuring smile. "He had a few bruises that will take a while to heal, but otherwise he is as good as always."

Arabella sat on one side of the chatelaine. Samuel sat on the other and greeted their sister with smiles. "We are happy to see that you are safe as well. We heard about what happened."

"Garrick is dead. He won't ever hurt any of us again."

When Callum and Lottie joined them in the chamber, Gwendolyn frowned at the bandages around the young man's head and shoulder. "Oh, Callum, not you too."

He nodded, returning a shy grin. "My first real battle and I fared not so well. Lottie says the gash on my head will leave a scar." He shrugged. "All warriors have them. I guess that makes me one of them now."

"We will definitely be accelerating your battle training," Alastair replied. "And yes, all warriors have scars. Some of them are visible, others are not."

Gwendolyn frowned, wondering what he meant. Before she could ask him to explain, a familiar mist gathered beside the wall near the hearth as the Grey Lady took form. Orrick and Rowena entered the chamber at the same time, through the doorway.

If such a thing were possible, it appeared as if the tear upon her cheek had vanished. The Grey Lady moved from Alastair and Gwendolyn to Tormod, Orrick, Rowena, and Callum.

My children. All home at last. Are you safe and finally at peace?

"Garrick MacDonald is dead," Alastair informed her as his gaze connected with Tormod's. "What happened after I left the battle? You returned so quickly. Did you decide not to fight Alexander MacDonald?"

"We fought, briefly," Tormod replied. "Within minutes I injured Alexander MacDonald, not fatally, but the wound in his thigh was deep enough that he will most likely have a permanent limp."

"After their leader was injured, the others fled, knowing that our numbers and our weapons were no match for them," Orrick added. Alastair's lips pressed thin. "You both did well today. Now we must prepare the men for the usual retaliation that will come."

"Perhaps this time will be different," Orrick said. "We don't know that the MacDonalds will strike back."

"Three hundred years of our two clans warring with each other says that they will. It is only a matter of time." The words had barely left his mouth when Alastair groaned. "Good God! I sound like my father."

You are nothing like that man. The Grey Lady came close

to her eldest son, until he was partially enveloped in her mist. *That you want to keep those whom you love safe is an admirable trait. Your father would have been wise to listen to your counsel more often.*

Alastair smiled. "Thank you for your confidence, Mother. But our battle today with the MacDonalds and killing Garrick leaves me in a tough situation. As a member of the isle council it is my duty to try and cultivate peace amongst our clans." He sighed. "Peace was the last thing I wanted to maintain with the MacDonalds today. They have abused us too many times to let their attacks to go unpunished."

"You did the right thing for our clan. As heir to the MacLeods your first obligation is to the safety and welfare of your people," Orrick said.

Alastair nodded. "I shall take that obligation seriously, I promise you."

"Just remember, you will always have our support." Tormod's gaze passed between Alastair and Orrick. "You did not come into this world alone. You will not walk through life that way either. Orrick and I can assist."

"I can help as well," Callum chimed in.

"I'd be glad of the help. Dunvegan Castle must undergo massive security enhancements," Alastair noted, his gaze not on his brothers but on Gwendolyn.

She offered a shy smile. "Since you are making improvements, might I suggest you focus some of your attention to replacing the roof in the old keep. In case you hadn't noticed, there are men everywhere. We will have to find places for all of them to shelter, and for their horses."

"I would be more than happy to bring in the necessary supplies—wood, stone, whatever is needed—right to your shore," Marcus offered.

Rowena left her brother's side to stand beside Marcus. "That you are in the chamber with the rest of my brothers gives me great hope for our future. But where and how, might I ask, did you acquire a ship?"

Alastair slanted a glance at Marcus. "That is something we would all like to know."

A long moment ticked past, then Marcus softly replied. "It became obvious to me at my first meeting with Alastair upon his arrival home that I had nothing to offer you, Rowena. And after all that has transpired, I have even less. I have no clan. No home. No income." He took her hand in his. "I would never ask you to live such a life of uncertainty with me."

"At least the young man is a realist," Tormod commented. "You have to give him credit for that."

"But what about the ship?" Rowena pressed.

"I sold everything I had to buy it. I've only had it in my possession for two days. The crew is working for me for a promise of a cut of all we will earn in the year ahead."

"The year ahead?" Rowena's eyes widened. "What do you mean?"

"I must part with you for a time to sail to faraway places

and bring back goods I can sell. With luck, I'll secure enough funds to support you and our family for the rest of our lives."

Rowena shook her head. "Take me with you. I am not averse to the sea or to going without. I've had plenty all my life. I could use a little austerity to help keep my perspective on the ways of most men and women in this country."

Marcus's jaw firmed. "'Tis too dangerous for a woman at sea. My goal is to return in one year a wealthy man. Promise you will wait for me." He moved to the side table and picked up a folded document, carrying it back to Rowena. "I had this drawn up for you."

Alastair surged forward and took the document from Marcus's hand. He unrolled the sheath of paper. "While your actions are admirable, I'll not allow her to sign a betrothal while you are gone." He inspected the contents and frowned.

"As you can see, the document is not a betrothal. It is my last will and testament. Should anything happen to me, God forbid, I have seen to it that all my worldly possessions transfer to Rowena."

"Nay, Marcus. I want nothing but you at my side."

Gwendolyn moved to Rowena's side and wrapped an arm around her shoulders, pulling her close. "What Marcus is doing to secure your future together is remarkable. He's obviously put a lot of thought into the kind of future he wants to have with you."

"But a year. . ." Tears formed in Rowena's eyes.

"Is no time at all. And with the promise of a betrothal when Marcus returns, you'll have much to look forward to."

Rowena turned her tear-bright eyes on Alastair. "Does this mean you'll agree to our marrying when Marcus returns home?"

A muscle worked in Alastair's jaw for a moment before he finally nodded. "I will agree."

Rowena smiled and her tears evaporated as she threw herself into Marcus's arms. "You absolutely must not die while you are away. For I would never forgive you."

Marcus grinned as he looked up. "Do you hear that, Lord? I am under instructions not to perish. By all that is holy, do your part to see me safely returned to my future bride."

Alastair returned the papers to Marcus. "If you'll accept my coin, I would ask that you secure supplies for me to repair this castle."

Marcus smiled as he slipped his arms around Rowena's waist. "It would be an honour to assist you in any way."

While the others congratulated the happy couple, Gwendolyn noted that Callum shifted away to stand before the spectral image of his mother. When the others noticed, the room became silent. "Why are you still here, Mother? You died so long ago."

My children. I had to see you protected.

"We are all safe now. We are all back together. Yet you are still here," Callum mused.

"Most ghosts are tied to a place because something in

their life is unresolved," Orrick offered. "I've read stories about how other spirits were finally set free."

"Perhaps we could determine why Mother is still here and find a way to release her." Rowena reached out and let her hand slide right through the coiling mist that made up her mother's spirit. "She's here, and yet she is not."

"After all that you have suffered, you deserve to rest in peace," Alastair said with a catch in his voice as he stretched up to kiss what would have been her cheek. "We love you, Mother."

And I love all of you. Janet MacLeod, the Grey Lady, drifted closer to Gwendolyn, to Arabella, and Samuel. *I love all of you as well. I couldn't do much to save you from your predicament, but I did my best to keep you safe until you were found.*

Gwendolyn's lips curved. "We are so grateful to you for everything. Thank you for bringing the three of us back to life."

The Grey Lady nodded. *I do wonder what will happen now*, she said with a pointed look at Alastair.

Alastair grinned as he slipped his arm through Gwendolyn's. "You'll learn that soon enough. For now, I'd like to take care of a few other important matters, in private." He smiled down at Gwendolyn, then, ignoring the eyes that watched them, bent his head and kissed her. Still grinning, he drew back and met her gaze.

Gwendolyn's chest felt unaccountably tight. "I have things I must say to you as well."

CHAPTER TWENTY-TWO

T WILIGHT HAD TAKEN hold by the time Alastair took
Gwendolyn's hand and led her upstairs to the laird's
bedchamber. Mrs Honey had insisted on feeding everyone a
simple meal of cock-a-leekie soup with crusty bread and
thick slices of cheese before letting them settle for the night.
Alastair allowed no one to sleep in the spaces between the
walls. He wanted no one else to know of the secret passageways for the safety of everyone at the castle. Instead the
warriors would bed down in the great hall, the solar, the
library, the drawing room, and even the chapel until the new
roof could be built.

Gwendolyn's heart thundered in her chest as Alastair
closed the door behind them. Leaning against the door he
turned his gaze on her. "I was so afraid I had lost you forever
today," he admitted, allowing her to see the fear in his gaze,
fear he usually kept hidden from everyone. "I could not have
survived losing you again. I am sorry, Gwendolyn, to have
failed you. I promise to keep you safe, to protect you and
your siblings in every way possible from this day forward.
You are precious to me and I never want to lose you."

"I forgive you, Alastair." Her lips turned up with happiness. "But you must know by now that I am a fighter."

"That you are." He leaned forward and kissed her.

Sharp and bright, a thrill of expectation flashed through her as his kiss grew hungrier, more demanding. She gripped his shoulders for support as instinct took over. Her desire for him was simple, and yet complicated by all that they'd lived through. Brought together on their wedding day with great expectations only to have them ripped away, then restored years later when they were both older and more prepared for what life held in store for them. Her heart was beating so hard now she could feel it in every part of her body. "I never wish to be parted from you again," she said boldly against his lips.

He pulled back. The emotions in his eyes shone bright. Faith. Hope. Love. Beacons that would guide them through the years ahead. "I love you."

Those three words rippled through her, wrapped around her heart. "And I love you."

He lifted her into his arms and carried her to the bed. There, with only golden candlelight bathing their skin, they celebrated all they had, all they had reclaimed. Life had not been easy for either of them, and still they realised the gift they had been given in each other and this second chance at love.

With their hands, lips, and bodies they scaled the peak of their bliss, loving each other as only they could. Love drove them, racked them, enfolded them in its grace. And finally, when at last they lay together in a tangle of limbs, with the bedsheets tousled, and the warmth of satisfaction heavy in their veins, their new reality crept around them.

Alastair perched up on his elbow, glancing down at her. "My dearest, I believe there is something I forgot."

Gwendolyn thought back over their lovemaking and laughed. "Nay, I'm fairly certain you covered it all, and quite well I might add."

His lips twitched. "Once you answer a simple question for me, I'd be happy to cover everything again."

She arched a brow. "And what question is that?"

He leaned closer, lowered his head and brushed his lips across hers. "Will you marry me, Gwendolyn Harris?"

Tears of happiness she'd never expected to feel all the days she'd been locked away in the tower filled her eyes. The same emotion swelled in her chest, filled her heart to over-flowing as she struggled to find her voice. "Nothing would make me happier."

"On the morrow?"

Gwendolyn laughed. "So soon? Mrs Morgan and Mrs Honey will not be well pleased at that, but aye. Tomorrow."

He smiled slowly, his dark eyes finally peaceful and calm, as he kissed her again and made good on his earlier promise.

CHAPTER TWENTY-THREE

T HE NEXT MORNING, dressed in a gold silk gown the dressmaker had finished only an hour earlier, Gwendolyn waited at the doorway of the chapel surrounded by Tormod, Orrick, and Callum. Making good on his promise to protect her, Alastair had asked his brothers to guide her journey down the aisle until she stood before him. When finally the short walk was achieved, Alastair took her hands in his.

"You're trembling." His hands tightened on hers and he offered her a soft smile. "There is nothing to be frightened of. We have made it farther down the aisle than last time. I dare say we will take this all the way to the end."

Gwendolyn laughed. In this moment, she felt like the luckiest person in the world. She'd never dreamed she would possess a love so powerful or as passionate for the strong, honourable, and courageous man before her. "I love you, Alastair, with all my heart."

He leaned forward and brushed his lips at her temple. "And I will always love you." He pulled back and smiled, and she was filled with a sense of wonder. It had taken them a long time to finally make this journey, and much had happened to them along the way. But life and love were like that she suddenly realised. There were darker moments, and splendid ones, with peaks and valleys in between.

It was the moments of true bliss that were remembered and treasured, but the pain and the turmoil of life was what made these moments matter, what made these moments special.

Gwendolyn shifted her gaze out across all those who gathered in the chapel with the two of them today. They were all very lucky, in a sense, to have each other.

Arabella and Samuel both looked healthy and happy, and once she and Alastair said their vows, her family would be blended with the MacLeods, and joined together for a lifetime.

Rowena and Marcus stood close, holding hands. Perhaps dreaming of their own wedding in the future.

Graeme, Mrs Morgan, Mrs Honey, and Becks smiled at her and Alastair. Happiness reflected in their eyes.

Tormod and Orrick nodded to her and then Alastair as they guarded those at the altar, prepared to defend the entire assembly if necessary.

And, at the back of the chamber, with a peaceful expression on her spectral face, was the Grey Lady, Alastair's mother, and her protector.

Bringing her gaze back to the man beside her, Gwendolyn's lips curled into a radiant smile. She had suffered at times in her life, but the reward she'd gained was far greater than she ever could have imagined. She had gained a husband and a protector. She had also gained a family of people who loved her in return.

She was safe. She was home. She had a place in this world where she belonged.

A WEEK LATER after Marcus had brought supplies to the shores of Dunvegan which would be used to refurbish the castle, he prepared to make sail once more. Alastair's arms went around Gwendolyn from behind as they stood on the shores of the loch. In the distance, Marcus's ship waited for his goodbyes.

"My heart goes out to Rowena." Gwendolyn's voice was thick as she fought back tears. "Do you believe we will ever see Marcus again?"

"I do not know." Alastair's lips gently brushed her temple.

"I care for Marcus."

Alastair turned her in his arms. His gaze was a warm caress. "I do, as well, despite his family origins."

"He is our family now."

Alastair nodded, his smile broadening. "That he is."

After pressing a kiss to Marcus's lips, Rowena gave Marcus what appeared to be a hatbox. He opened it, peered inside and smiled.

For a moment, Gwendolyn thought she saw a splash of familiar yellow silk. But how could that be when the Fairy

Flag had been returned to its home in the Dunvegan drawing room? She would have to ask Rowena about her parting gift sometime, but for now, they simply needed to lend the young woman their support as her heart's desire sailed off into the unknown.

Gwendolyn pulled Alastair's arms more tightly around her as Rowena and Marcus shared a last kiss before he waded into the water, pushing the small boat past the waves before he got in and rowed towards his waiting ship. Rowena waited at the edge of the surf, her hair and dress flapping wildly in the wind.

Rowena came to join Gwendolyn and Alastair and the three of them linked their arms around each other, watching as Marcus climbed the rope ladder and onto his ship. His men lifted the small boat and the anchor before unfurling the sails. The ship started forward.

The three of them stayed there on the Dunvegan shores until the ship was barely visible in the distance. "He's sailing into the unknown," Rowena said through her tears.

Alastair and Gwendolyn shared a look, as they each remembered their journey to each other. "There will be struggles for both you and Marcus in the days ahead, but there can be great rewards in the unknown," Alastair said, and as if accentuating his point, an errant beam of sunlight broke through the clouds, bathing the three of them in radiant light.

Rowena tipped back her head, letting the warmth caress her face. She reached up and brushed the tears from her cheeks. "You are right. I believe the power of the Fairy Flag goes with Marcus. It will protect him as it protects those of us here at Dunvegan."

"That is a lovely thought, Rowena," Gwendolyn said, and yet she found herself frowning. To Alastair she asked, "Do you think the MacDonalds and the clans who have joined them will ever leave us in peace?"

Alastair's features sobered. "The true battle of the clans has yet to begin, but with Tormod, Orrick, and Callum here at the castle, and the Fairy Flag once more in our possession, we are well-prepared for whatever comes our way." Then his expression cleared. "Until that happens, and even through the tough times ahead, it is our task is to be gloriously happy for the rest of our lives. Can you commit to that, Lady MacLeod?"

Gwendolyn didn't think she could ever be happier than she'd been on the day of their wedding. But she'd been wrong. Joy beyond compare filled her. It seemed in this moment as if her happiness would increase proportionately every day she spent in Alastair's arms.

"Aye, my love. I can commit to that."

THE END

Want more? Check out the next book in the Guardians of the Isles series, *Only a Highlander Will Do*!

Join Tule Publishing's newsletter for more great reads and weekly deals!

Author's Note

Myths and legends are rarely without some basis in historical fact. People tend to pass these stories down from one generation to the next because they help explain the origins of things that might otherwise be unexplainable. The Guardians of the Isle series is based on one such tale that is connected to the Clan MacLeod of Scotland. This clan possesses several artifacts from various times and events in history, but none more precious than the Fairy Flag.

Probably originating in Syria or Rhodes and woven in silk in the fourth century AD, legend has it that this sacred clan banner has miraculous powers. When unfurled in battle and waved three times, the clan would invariably snatch victory from the jaws of defeat.

Traditional tales about the Fairy Flag's origin have two themes—crusaders and fairies.

The crusader version tells the tale of when a MacLeod, on a crusade to the Holy Land, received shelter and food from a hermit in a mountain pass. The hermit warned him that an evil spirit, a destroyer of true believers, guarded the pass and that he needed a piece of the True Cross to proceed.

When the MacLeod came upon the spirit, he slew her, the Daughter of Thunder, *Nein na Pheupere*. Before she died, she revealed to him the future of his clan, directing him to take her girdle and make a banner of it and to make a staff of her spear.

There is also scientific evidence that could explain the Fairy Flag's origins as that of the famous banner of the Norseman Harald Hardrada, one of the early ancestors of the chiefs of MacLeod. It is said Harald brought a silken banner back to Britain from the Middle East which fits with the dating of the flag and the location in which the fabric was most likely produced.

However, the MacLeod clan prefers the Fairy Tower version of the flag's origin which I used in this story. It is the tale of Iain Cair, stumbling upon a fairy dwelling where he met a fairy princess. The two fell in love, married, and had a child. But after a year in the mortal world, the fairy princess had to return to Fairyland. After promising his wife never to let their child cry, the laird did just that. Hearing her son's cries from the fairy world, the fairy princess returned to her son, wrapped him in a fairy shawl, and sang him a fairy lullaby. Years later, the child told his father that the shawl his mother had given him had magical powers. That magic could be used at a time of great need, but only three times, before the flag, and the flagbearer would return to the fairy world.

Yet another version of the tale is that of the Fairy Bridge, wherein a fairy married a MacLeod chief. They lived together for years in the fairy world. One day, the chief felt he had to return to his people, so they parted at the Fairy Bridge, three miles away from Dunvegan Castle. As a farewell present, the fairy gave him the Fairy Flag, telling him that when he was hard-pressed in battle, waving it would bring his clan victory whatever the odds. However, she warned that the magic could only be used three times.

Whatever version of the story is true, or partially true, the MacLeod clan has believed in the Fairy Flag's magic over the centuries. During two major clan battles in the past, the clan chief waved the Fairy Flag when his clansmen were close to defeat and it brought about miraculous victories. Belief in the power of *Am Bratach Sith* to save the clan from disaster remains strong to this day.

In 1939, a fire in the south wing of Dunvegan threatened to destroy the entire castle. When the Fairy Flag was carried to safety, the wind dropped and the flames seemed to abate. During World War II, pilots from the clan carried a picture of the flag as a talisman. During that same time period, Dame Flora MacLeod offered to wave the flag from the cliffs of Dover should the Germans attempt to invade Great Britain, but fortunately Clan MacLeod did not need to call upon the magic of the flag, and so according to legend, the MacLeods can call upon the Fairy Flag and its magic one last time.

Also in the pages of this book I use an illusion technique that is nowadays known as the Pepper's Ghost effect that has been used in theatre, amusement parks, museums, television, and concerts. But the technique goes back farther in time than the effect popularised by Henry Pepper in 1862.

Leonardo da Vinci invented this technique which he described in his work *Magia Naturalis* in 1584 and called it "How we may see in a chamber things that are not." In the sixteenth century, a Neapolitan scientist and scholar called this technique camera obscura.

The basic trick involves a stage that is basically in two places, one people can see, and one that is hidden to the side. A plate of glass is placed in the main stage at an angle that reflects the object or objects on the hidden stage.

When the lights are bright in the main stage area and dark in the hidden area, the reflected image cannot be seen. When the lighting in the hidden area is increased and the main area dimmed, the reflection becomes visible to those viewing it.

In 1742, the entrance to Dunvegan Castle was through the sea gate in the outer wall surrounding the castle. The main entrance to the castle on the landward side was created in 1748. For this series, I took creative license and decided to use the landward entrance to the castle before it existed six years later.

If you enjoyed Gwendolyn and Alastair's journey in *The Return of the Heir*, be sure not to miss the continuing tale of the Fairy Flag in *Only a Highlander Will Do*, featuring Tormod MacLeod, *To Win a Highlander's Heart*, featuring Orrick MacLeod, and *To Claim His Highland Bride*, featuring Marcus MacDonald.

If you enjoyed *The Return of the Heir*,
you'll love the next books in the...

GUARDIANS OF THE ISLES SERIES

Book 1: *The Return of the Heir*

Book 2: *Only a Highlander Will Do*
Coming in April 2022

Book 3: *To Win a Highlander's Heart*
Coming in June 2022

Available now at your favorite online retailer!

More books by Gerri Russell

All the Kings Men series

Book 1: *Seven Nights with a Scot*

Book 2: *Romancing the Laird*

Book 3: *A Temptress in Tartan*

Book 4: *A Laird and a Gentleman*

Book 5: *Much Ado About a Scot*

Available now at your favorite online retailer!

ABOUT THE AUTHOR

Barbara Roser Photography

Gerri Russell is the award-winning author of historical and contemporary novels including the Brotherhood of the Scottish Templars series and *Flirting with Felicity*. A two-time recipient of the Romance Writers of America's Golden Heart Award and winner of the American Title II competition sponsored by *RT Book Reviews* magazine, she is best known for her adventurous and emotionally intense novels set in the thirteenth- and fourteenth-century Scottish Highlands. Before Gerri followed her passion for writing romance novels, she worked as a broadcast journalist, a newspaper reporter, a magazine columnist, a technical writer and editor, and an instructional designer. She lives in the Pacific Northwest with her husband and four mischievous black cats.

Thank you for reading

THE RETURN OF THE HEIR

If you enjoyed this book, you can find more from all our great authors at TulePublishing.com, or from your favorite online retailer.

TULE
PUBLISHING

22186021R00198